DEATH
BY
DUMPLING

"Vivien Chien serves up a delicious mystery with a side order of soy sauce and sass. A tasty start to a new mystery series!"   —Kylie Logan, bestselling author of *Gone with the Twins*

"Vivien Chien brings a fresh new voice to cozies. *Death by Dumpling* is a fun and sassy debut with unique flavor, local flair, and heart."
—Amanda Flower, Agatha Award-Winning author of *Lethal Licorice*

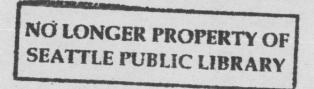

St. Martin's Paperbacks Titles by Vivien Chien

DEATH BY DUMPLINGS
DIM SUM OF ALL FEARS
MURDER LO MEIN
WONTON TERROR
EGG DROP DEAD
KILLER KUNG PAO
FATAL FRIED RICE
HOT AND SOUR SUSPECTS

DEATH BY DUMPLING

VIVIEN CHIEN

St. Martin's Paperbacks

This is a work of fiction. All of the characters, organizations, and events portrayed in this novel are either products of the author's imagination or are used fictitiously.

DEATH BY DUMPLING

Copyright © 2018 by Vivien Chien.
Copyright from *Dim Sum of All Fears* copyright © 2018 by Vivien Chien.

For information address St. Martin's Press, 120 Broadway, New York, NY 10271.

ISBN: 978-1-250-12915-4

Our books may be purchased in bulk for promotional, educational, or business use. Please contact your local bookseller or the Macmillan Corporate and Premium Sales Department at 1-800-221-7945, ext. 5442, or by e-mail at MacmillanSpecialMarkets@macmillan.com.

Printed in the United States of America

St. Martin's Paperbacks edition / April 2018

St. Martin's Paperbacks are published by St. Martin's Press, 120 Broadway, New York, NY 10271.

10 9

For Paul,
father and best friend

Thank you for always believing.

CHAPTER
1

You know in the movies where someone says "You can't fire me, I quit!" . . . maybe don't do that in real life. Unless you don't mind working as a server in your parents' Chinese restaurant for the rest of your life.

Turns out finding a new job wasn't as easy as I thought and my portion of the rent wasn't going to pay itself. My roommate and best friend, Megan Riley, didn't have the extra funds to cover my half of the bills, so there was no time to waste being "in between jobs." And to top it off, those pesky credit card people kept calling me day and night. Without any other options readily available and an ever-so-conveniently open spot at my parents' restaurant, Ho-Lee Noodle House, I gave in.

My parents were thrilled that I needed them for something again. However, I was not. At twenty-seven, depending on my parents was not my idea of a good time. Especially since they had been trying to convince me that working at the noodle house was my destiny well before I went to college. Somehow, I had always managed to escape that reality, until now.

Lana Lee, at your service. Literally.

Things to know about me: I'm half English, half Taiwanese, and no, I don't know karate. I'm definitely not good at math and I don't know how to spell your name in Chinese.

The last time I had straight-up black hair, I was in high school. Since then, I've spent a lot of time bleaching and dyeing my hair this color or that. Currently, it's chestnut brown with some golden peek-a-boo highlights. My mother had repeatedly assured me that one day dyeing my hair wasn't going to be fun anymore, and I should enjoy life without graying hair while I still could. But, what can I say, I get bored.

Leaving the house without putting on makeup means there's an emergency. Or that I've been forced out of the house against my will. If that's the case, send help.

I still have hope that the world can be a better place. This last bit has led some to call me an idealist once or twice. As far as name-calling goes, I'll take it. We've all been called worse, right?

Oh, and I have a problem with doughnuts. I love them and they love me. My older sister, Anna May, is always warning me that it's going to catch up with me at some point. That day may come, but for now, pass me the Boston cream.

And that's really the important stuff.

Aside from that, it had been six excruciating months since I started working full-time for my parents. Several factors came into play, helping this particular pursuit of employment along. We start with a foul breakup, then the previously mentioned quitting of former job, and my parents' sudden loss of their only full-time day-shift server, Lily. Really, Lily couldn't have picked a better time to walk out. I've considered sending a card of thanks.

I'm not the biggest fan of the restaurant business. That might have something to do with spending most of my childhood trapped in the back room of my parents' restaurant. As a child, I came to the restaurant every day after school where my mother would keep me stowed away in the back room near her office. She had set up a makeshift living room of sorts with a TV and couch, even a small desk where I could do my schoolwork. It wasn't until Anna May was old enough to babysit that I was allowed to go home after school. Then that started a whole new saga of my life. I called it "Stuck with Miss Know-It-All."

When I agreed to start working at the restaurant, my mom was so excited that she let me make up my own schedule. And if I was short on money, I was able to pick up extra shifts without any trouble. It didn't solve all of my money problems, but it got the bills paid, which was priority one in my life right now.

So, things could have been worse . . .

I counted the ways that life could be worse as I made my way down to Mr. Feng's office with his lunch order.

Our family's restaurant, along with Mr. Feng's office, is located in the charming plaza of Asia Village, a quaint shopping center filled with what I liked to refer to as "Asian stuff and things." You name it, we got it. Need Asian food, drinks, or candy? We got it. How about a stuffed Hello Kitty for your granddaughter? We got it.

Maybe you miss KTV or need some old Chinese movies? We have that too. In all, there were thirteen stores, a giant Asian grocery, my parents' restaurant, and a new karaoke bar, the Bamboo Lounge.

Northeast Ohio—more specifically, Fairview Park—isn't what you'd typically consider "Asia Central"; the original Chinatown area started out on the east side of Cleveland. It grew as Asians started to flock to the surrounding areas, and then for a time, it began to diminish. Right now, however, it was on the upswing.

Clevelanders tended to gravitate toward their own part of town despite the fact that the *other* part of town wasn't even that far. Mr. Feng, our property owner, who happened to be a dedicated west-sider, craved a more convenient location. And thus Asia Village was born. Though small, it has both charm and character. At the entrance to the parking lot is an ornate, arched entry gate decorated with gold dragons wrapping their scaly bodies around vibrant red poles. Beyond that is Asia Village itself, a tiny city of pagodas all in a row.

Inside, cobblestoned walkways wind around a large koi pond smackdab in the center of all the stores. There's a footbridge that crosses over to the other side, and if people feel like lingering by the water, they can feed the koi fish. Strung from the ceiling are red paper lanterns wishing good luck and long life, and above those are massive skylights that fill the plaza with so much natural light, you could swear you were still outside.

Some of the shop owners made their storefronts as authentic looking as possible. They kept to the traditional colors of red, gold, and black, adding Asian characters and symbols however they could. Other shop owners decided to use metal and wood textures, taking the more modern approach. For a sampling of Asian styles from past and present, Asia Village was without a doubt the place to go.

I stood now in front of the meager office of Feng and Sung. It was the most plain of all the storefronts, with two large windows, one on each side of the door, covered with miniblinds. Their names in both English and Chinese were emblazoned on the right window in gold lettering. A gold dragon sat between the words, separating their names.

Just as I was about to reach for the brass door handle, I heard yelling from inside. I stepped back, rethinking my entry, and stared at the door, miniblinds staring back at me. Well, this was awkward. The blinds were closed for privacy, and I had no idea who was in there and whether or not I should go in. I didn't want to interrupt whatever was going on.

Before I could overanalyze the situation, the door whipped open and a chubby Asian face glared at me, her cheeks red with anger. It was Kimmy Tran, and it was safe to say she was a little ticked.

Kimmy was my age and we had known each other since we were toddlers. The Tran family ran a shop called China Cinema and Song, an Asian video and music store; they'd had it for about as long as my parents had owned the restaurant. And because our parents were friends, we spent a lot of time together in our youth. As adults, we weren't terribly close friends, but there's a certain bond that develops after you spend hours together contemplating Barbie life scenarios, so we'd kept in contact despite our lives going in different directions.

She slammed the door behind her. "What a selfish jerk!" she yelled.

At a loss for words, I hugged the bag of takeout. Heat from the freshly cooked food seeped through my shirt.

"Do you have any idea what that slimeball is up to?" she asked, pointing furiously at the door. Her hair was wrapped in a sloppy bun on the top of her head, and it shook with each word.

I shook my head. "No . . ."

She began to pace in front of me, clenching her fists. "He's raising the rent fifteen percent!" She stopped briefly to gauge my reaction. When I didn't respond, she began to pace again. "Fifteen percent! Can you even believe that? My parents can't afford what the rent is now! It's high enough already!"

This was the first I'd heard of Mr. Feng raising the rent. I would have to ask my mother if she'd heard the same thing. "How did you find this out?" I asked.

"He slipped it in while he was telling my mother about this great plan he came up with to make Asia Village better." She stopped to face me, placing her hands on her hips. "Better for who? For him and his wallet?"

"Well, maybe there is more to—"

"No, Lana. There are no 'well, maybes.' He's a jerk and he's selfish and someone has got to stop him before he runs us all out of here," she said, waving her arms in the air. "He forgets that our parents were the ones who backed him up in the beginning and stuck with him through all the rough times. Now this is how he's going to treat the people who were there for him? It's absurd."

She had a point with the whole parent thing, but I wasn't sure if I should egg her on. She seemed pretty fired up on her own and I didn't feel like getting into this discussion so early in the day.

"I'm telling you, Lana, that man is asking for it. One of these days he's going to make the wrong person mad." She gave a final huff and stormed off.

Well, that was bracing.

Shaking off her negative vibes, I repositioned the food in my arms and headed inside.

Mr. Feng's office was always dimly lit and a little on the dusty side. There were two desks at opposite sides of the small, rectangular room. On both of the desks sat those small banker's lamps with the plastic green lampshades and gold chains. Did anybody even really use those anymore? I'm pretty sure that Mr. Feng owned the last two in existence.

He had his back turned to me and was organizing something in a drawer. I purposely cleared my throat and he jerked up, turning around. Thomas Feng was not just our landlord, but a close friend of all the people who worked in Asia Village. He was a softspoken man in his mid-fifties, with salt-and-pepper hair and pronounced wrinkles around his eyes, which I'm guessing came with running a large property—and having two teenage daughters.

He kept this small office space for himself and his partner, Ian Sung, so they could have a quiet place to work on-site when necessary. I also suspected that Mr. Feng liked to have someplace away from home that he could claim as his own. Ian rarely showed up and the other desk seemed to be a courtesy, if anything.

Mr. Feng and Ian owned a couple other small properties in neighboring suburbs. Ian handled the other properties, which included a few small apartment buildings, a stand-alone Chinese grocery, and three duplexes. Asia Village—the first piece of real estate that Thomas had ever owned—was his pride and joy, and so he spent most of his days walking the plaza and checking in with the people he'd known for so many years and considered family.

"Lana . . . what are you doing here?" he asked me.

"I came to drop off your lunch."

He looked at the bag in my hands and back up at me. "Where's Peter?"

"Oh, he had a large takeout order to finish up and couldn't leave the kitchen. He asked if I could drop it off instead."

Mr. Feng furrowed his brow and seemed to forget I was there. I inched up to the desk and set his food down. "Is everything okay?" I asked.

"Yes, I'm just . . . yes . . . everything is fine, Lana."

"I ran into Kimmy Tran on my way in." I nodded toward the door.

He sighed. "I have learned the hard way that you cannot make everyone happy."

"I'm sure it'll blow over. You know how Kimmy can be."

Mr. Feng chuckled as he pulled his wallet out of the back pocket of his pants. "How is business at the restaurant? Are your parents doing okay?"

I nodded. "Things are going good enough that I don't hear any complaints from them."

"Do you enjoy working with them?"

I inhaled deeply, grasping for an appropriate answer. "It's not as bad as I thought. I didn't see myself here, but you never know where life is going to take you, I suppose."

He handed me the money and sat on the edge of his desk. "Appreciate your parents while they are still here. One day you will want them here and it will be too late."

I gave a polite smile as I accepted the money and said my good-byes.

CHAPTER
2

Our family's restaurant has been around since the plaza's beginning. My mother, ever the traditionalist, insisted that our restaurant be decked out in red, black, and gold. Gold lettering above the door let you know that you were about to dine at Ho-Lee Noodle House, Number One Noodle Shop. And that is the only thing that has stayed the same for the entirety of its existence.

The inside followed the same theme with black lacquer tables, red walls, and gold accents. Even though the restaurant has been slightly updated a few times in the past thirty-odd years, the dining room was still partially separated into two sections. The smaller section used to be for when restaurants still had smoking sections. A portion of the restaurant was enclosed with an intricately designed wall of carved wood, with a doorway that led to the area we used for private parties.

A walkway separating the two areas takes you

straight back to the kitchen. I had spent most of my childhood running up and down that aisle. And now, here I was running up and down it again, but in a completely different context.

The rest of the morning flew by and I was at the end of the lunch rush. The dining room was almost completely cleaned up and I focused my attention on wiping down a freshly vacated table. Dried sweet-and-sour sauce on a lacquered tabletop could be a real pain.

"Excuse me, young lady?" an elderly customer called from a few tables over.

Leaving the wet rag behind, I wiped my hands on my apron and gave a smile to the two elderly ladies looking up at me, their hair freshly permed with not a strand out of place. They must have been visiting the hair salon. "Did you need more tea, ma'am?" I glanced at her empty cup.

"Oh, no, thank you, dear. I've had so much tea, I'm ready to burst," she replied, chuckling to her friend. "If you could, would you bring us the check?"

"Sure thing." I headed for the front counter and printed a copy of their bill, placing it squarely on a little black tray with two fortune cookies. I placed it in the middle of their table with another sweet smile.

"Beverly," the little old lady said, her eyes lighting up, "pick which fortune cookie you want. I think it's going to be a good one." She looked up at me and winked. "I do love these little things. You Orientals have the cutest traditions."

I groaned inwardly. That term is totally outdated, except when it's used to describe a vase or rug. Of which I am neither. I mean, don't get me wrong, I am far from politically correct, but everybody has their pressure points.

However, in this unfair world, the customer is always right. So, instead of correcting her, I kept my smile securely in place and walked away.

The two women were the last of the lunch crowd, and I had an opportunity to lounge up front for a while. On my little perch at the hostess booth, I looked out the glass double doors and watched the shoppers shuffle through the plaza with their bags and takeout packages, probably enjoying a day off from work. Lucky ducks.

Five shop lengths down, I saw my mother's best friend, Esther Chin, running through the plaza faster than I've ever seen her move. Within no time, she was thrusting open the double doors to our restaurant.

"Lana!" Esther's hands flailed in the air, her gold bracelets jingling with each movement. "Where is your mommy? I need her . . ."

Esther was a tiny woman in her mid-fifties with cropped black hair and a deep love for floral prints. Today's ensemble consisted of a black silk top with bright pink chrysanthemums that perfectly matched her lipstick.

I looked at her, bewildered. "She's in the back room . . ."

Without another word, Esther flew past me screaming, "Bettyyyyyy!!!"

What on earth was going on?

Before I had time to follow her, a family of four walked in. I plastered on "the smile" and grabbed some menus, leading them to a corner booth, far from the kitchen where potential action was about to take place. After getting them situated, I hightailed it to the kitchen to grab them water and see if eavesdropping was a possibility.

Our cook, Peter Huang, looked up at me as I walked through the swinging doors. "Dude, what the heck is going on? Esther just flew through here like she was on fire!"

Peter, the son of one of my mother's good friends who was our other full-time waitress, had worked for the restaurant since he was eighteen. Now, at the age of thirty, he'd established himself as our head chef and did a bang-up job, if I do say so myself.

For a cook, he was a toothpick. There goes that saying about not trusting skinny cooks, but if you wanted someone to make the best noodles you've ever had in your life, you'd want Peter behind the wok. Once my mother saw how well he did in the kitchen, she did not second-guess promoting him over our other cook, Lou, who still tore more dumpling wrappers than the rest of the staff combined.

Today Peter was dressed in his usual outfit of solid black. Instead of a chef hat, he wore a black baseball hat to cover his shaggy hair. Since I've known him, he's always kept his hair long, in a Brandon Lee sort of way.

"I have no idea. I was wondering the same thing." I grabbed four water goblets from the stacked trays of clean dishes.

"It's got to be something serious, I've never seen Esther run anywhere in my life."

We both laughed.

I filled the glasses with ice and water, as slowly as possible, hoping the door to the back room would open and we'd get some answers. No such luck. I headed back out into the dining area disappointed. How exciting could it really be? I asked myself, trying to pacify my curiosity. I mean, it was Esther. The highlights of her life were mah-jong and shopping for new floral prints more chipper than the last.

After I had taken the family's order and given them their drinks, I slipped back into the kitchen, and stood outside the door to the back room with my ear pressed up against it. Peter watched in anticipation.

Without warning, the door swung open, nearly knocking me over. Thanks to my ninja-like reflexes, I caught myself before kissing the floor.

My mother jumped, startled by my proximity. "Ai-ya! Lana! What are you doing?"

"Nothing . . ."

She stared impatiently at me, her arms folded over her chest. Even at five feet two inches she was intimidating. Don't let my mother fool you. Sure, she looks sweet enough in her cute pastel blouses, and her chubby cheeks give her a warm, friendly look that's deceivingly trustworthy. She looks innocent enough, but like the pagoda walls outside, it was just a façade. She could crush a man like a bug if she had to.

Esther rushed past us, exiting through the swinging doors back into the dining room.

"What is Esther's deal?" I asked, pointing toward the dining room, and pretending my mother wasn't giving me "the look."

"Do we have customers?" my mother asked, ignoring my question.

"Just one family, they're waiting on their food." I glanced at Peter who had slipped back into cooking mode.

"Okay, good. Lock the door. No more customers today. Mr. Feng died."

My stomach dropped. "What?"

In the background, I heard Peter drop his metal spatula.

"Esther called the police already, they are coming now." She waved her hand toward the dining room doors. "Now go, lock the door, no more customers today."

I got the family of four paid up and out the door. The CLOSED sign was facing out, and I dead-bolted the entrance. During that time, the police had shown up along with an ambulance. I saw the gurney go by and all eyes followed the procession down to Mr. Feng's office.

I could see Esther standing outside the office door, wringing her hands. Cindy Kwan from the bookstore was standing next to her, and I wondered why she was there.

My mother had called my dad to inform him of the news and he arrived in record time. They came out of the kitchen with Peter in tow. My mother looked solemn, and I didn't have the heart to ask what happened. They joined me at the entrance and the four of us stood lumped together at the glass doors staring out at the circus of people starting to congregate outside the property office. None of us said a word or even seemed to breathe for several minutes while we watched the commotion outside our doors.

My dad broke the silence. "Cindy from the bookstore was meeting Tom for a business meeting and found him slumped over his desk. She tried to wake him up, but when he was unresponsive she ran over to Esther's and they called the police." My dad shook his head. "I can't imagine what his wife must be going through right now."

My dad, William Lee, is a big ole white guy. Looking at my sister and me, people assume both our parents are Asian, especially because the name Lee throws people off. They usually assume it's attributed to an Asian background but actually is thanks to my dad's English background. My dad doesn't have a neat accent, but my grandparents do. They call me things like *love* and taught me about scones. Anyway, it's always fun watching the reaction on someone's face when they meet my dad for the first time.

He is extremely white. There's no two ways around it. Sometimes, he reminds me of those posters you see in a bank of some guy shaking hands with overly excited homeowners. Which isn't too far from reality because he's a Realtor. He even comes with his own million-dollar smile and crisp, well-fitted suit.

He does pretty well for a guy in his mid-fifties. At first when his hair started to go gray, he had a panic attack and bought an entire case of Just for Men, but eventually he came around and concluded that it gave him a more "distinguished" look and might even help him in the realty business. My mom hated to see all that dye go to waste, so now she uses it to touch up her roots. Hey, I don't judge.

"According to Esther, she thinks he's been like that for a little over an hour," my dad informed us.

I looked up at him; he towered over me at six feet. "What makes Esther think that?"

"He was lying next to a takeout box . . . there was still food left."

I gulped. His lunch . . . the lunch that I brought him.

I contemplated that statement and the timing of my visit. I believed in timing. Kind of like when you see a major car accident that just happened and you were running five minutes late that morning. Suddenly, you're not so upset about being late, almost as if it were a favor in disguise.

My mother, who hadn't spoken a single word, lifted her tiny hand and unlocked the dead bolt. Softly she said, "Let's see what's going on."

"Betty." My dad reached a hand for her shoulder. "Maybe we should stay here."

"No . . . I want to go."

My father didn't argue. My mother pushed open the door and instantly we were exposed to a clamor of voices. Following behind her, my dad kept a protective hand on her back and Peter and I brought up the rear of our little procession.

There must have been around a hundred people standing outside the office. Shoppers hung around waiting to see what the commotion was about and fellow shopkeepers had abandoned their posts to get a closer look.

We stood at the edge of the crowd. My mother, curious but not wanting to go any farther, secured her space and stared intently in the general direction of the office.

Time dripped on and just when I thought I couldn't take any more, the door to the office sprang open and two paramedics came out with a gurney carrying a rather human-shaped body bag. Behind them appeared two uniformed officers and a grave-looking man in a charcoal-gray suit.

One of the paramedics shouted, asking the crowd to move aside and let them through. Like migrating birds, the cluster of people moved as one, making room down the center, letting the gurney pass.

As they passed us, I couldn't take my eyes off the body bag. My brain worked overtime trying to acknowledge that someone I knew and cared about was in there. I had never seen a dead body in this scenario before. Although I suppose not many people my age really do.

Esther came fluttering over. She hugged my mother, and they shared a moment of hurried Mandarin together.

Esther glanced among the four of us. "I heard the man in gray say that maybe Thomas died from allergies."

"You mean an allergic reaction?" my father asked to clarify.

She nodded slowly. "Yah, yah, yah . . ."

For a minute, my attention was taken away from the gurney as what Esther said registered in my mind. The whole Village knew that Mr. Feng had a shellfish allergy. And it wasn't something that he trifled with. He was always very careful about what he ate and how he ordered food. Even at our restaurant, we had special instructions for preparing his orders. On top of that, he always carried an EpiPen as a safety precaution.

Now that I thought about it, I remembered seeing the tip of it sticking out of his shirt pocket.

It was possible that Esther had heard wrong. She was in shock after all. We all were.

The paramedics had crossed the plaza and we watched as they exited through the main entrance on the other side of the building. As the doors shut, my mother burst into tears.

CHAPTER
3

After Thomas had been . . . *taken* from the plaza, many of the smaller shops closed for the remainder of the day. Ho-Lee Noodle House was one among the many who decided the rest of the workday would just be absolutely unbearable. Once calls were made to the rest of the staff, and everything was situated, my parents sent me home.

My mom had left almost immediately to call on Donna Feng to give her condolences and see if she needed anything. My dad, Peter, and I settled the loose ends at the restaurant. I offered to go over to my parents' place and sit with them for a while, but my dad insisted I go home and get some rest.

The place I call home is a two-bedroom, garden-style apartment in North Olmsted, and the drive to and from work isn't a long one. Fifteen minutes tops. The apartment that Megan and I picked out wasn't glamourous by any means. It was your basic cookie-cutter apartment with off-white paint and that funky brown carpet that no one ever likes.

Megan and I, both unsatisfied with the look of things, took it upon ourselves to redecorate the apartment, hoping to give it a warmer vibe, something more homey-looking. Megan, who was the real decorator of the two of us, did most of the work. I helped with the shopping and painting.

The apartment as a whole was still a work in progress, but the living room, now covered in soft grays and lavenders, felt comfy yet elegant when you walked in. Our next project was the bathroom and I knew that long hours of picking out paint swatches at Home Depot were in my near future.

When I got inside, my dog, Kikkoman, was waiting for me at the door, her curly black tail wiggling in excitement. Kikko, my black-as-soy-sauce pug, looked up at me, her tongue hanging out of her mouth. She looked as if she were grinning and it forced a smile out of me. At least someone was having a good day.

Megan was sitting on the couch, chatting away on her cell phone. Her blond hair was swept up in a tight ponytail on top of her head and her casual outfit—black T-shirt and skinny jeans—gave me the impression that she was heading to work. She told whoever she was talking to that she had to go and hung up as I was shutting the door.

She looked me up and down, her hazel eyes scrutinizing my appearance. "You look like hell, woman."

"Gee, thanks," I mumbled under my breath.

"What happened today? I texted you a bunch of times and you never responded."

I dug in my purse and pulled out my phone. Five missed text messages. "Oops, sorry."

"I was going to stop by and see you today, but then Nikki called and you know how she can just go on forever. I've been on the phone with her for like three hours talking about her relationship issues with Kyle, and it just went on and on. I swear, she doesn't take a breath sometimes . . . and hey, what are you doing home from work already?" She looked down, checking the time on her phone and back up at me.

I felt my lip quiver, and the tears welling in my eyes. Megan's expression changed from quizzical to concerned and then she said those magic words, *"What's wrong?"* and I burst into tears.

Sitting on the couch with Kikko between us, I went through the whole story from Esther running in to tell my mother the news, to my dad informing us that Mr. Feng died almost right after I saw him, and finally to the body bag being wheeled through the plaza.

Megan, in the meantime, had grabbed a box of tissues and balanced it on her knee. "Wow . . . that's intense. And, kind of scary. I mean, what, the guy was in his fifties, right? Seems so young."

"I know." I sniffled into my tissue. "I keep going back to our conversation, it was so trivial." Kikko put a paw on my leg and huffed as if she sympathized.

"What did you talk about?"

"Dumb stuff, you know? Like, how business was going and did I enjoy working for my parents. That kind of stuff."

Megan nodded. "That's natural though, that's what people normally talk about. It's not like you knew it would be the last time you'd ever see the guy or anything."

I took a fresh tissue from the box. "I just wish I would have said something better."

"Well, you know, hindsight and whatever," she responded, flipping her hand nonchalantly. "We would all say something better if we knew that we weren't going to see someone again. But, most of the time, we don't have that luxury."

"What's even stranger is that Mr. Feng talked about that. About appreciating people while they're still around. Who would have thought he'd be the one that wasn't around anymore?" I thought about his wife and two teenage girls. They'd never get the chance to see their father again. What had their conversations been like the last time they spoke with him?

"So make a change," Megan said matter-of-factly.

"What do you mean?" I wiped a stray tear from my cheek.

She put the tissue box on the coffee table and stood up to face me, hands on her hips. "Life is short; we hear it all the time. So, instead of moping around, let's both take life by the proverbial horns. Let's live and appreciate each other and what we have in our lives. Maybe the loss of Thomas can help shape a new outlook on life."

I knew she was right, but I didn't have it in me at the moment to take on such a positive attitude. "Maybe we can start tomorrow?" I asked, looking up at her.

She let out a heavy sigh. "How about I call in sick from work and we can watch movies?"

"Scary movies?" I asked.

"Sure."

The idea of a movie binge cheered me up a smidge. "I'll get the ice cream."

The following morning, I woke up to what appeared to be another day of mild weather. November in northeast Ohio is hit-or-miss. By this time of year, it had usually started snowing, but sometimes we lucked out with a sprinkling of seventy-degree days throughout the beginning winter months. So far, we'd escaped an early snowfall, but who knew what tomorrow would bring. Content with my light winter jacket, I was keeping my fingers crossed that snow would show up right in time for Christmas . . . and then it could go away again.

The atmosphere upon arriving at Asia Village was extremely somber, and a sadness filled the air. I couldn't bring myself to look up at Mr. Feng's office, so I kept my eyes down and slithered by unnoticed. There were only a few people opening up when I arrived and no one said a word to me as I passed.

I opened the door to the restaurant and locked it behind me; Peter wouldn't be in for another thirty minutes.

On a normal day, the quiet didn't bother me, but the silence was overbearing and I had a sense of loneliness I couldn't quite shake. I turned on the sound system and switched the setting to a rock station, hoping it would lighten the mood.

As I busied myself with the tasks I usually dreaded, like refilling condiment bottles and double-checking the tables for flaws, my mind drifted back to the Feng family. I thought again about their two daughters and couldn't imagine what this whole ordeal was like for them. It made me think about my own life and what it would have been like had one of my parents not been there.

Despite my uneasiness, time flew by as I tidied up the restaurant, and before I knew it Peter was tapping on the glass to get my attention.

"Good morning," I said as I let him in.

"Dude, is it just me, or does it feel like we work in a funeral home today?" He looked back at the plaza, shaking his head. "It's so gloomy out there."

I shrugged, locking the door again. "I think it's going to be that way for at least a few days. His death was so unexpected."

Peter looked away. "Do you know what's going to happen to us?"

"What do you mean?" I asked.

He shrugged. "I don't know, now that Mr. Feng is gone, will his wife take over? Or, do you think it'll be his partner? Ian Sung has always run the residential properties. He doesn't seem very interested in the plaza. You don't think he'll sell the place, do you?"

"I don't know . . . I'm sure Mr. Feng left a will," I said, hoping that was true.

We talked as we walked back into the kitchen. Peter hung up his coat and ran his hands through his hair before putting on his hat. "I hope we don't have to get new jobs."

My eyebrows furrowed. "Worst-case scenario, my parents would find a new property for us to move into. We wouldn't actually shut down for good." The thought was absurd. My parents, especially my mother, loved this place. "Maybe we'd move over to the east side near old Chinatown."

"Yeah, but Asia Village, it's like . . . a staple, man. It's like, so many things are leaving the west side lately. There's too many empty businesses . . ."

"I'm sure everything's going to be fine." I wasn't sure if I said it more for his benefit or my own, but either way, I didn't have time to think about it. I looked up at the clock. "I better get out there and finish prepping the dining room. You know the Mahjong Matrons like to come in for their rice porridge first thing in the morning."

He laughed. "At least one thing in our day will be normal."

As predicted, the Mahjong Matrons—one of the many teams at the Village—were our first customers of the morning. Every day at 9 A.M. sharp, the four widowed women—whom you hardly saw without one another—would come in for the same breakfast of rice porridge, pickled cucumbers, century eggs, and Chinese omelets with chives. While they ate, they enjoyed looking out into the plaza, people-watching and gossiping about anything juicy they could come up with. They were a sassy bunch and some of my very favorite regulars.

I seated them at their usual table by the window. All four women looked somber and lacked the pep they usually brought in with them.

"I'll get your tea, and put your order in, ladies," I told them as they shuffled into the booth.

The smallest one, Opal, looked up at me. "Oh, thank

you, Lana," she said in her soft voice. "This is a sad morning for us, we are grateful for your kindness."

The others nodded and I hurried to the kitchen to get their tea. It was hard to see the four of them so out of sorts.

Breakfast came and went. The Mahjong Matrons barely spoke two words as they picked at their food. The rest of the morning crowd was light and most everyone that came in already had heard the news that Mr. Feng passed away. I tried my best to remain cheerful for their sakes, but whether or not I was successful was another story.

My mother showed up around 11 A.M. and didn't say much as she passed by. She mumbled something about going to look over the books and was gone before I could ask how she was holding up.

A little after noon, I made a cup of tea for her and knocked on her office door. She didn't respond, but I decided to go in anyway. I opened the door a crack and poked my head inside. "Mom?"

"What?" She kept her eyes fixed on the ledger in front of her.

"I brought you some tea." I held up the cup, inching my way through the door. "Do you want me to ask Peter to make you something?"

"No, I am not hungry." She glanced up briefly. "You eat?"

"Yeah, I had some noodles for lunch." I stepped farther into the office, setting the cup of tea on the edge of her desk away from her stack of papers.

She eyed the teacup. "Good."

"Are you okay?" I asked.

"I am sad for Donna," my mother explained. "She is too young to lose her husband this way. Now life will be hard for her, she has two kids and no husband to help her."

"We can help her though." I attempted an upbeat tone, hoping it would rub off on my mother. "She has lots of friends."

She shook her head. "It's not the same, Lana."

"I know . . . I'm just . . . Who do you think will take care of the plaza now?" I asked, thinking about Peter's concern.

My mother looked up at me and the blank expression on her face told me that she hadn't thought of it either. "Maybe Donna . . ."

"What about Ian Sung?" I suggested. "Maybe he'll take over?"

She made a face. "I don't know if he is good for this plaza."

"Why do you say that?"

"Don't worry about it." She reached for the teacup. "You are too young to understand. You just worry about you, take care of yourself."

I sighed. "I'm fine, Mom."

"Yeah, yeah, you always say the same thing, you are fine." She waved her hand with exasperation.

"Well . . . I am," I replied defensively.

"You don't have boyfriend . . ."

I groaned. She liked to remind me of this fact more than necessary. "Mom . . . I don't need a boyfriend to be fine. I'm perfectly fine alone."

"You can't be alone all the time."

"Don't worry about it. Being single is no big deal."

"You need to be more like your sister. If you were more like your sister, I wouldn't worry." She said this as if it were common sense.

"She doesn't have a boyfriend either. How come you don't nag her about the same thing?"

"She's busy with her schoolwork. When she is done, she will be a lawyer. Then she can worry about a boyfriend. You are not that busy."

"I had a boyfriend, who was a jerk, remember?" I cringed at the memory of finding my ex-jerk strolling through the mall with his "other" girlfriend. "I need some time by myself to clear my head."

"You clear your head for nine months now. Mommy can pick a good boyfriend for you to marry one day." She pointed at herself. "You are getting too old to keep waiting."

"Mom! I'm twenty-seven . . . Anna May is thirty! How am I the old one?"

"That is different . . . she is busy . . ."

"Yeah, busy with her schoolwork. Isn't she just so great?" My voice rose an octave. "Well, you know what?"

My mother looked at me expectantly, daring me to challenge her.

"Never mind. I gotta go check on the front." I shut the door behind me and stomped through the kitchen.

Before I even had a chance to cool down, I realized there were customers waiting for me. Or, at least, that's what I thought until I made my way to the hostess station. Two men stood waiting for me in the front lobby. One was drop-dead gorgeous and looked to be in his mid-thirties with eyes that reminded me of vibrant jade.

And the other was a borderline attractive man in his early forties with thin lips. The handsome one, standing a little bit in front of the other man, looked around absorbing the room, almost as if he were cataloging everything in sight. Aside from being cute, he was well dressed in a dark blue suit and matching tie. His short reddish-brown hair was slicked back and the color complemented the green of his eyes.

He noticed me approaching the podium and our eyes locked on each other for a brief moment. I could feel the heat rising in my cheeks as a thought leaped through my mind. Now him . . . I wouldn't mind making *him* my boyfriend . . .

"Excuse me, miss?" His voice was deep and gravelly; there was no smile on his face or in his voice. The way he watched me made my hands tingle. I hadn't experienced such an intensity since . . . well, okay, I was having a hard time focusing right now. But it had definitely been a long time, if ever.

My voice struggled to find itself. "Yes, can I help you?"

"We need to speak with the owners." He looked behind me toward the back of the restaurant. "Are they here?"

"My mother is here. Is there a problem?"

He handed me a business card without saying another word. It read: DETECTIVE ADAM TRUDEAU, FAIRVIEW PARK POLICE DEPARTMENT.

I looked up at him, confused. "Is everything okay?"

His partner stood next to him with his hands folded in front of him. He didn't offer an explanation and he wasn't smiling either.

"I think it would be best if I spoke with your mother first, miss."

"I can take you to the back." I pointed to the kitchen door. "She's in her office."

He nodded and the two men followed behind me as I led them through the dining room. I felt like I was being escorted on a death march. The air hung heavy with tension and my mind raced with such potential disasters as unstoppable fires, public shootings, and fatal car crashes.

As we passed through the kitchen, Peter watched us, a question mark on his face. *Who the hell are they?* he asked with his eyes.

I shrugged and opened the door to the back room. Whatever was going on, my mother was not going to be happy.

After I introduced the two men, his partner, the one who hadn't spoken yet, turned to me. "Miss, we need you to go back to your hostess booth for the time being."

Without waiting for me to respond, the two detectives piled themselves into my mother's tiny office and shut the door.

Fifteen minutes later, the two men came out of the kitchen with Peter in tow. He had his head down and refused to look at me. "What the heck is going on?" I asked as they proceeded toward me.

The officers remained stone-faced, neither one of them bothering to answer my question.

As they walked past me, Peter, still with his head down said, "Call my mom and let her know that I'm down at the police station."

Detective Trudeau stopped while his partner and Peter left the restaurant. He looked down at me, the expression on his face all business. "I'm going to need you to come down to the station in a little while."

"For what exactly?" I asked.

"We're looking into the death of the property owner, Thomas Feng, and we'd like to ask you a few questions. Shouldn't take too long."

"I'm not sure how I can—"

"We can discuss it further when you get there," he said, interrupting me. "I already let your mother know that you would need to leave work for the rest of the day. You'll probably need time to wrap up. Can you be there in an hour?"

My mouth went dry and I could feel my teeth sticking to my lips. I nodded without saying anything.

"Good. I'll see you then." He gave a curt nod, and left.

I stood there in a daze for a solid five minutes. What just happened?

The tinkle of the door chimes shook me out of my trance. Charles An from the Painted Pearl, an Asian art store, poked his head in the door. He looked around the empty room. "Is everything okay? I just saw two men leave with Peter." Though his English was good, his accent was thick and he spoke with care.

Shaking my head, I responded, "I'm not sure."

He stepped into the restaurant, letting the door close behind him. He was a short man, and age was heavy on his face. The tan short-sleeved, button-down shirt he had on made him look old-fashioned and kind of washed out. Concern was set in his features as he neared me. "Do you need to sit down?"

"Maybe . . ." I glanced at the hostess stool, and decided he was right. I hoisted myself up, leaning my body weight on the podium.

"Is Peter in some kind of trouble? He did not look so good."

"They didn't say much," I told him. "I have to go down to the police station for questioning. I guess I'll find out more then."

He nodded. "I should not bother you right now. Please let me know if you need anything." With a small bow of his head, he left the restaurant.

I stared at the bells above the door as they slowly stopped swaying back and forth. All I could think was, This can't be real.

CHAPTER
4

About a half hour later, I made it to the police station. I had only passed by, had never had reason to go inside, and I wasn't looking forward to it now.

An attractive-looking woman in uniform greeted me as I walked in, and after I told her who I was, she led me to a room down a hallway where I was instructed to wait for the detective.

I stood near the doorway, tapping my foot, until he came in.

"Have a seat, Miss Lee," he said, gesturing to the chair as he shut the door behind him.

"You can call me Lana." I sat down on the edge of the metal chair. "What is this about, Detective?"

He sat down across from me, placing a pad of paper and pen on the table. "There's been an unfortunate situation that's come up with Thomas Feng's death." He stared at me as he said it.

I matched his stare. "What type of situation?"

"From what I understand, you were working the day of the incident, along with Peter Huang. Is that correct?"

"Yes, I was there. What type of situation?" I asked again.

The detective pulled a zipped plastic bag out of his pocket and laid it on the table, smoothing it out. He slid it toward me. "Does this look familiar to you?"

Inside the bag was a copy of a takeout receipt from the restaurant. It read: *steamed pork dumplings, chicken and broccoli with white rice, and one spring roll.* I stared at the receipt, my mind spinning in a million directions. It was Mr. Feng's receipt, he ordered the same thing every week so it was forever ingrained in my memory.

"Do you recognize this?" Detective Trudeau asked again.

I nodded and looked up at him in confusion. "Yes, this is the receipt that we staple to the takeout bags. But I don't understand why—"

He scribbled a note on his pad. "Miss Lee, were you aware that Thomas Feng had severe allergies to shell-fish?"

"Lana," I reminded him. "And yes, everyone in the plaza knows that."

"So that would imply that Mr. Huang is also aware of this same fact?" His tone went rigid as he questioned me about Peter.

"Yes . . ." I could hear the intimidation in my own voice.

"And are you aware that the dumplings you delivered

were not actually pork dumplings like it says on the receipt? The ones you delivered contained shrimp in them. Were you aware of that?"

I think my eyebrows must have touched. "Excuse me? Can you say that again?"

"The dumplings you delivered to Thomas Feng . . . had shrimp in them." He paused. "This caused Mr. Feng to go into anaphylactic shock."

"That's impossible!" I protested, leaning forward against the table. "There's no way that anyone at our restaurant would ever dream of giving Mr. Feng anything with shellfish of any kind."

He scribbled on his pad. "So, you're saying that you were not aware that the bag you brought him contained shrimp dumplings and not pork dumplings?"

"Of course not!" I screeched. "The dumplings I brought him were most certainly not shrimp dumplings."

He jotted down another note. "I can assure you, Miss Lee, that Thomas Feng did have shrimp in his stomach contents. And I can also assure you that the dumplings in the takeout container had shrimp in them." He stopped writing and looked up at me. "Is it a possibility that you accidentally picked up the wrong to-go order?"

"No, Peter handed me the order." I folded my arms over my chest. "Besides, Mr. Feng's orders are always specially marked. We use different cookware for him and everything."

"Is it possible that Mr. Huang made a mistake and put the wrong order in the bag?" he suggested. His pen hovered over his notebook, waiting for my reply.

"No," I said with resolution. "Peter is without a doubt

one of the most meticulous people I have ever worked with. There is no way that he would make that kind of mistake."

"Accidents can happen," he replied.

I stood my ground and refused to argue the point. I stared back at him, waiting for him to ask a different question.

"Were you aware of any verbal altercations between Thomas Feng and Peter Huang?"

"Verbal altercations?" I repeated.

His lips pursed. "Yes, verbal altercations. You know, did you hear them arguing at any point in the recent past?"

My eyes narrowed and I could feel my nostrils start to flare. "I know the meaning of verbal altercations, Detective. And no, I was not aware of any verbal altercations between the two of them."

Again, he scribbled on his notepad, flipping the page carelessly and then continuing to scribble some more.

My body tensed in the chair. "Detective," I started. "Can you please tell me what exactly this is all about? Why did you need me to come down here? Am I being accused of something?"

The detective put down his pen and folded his hands neatly in front of him. "Right now we're just asking a few simple questions to figure out what exactly happened that day."

"These don't seem like simple questions."

"Trust me when I say that they could be a lot more difficult." His expression remained flat.

"Are you saying that Mr. Feng was murdered?" By the time it came out of my mouth, I wished I hadn't said it.

He closed his eyes for a few seconds. In his head, I imagined him counting to ten. "On Tuesday afternoon, Thomas Feng died from anaphylactic shock caused by an allergic reaction. Originally, the coroner had assumed it was an accident, but when I went to talk with Mrs. Feng, she assured me that her husband would do no such thing. He was very careful with his allergies and always carried an EpiPen with him."

I nodded. "I remember seeing one in his shirt pocket when I dropped off the food. He did have it."

He scribbled that down in his notebook and then looked up at me. "No EpiPen was found on him or in the office. The death is being considered suspicious and we're looking into a few things while we wait for the rest of the autopsy results to come back. Can I say conclusively that he was murdered intentionally?" He flattened his hands on the table, spreading out his fingers. "No, but I intend to find out."

"So all of this somehow naturally makes Peter and me the guilty ones?" My voice peaked with defensiveness. I was definitely not a killer. And I had known Peter for way too long to ever suspect him of something this horrible.

"Between the receipt and our conversation with Mrs. Feng, we are led to believe this requires a bit more attention. And you and Mr. Huang directly handled the dumplings," he stated. "Like I said, we're checking some things out."

"I see." My shoulders relaxed a little bit. It was just procedure. Just something they had to do while they waited for the rest of the autopsy results. This whole mix-up would be behind us before we knew it. Then why did I feel so bad?

"Can you tell me if anything out of the ordinary happened that day?" He picked up his pen and positioned it back on the paper.

"Like what?"

"Was Peter acting strangely, or did he seem angry about anything?" The detective gestured with his hands as he spoke.

I shook my head. "Nothing that I can think of . . ." I stopped myself and thought back to that day.

The look on my face must have given me away because the detective said, "Miss Lee, if you know something . . ."

"It's nothing really," I said. When the detective refused to stop giving me the look of death, I continued. "I don't normally deliver the takeout orders, that's all. And that day, Peter asked me to deliver Mr. Feng's food so he could keep cooking. He was working on a big rush order that just came in for another takeout request."

The detective scribbled away. "Did he deliver that order himself?" He glanced up at me. "Or did you deliver that one as well?"

I sat silently, inspecting my fingernails. I knew that what I would tell him next wasn't going to sound good.

"Miss Lee . . . Lana . . ." Detective Trudeau urged.

"Like I said before . . ."

"No," I mumbled.

"No?"

I shook my head. "I didn't deliver that order."

He stared at me. "So, Mr. Huang delivered it himself?"

"I'm not sure," I mumbled.

"So you're saying that it's possible the other order was never delivered?" His pen flew across the paper.

"Well, I'm not really sure. I didn't think anything of it at the time."

"That's all right, I've requested that day's order slips from your mother. I just haven't had a chance to go through them." He jotted down another note and closed the pad. "I think that's all for today, Miss Lee."

"But . . ." I started to say.

"Thank you, Miss Lee," he said, dismissing me. "If I think of anything else, I'll be in touch."

We both stood up, our eyes never leaving the other. He studied my face as if he were trying to figure out whether or not I was a killer. He blinked, looking away, and gestured toward the door. "I'll walk you out."

He followed me out, leading me the way I came in. I left without saying anything more, a pit at the bottom of my belly. I held my stomach as I got into the car. Deep breaths, Lana, deep breaths. Everything was going to be fine. Right?

I drove back to Asia Village to meet my mother at the restaurant. She'd instructed me to come back after I left the police station so I could tell her what happened. I found her sitting in the dining area, staring off into space.

"Mom . . ." I whispered. She seemed deep in thought, and I didn't want to startle her.

Her head turned slightly, but she didn't respond.

"There's no way that—"

"I know you did not do this . . ." She slowly turned to face me, and I could see the worry etched in her eyes. "Lana . . . this is big trouble for us."

"But no one can seriously believe that anybody here would do something like that. It wasn't me, and it definitely wasn't Peter. He's not that kind of person." I stopped. "You don't believe it, do you?"

"No, but Donna thinks so," my mother replied.

"Why? How could she think that?" I sat across from my mother. "What has ever happened to make Donna think that Peter had a problem with Mr. Feng?"

She looked away. "People will surprise you, Lana. When they are hurt, they will blame anybody for anything. Remember that."

CHAPTER
5

It felt like an eternity since the morning and my mother decided she wanted to eat after all. Since everything was still on in the kitchen, she did what she did best when her mind was heavy and cooked us a feast. To the corner booth, she brought out a large bowl of white rice, spinach sautéed in garlic and sesame oil, a Chinese omelet with extra scallions, a pan-fried fish that still had its head (yuck), fried tofu, turnip cakes, wonton soup, and a plate of Shanghai noodles with ground pork. By the looks of it, you'd think there was more than just the two of us having lunch.

While we were eating, Megan showed up at the door and tapped on the glass, waving me over. She pointed at the door with a confused look on her face. "What's the deal with the door?" Megan asked as I let her in. She glanced around the empty restaurant. "Did you guys close early again?"

My mother stood to greet her. "You look too skinny," she said, giving her a once-over. "You work too hard."

Megan hugged my mom. "You can never be too skinny," Megan teased. "I started working out last month and I've been trying to get your daughter to come with me." She gave me a sideways glance. "But she keeps fighting me on it."

My mother snorted. "Ha! Lana, exercise?"

"Hey!" I protested. "I'm right here."

Megan elbowed me and winked. "Well, I just came by to see how you were doing." Turning to my mother, she said, "And to tell you that I was sorry to hear about Mr. Feng. I didn't know him well, but he seemed like he was a very nice man."

My mother nodded solemnly. "Thank you, Megan, he was a good friend. I will miss him very much."

"So what's the deal with the lack of business?" Megan pointed toward the front. "And the locked door?" She checked her cell phone. "It's not even three o'clock yet."

"We have more trouble now," my mom said, returning to her seat.

I sighed. "Come sit with us and have some lunch. I'll tell you all about it." I started from the top and worked my way through all the events that had happened up until I got back to the plaza a half hour ago.

When I was done, Megan let out a deep sigh and sat back in her seat. "That's pretty crazy. Does this guy even know what he's talking about? I mean, it's Peter . . . and you . . . you're uncomfortable hanging up on telemarketers. Not exactly murderer material."

I nodded in agreement. "I know, that's what I said.

The whole thing doesn't make any sense, but supposedly Peter and Mr. Feng got into a 'verbal altercation,'" I said, using sarcastic air quotes. The more I thought about it, the madder I got. What a ridiculous accusation.

"He's probably jumping the gun . . . he's probably some young guy who doesn't know what he's doing. Was he a young guy?" Megan asked. "I bet he was a young guy."

"Maybe mid-thirties? It was hard to tell . . ." I said, picturing the detective in my head. "He was attractive though. Nice eyes . . ." I responded absently as I piled more noodles onto my plate. Being questioned by the police sure worked up my appetite.

Megan's eyes narrowed. "He was attractive?"

"Yeah," I said.

"He was very handsome," my mom said matter-of-factly. "The young one. The older one did not look as nice."

We both looked at my mother with surprise.

Megan turned back to me. "Nice eyes?"

"Yes . . ." My chopsticks stopped in midair. I eyeballed her. "Are we deaf today?"

She clucked her tongue at me. "No, it's just that this is the first time you've said anyone's been attractive since—"

"Don't." I held up my index finger, pointing at her. "Don't say his name."

My mother looked at me and then back at Megan, noodles hanging out of her mouth as she watched our exchange.

She held up her hands defensively. "I wasn't. I was going to say 'since jerk face.'"

"Oh. Well, yeah, 'jerk face' is fine."

"So you like this detective then?" Megan prodded. "Even though he thinks you and Peter might have offed someone?" A perfectly penciled brow rose at the end of her question.

My mother snorted. "No, Lana is clearing her head."

"Mom!"

My mother shrugged.

Megan rolled her eyes. "That again?"

I set my chopsticks down on my plate. "Are you guys ganging up on me?"

Neither one of them answered me. My mother looked down, suddenly very interested in her noodles. Megan stirred the soup in her bowl, focusing on the one wonton still floating around.

"Well?" I asked, waiting for one of them to respond.

Megan cleared her throat. "Well, I think you need a night out after everything that's been going on, and you can*not* possibly sit in the house and mope another night. So . . ." She chanced a peek at me. "You should come to the Zodiac tonight. I have to bartend until close and some of the guys will be there. You'll forget everything that's going on."

"I don't think I can tonight," I said, picking up my chopsticks. "I'm just not in the mood to be social."

"You shouldn't sit at home by yourself either. What's that going to do?" she asked, her courage clearly restored. "Plus, maybe if you talk about it, you'll feel better."

I gave an apologetic smile. "I'm going to sit this one out, okay? Maybe tomorrow night . . ."

She pushed her empty soup bowl aside. "Fine, suit

yourself. If you change your mind, you know where to find us. Drinks are on me if you decide to show up."

After Megan left, my mother said, "Tomorrow, you and Anna May will go see Donna at her house, okay? Bring egg rolls or something nice for her."

"Aren't you coming?"

"I already talked to her by myself."

"Mom . . . what if she says something about Peter? Or me?" I asked. "I don't know what to say."

"Just let your sister talk. She is good at that."

Pfft. Yeah, she had that right.

By the time I left the restaurant, I was in full-blown tizzy mode. Something about the way Megan had questioned me about Detective Trudeau was nagging at me. "He thinks I offed someone," I said out loud to myself in the car. How absurd. As if I were some sort of casual killer . . . as if Peter and I plotted to get Mr. Feng out of the way for our own selfish purposes. And what purposes would those even be exactly? Had the detective even thought of that?

I squeezed the steering wheel, the heat rising in my cheeks. No, I couldn't let myself or Peter get blamed for something we weren't responsible for.

Parking the car outside of my apartment, I took a deep breath and nodded with resolve. If that meant I had to figure this out myself, then so be it. I'd start tomorrow . . . a fresh day. Tomorrow had to be better. They even made a song about it. The sun comes out and all that junk.

CHAPTER
6

"Looks like someone else is here," Anna May said, parking behind a silver Honda Accord in the Fengs' driveway.

"I think that's Kimmy Tran's car," I said, recognizing the beat-up car from the plaza parking lot.

Anna May flipped down her car visor and opened the mirror, dabbing at her lipstick. I watched as she primped. We didn't really look alike, but you could tell we were related. My sister's face was flat and oval shaped, and mine was more pronounced and round. Her lips were on the thinner side and when she smiled I swear you could see every tooth she had in her mouth. My nose has a good bridge and I'm pretty sure that comes from my dad.

And even though Anna May was only three years older than me, she looked like it was about ten. But not in a bad way or anything; I chalked it up to her conservative fashion sense and the way she carried herself. Meanwhile, I still got carded at bars.

"Can you grab the egg rolls from the backseat? I'll carry the flowers," she said, inspecting the pale taupe shadow on her eyelid. She gave her long hair a good toss, and we both reached in the backseat to grab our respective items.

No matter what culture, food is always an important staple when someone is grieving, so we brought a platter of homemade egg rolls. Along with that, my sister chose a bouquet of white orchids, a symbol of respect.

The Fengs lived in a massive house in Westlake, a few cities over from Asia Village. To say that their house and land was sprawling is not an overstatement.

We walked up the long drive to their oversized brick Colonial, though to me, it looked like a mansion. As we walked up the stone steps to the front door, I wondered to myself if Mrs. Feng would be able to take care of all this property on her own. Maybe they had "people" for that. It's not like they were hurting for money or anything.

Anna May rang the doorbell and we only had to wait a few seconds before someone opened the door. A short Asian woman with graying hair in a tight bun looked up at us, caution on her face.

"Can I help you?" she asked, her accent thick.

"We're here to pay our respects," my sister said pleasantly.

"Everyone is in the living room. You can go there." She stepped back from the door to let us pass. After she shut the door, she disappeared up the staircase without another word.

When we reached the living room, Mrs. Feng stood up with a sorrowful smile. For a widow, she still looked beautiful. Donna Feng was dressed to the nines at all times. I admired a woman who looked her best no matter the circumstances. She was decked out in a bold blue pantsuit and nude high heels. Her hair was wrapped in a French twist, not a hair out of place. She greeted us both with a hug. "Oh, the Lee girls, it's so nice of you to come." Like her clothing, her English was immaculate. It was a far cry from the broken English my mother and most of her friends spoke.

After we all hugged, Kimmy Tran and her mother, Sue, rose to greet us. Kimmy stood slightly behind her mother looking annoyed. I'm sure that my assessment was spot-on after the way she had acted the other day. She wasn't exactly Mr. Feng's biggest fan. I didn't know how long they'd been there, but Kimmy still had her coat on and looked like she was ready to run out the door any second.

"I see you met my mother," Mrs. Feng said, looking toward the hallway. "You'll have to forgive her for not joining us, she isn't much for strangers."

My sister smiled politely. "I hope we're not disturbing you at a bad time."

"Nonsense!" Mrs. Feng batted a hand as if to wave off the idea. "And look at these flowers! They're just beautiful." She took the vase out of Anna May's hands and held the flowers up to her nose. "Orchids are my absolute favorite."

"It was the least we could do," my sister replied. "We're so sorry about Thomas."

Mrs. Feng gave a tight-lipped smile. "Yes, I wish these flowers were for different circumstances. It's hard to believe that he's gone."

I held up the tray of egg rolls like a proud five-year-old in art class. "We brought some food too."

"Oh, you girls are just so thoughtful. Your mother raised you right." She took the egg rolls from me with her free hand and turned to walk away.

"Mrs. Feng . . ." I said, stopping her before she could walk away. "I just wanted you to know that . . ."

She turned around, a gentle smile on her face. "Lana, darling, I hope that you're not blaming yourself for anything. As far as I'm concerned, you could never harm a fly. I know without a doubt in my mind that you couldn't have possibly known what was in that bag."

I took what felt like a first breath since I walked in the door.

"If anyone is to blame, it's that Peter Huang." She shook her head in disapproval, her face hardening. "That boy is trouble. I'll never understand why your mother decided to hire him." She paused. "Well, I'm sure she did it as a favor to Nancy. That woman could never control her own affairs."

"I don't think that Peter would do anything to hurt Mr. Feng . . . or anybody."

"Well, we'll see about that when the coroner's report comes back with the full results."

We stood in an awkward silence for a moment. I felt marginally better about myself, at least. But now I worried about Peter's fate considering how convinced Mrs. Feng seemed to feel about his guilt.

Mrs. Feng switched gears and put on a bright smile. "I'm just going to put these things in the kitchen and I'll be right back."

While we'd been talking, Kimmy and her mother had

returned to the love seat, and by the placement of the teacup in front of the couch, I assumed Mrs. Feng was sitting there. I chose the chair off to the side and let my sister sit by Mrs. Feng.

Sue smiled, her plump cheeks rising underneath her eyes. She gestured to the teapot resting on a delicate blue and white porcelain platter. "Would you like some tea?"

My sister and I nodded and Sue poured two cups, handing one to each of us.

"How is business at the noodle shop?" Sue asked, turning to me. "I've been meaning to come see your mother, but I haven't had the time."

"It's going pretty good," I replied. "It's starting to pick up now that the holidays are right around the corner."

"We've been slow at the video store." Sue looked down at her tea. "Too slow."

"My mom had to get a second job delivering newspapers," Kimmy added. A hint of bitterness touched her words.

Sue clucked her tongue. "Kimmy, you don't need to tell everyone our business."

"Oh, Mom, who cares?" Kimmy said, rolling her eyes. "It's not like they're strangers."

Mrs. Feng came back and took her place next to my sister. "What did I miss?"

"Nothing important," my sister replied, beating the others to the punch. "Just business at the plaza."

"Oh, the plaza. Thomas did love that place . . ." Mrs. Feng sighed. "Asia Village was his pride and joy. It won't be the same without him. He'd dreamed about building an Asian shopping center ever since he was young."

"What's going to happen to the plaza now that Mr. Feng is gone? Are you still going to raise the rent?" Kimmy blurted out.

"Kimmy!" Sue gasped. "You shouldn't ask Mrs. Feng about that right now!"

"It's okay, Susan," Mrs. Feng answered good-naturedly. "I'm not sure yet, Kimberly. Thomas left instructions in his will on how he wanted things handled, but I haven't reviewed it with our lawyer just yet. There's so much to be done," she said wearily. "But I've never heard any talk about increasing the rent prices. It might be something he discussed with Ian."

"My parents can't afford a rent increase or we'll lose the shop. Then you'll have another empty storefront on your hands."

"Kimmy!" Sue set down her teacup. "Donna, I'm so sorry."

"No, no, Susan, it's really all right. Grief is different for young people. I understand."

My sister and I gave each other a look from across the coffee table.

"I think we should get going," Sue said to the group, her face a bright shade of pink.

"Really, please don't feel that you have to go," Mrs. Feng replied gently. "The Lee girls have just arrived."

Sue looked at her watch. "I should get back to the shop anyway. Daniel needs to get to his other job soon."

Kimmy stormed out without saying anything more and the rest of us just looked at each other, unsure of how to react. I set down my teacup and rose. "I'll just go check on her while you say your good-byes."

I found Kimmy outside, leaning against her car, staring out into the street. She'd lit a cigarette and puffed deeply on it. As I approached her, she glanced at me, smirking. "Sorry. I get so mad when my mom brings up business. She doesn't want people to know we're struggling, but then she goes on and on about it behind closed doors. Then I'm the bad guy because I'm not willing to sugarcoat things."

I leaned against the car next to her. "It's that bad?"

"Sales keep dropping and I have no idea how to help them." She took a long drag of her cigarette and let the smoke float lazily through her lips. "Both of my parents are working second jobs now. My mom has been devastated ever since she found out about the rent increase. We can't afford fifteen percent added to our rent. That's why I went to see him the other day. I wanted to convince him that he was making a mistake."

I remembered how angry she'd been that day. And even though she was clearly still mad about it, a part of her looked defeated.

As if on cue, she looked down at the ground. "I don't know what more can be done."

"I wonder how my parents will take the news. I mean, we're not doing too bad, but fifteen percent could really hurt us."

"Tell me about it. Meanwhile, look at this house." She jerked her head toward the Fengs' stately home. "Makes you wonder what they need the extra money for."

"I guess so."

She turned to me, smoke blowing in my direction.

"By the way, sorry all of this is falling on you and your family. You've always been good people. I saw the police leave with Peter yesterday."

I frowned. "You saw that, huh?"

"Oh yeah, I'm pretty sure the entire plaza saw Peter leave with the police." She shook her head. "How embarrassing for him."

"I know he didn't do anything. He doesn't have that kind of hatred in him." I looked back at the house, thinking about the anger I saw on Mrs. Feng's face as she'd talked about Peter. "Whatever may have happened between them, Peter would never do something that terrible."

"Listen, I wouldn't worry about it too much. There's nothing you can do about it."

That's where she was wrong. There *was* something I could do about it, but I wasn't going to tell her that.

She tapped her lip with the butt of her cigarette. "But if they think someone killed him then they should really look at his enemies . . . you know? People he's wronged."

My ears perked up. "People he's wronged?"

"Yeah, like I said to you the other day, he was going to make the wrong person mad."

"Are you thinking of anyone in particular?" After all, it couldn't hurt to pick her brain for ideas.

"Like poor Mr. An. He can't afford his rent either and I know for a fact he loves that store. It was really important to him to be a part of Asia Village. Especially after everything he's been through."

Mr. An and the Painted Pearl were fairly new to the plaza. He'd opened up about a year ago and at first he'd done really well. But, as time went on, he had fewer and fewer customers. He seemed like a nice enough man, so I couldn't really see him being capable of murder.

What Kimmy said was true though. He was closing his shop and from what I'd heard around the plaza, he'd thrown a full-sized tantrum over it. Now his front windows were covered with posters promising bargains for the store closing. From the looks of it, his sales hadn't helped much.

"What do you mean? What has he been through?"

She leaned forward off the car. "I heard my mother gabbing with the Mahjong Matrons about Mr. An and his big falling-out with someone or other . . . something to do with a woman, I think. So the store is really important to him, you know? Probably keeps his mind busy."

I looked at Kimmy skeptically. "You really think Mr. An would be capable of something like that . . . over a store?"

Kimmy nodded. "Without a doubt. The poor guy has to move his shop to one of those kiosks in a mall." She stared at me. "A kiosk, Lana. How do you even sell art properly from a kiosk? What a slap in the face."

"But he seems so nice," I pointed out. "I can't see him being the vindictive type."

"If you push people far enough . . ." She tilted her head. "Yeah, forget all the other stuff, just taking away someone's livelihood, that's enough to piss anyone off. If you ask me, I can't think of a better reason to kill somebody."

Before I could respond, Sue came outside with my sister. Kimmy flicked her cigarette across the yard and opened her car door. "See you around, Lana."

Anna May and I stood in the driveway and watched

them drive off. As their car disappeared around the corner, my sister turned to me and said, "Boy, she's turned out to be an angry little thing, hasn't she?"

I didn't do it often, but I couldn't help but agree with my sister.

CHAPTER
7

I woke up to Kikko staring at me. She was about five inches away from face, and when I opened my eye a sliver, she placed her paw square on my nose and grunted. I grunted in return and rolled over. It couldn't possibly be time to get up already. It was still dark outside.

Kikko continued to paw at my back, and with a giant sigh, I sat up in bed and looked at the clock. Crap. It was time to get up.

After walking the dog and starting up the coffee-maker, I found my way into the shower and stood under the warm water until my toes turned red. Our morning walk had been crisp, to say the least. Today was going to be a struggle. I could feel the weight of the past couple of days bearing down on my shoulders. Figures . . . here I'd thought that things were finally going back to normal.

I couldn't stop thinking about Mrs. Feng or the

expression on her face when she talked about Peter. And what about Mr. An? He'd been a regular at lunch a few days a week since his shop moved in, but since Nancy usually waited on him, I didn't know much about him. I knew he was soft-spoken and not entirely social. I'd never heard anything troubling about him until the announcement of his store closing. Even then, I didn't actually see any of it myself. The gossip mill worked double time at the plaza most days. The Mahjong Matrons were usually in the thick of it, and since I saw them first thing every morning, I'd hear things before everyone else did.

Megan was still sleeping when I left for work, so I stuck a Post-it note on the fridge telling her I'd be home around six.

The plaza parking lot was fairly empty when I pulled in and I found a decent spot in the employee parking area. As I got out of my car, I saw Ms. Yi, who ran Yi's Tea and Bakery with her twin sister. I smiled and waved a good morning. In a quick movement, she turned her nose up at me and turned away, hurrying inside. Okay . . . someone was grouchy this morning. Not that either of the Yi sisters were particularly pleasant people, but they were usually at least civil.

My usual morning routine flew by. After I'd gotten home last night and updated my mother on my and Anna May's trip to the Feng house, she informed me that Peter would be taking some time off and our night cook, Lou, would be filling in most of the mornings. My mother would work the evenings and Anna May would fill in whenever she was free.

It's not that I didn't like Lou . . . he just bugged me.

He was kind of a pain and his cooking wasn't as good as Peter's. But my mom liked him well enough, so I had to suffer with the adjustment until Peter came back to work. I asked my mother why she couldn't work in the morning instead. She laughed for about ten minutes.

There was a loud rap at the door, and I jumped, nearly dropping the handful of chopsticks I was holding. When I turned to see who was there, a bundled-up Lou stared back at me, waving eagerly with a gloved hand.

"Good morning, Lana!" Lou said with an overabundance of cheerfulness. He took his gloves off and ran a hand over his slicked-back hair.

I looked up at the clock; it was only eight-fifteen. "Morning," I replied. "You know we don't open until nine, right?"

His puffy black jacket rustled as he walked past me. "Nine sharp," he answered, tapping his watch. "I like to get an early start."

I watched him scurry into the kitchen. Great. A morning person. I could already tell this wasn't going to go well.

Nancy Huang walked in a little before noon with a pitiful look on her face. Under her normally cheerful eyes sat big black circles and her skin, which was usually milky and bright, looked ashen.

Aside from Esther, she is the only other Taiwanese friend that my mother has, therefore making the three of them the best of friends. Nancy had taken on the midday shift several years ago as a temporary solution to my mother's lack of employees at the time. But they had both enjoyed her working there so much, Nancy dropped her other job as a seamstress to work for my mother full-time. I liked having her around and considered her to be "the cool aunt."

Seeing her so unlike herself gave me a sharp pang in the bottom of my gut. Peter was all she had and I could hardly imagine what it was like for her to watch him go through something like this.

When I talked with my mother about Peter taking some time off, she didn't go into details about why or how long. Peter and I hadn't talked and I didn't know what was said to him at the station. I wanted to reach out, but I felt like I should give him some time first.

I met Nancy at the hostess booth and gave her a hug. "I'm so sorry."

"Thank you, Lana." She gave me a light squeeze as she returned the hug. "I don't know what to do," she whined. "Peter said he doesn't want to talk to anyone right now. How can I help him if he won't talk to me?"

Releasing her from the hug, I took a step back and looked her square in the eye. "Why did you come in today? Me and Mom could have handled your shift."

She half smiled in a brave sort of way, and shook her head. "It's better to work. I didn't want to sit at home any-more. If he won't talk to me, there's nothing I can do."

"What's going on exactly?"

Her eyes began to well up. "He would not tell me much. Just the way that the detective was talking to him sounded like he was guilty." She sniffed back her tears. "Peter thinks he's going to need a lawyer."

I sighed. "Do you know of any reason why Peter and Mr. Feng would get in an argument?"

She looked up at me from under her eyelashes and it reminded me of a Precious Moments doll. She shook her head. "I don't know. I don't know what's going on. Why would Donna blame him?"

"Have you talked to her at all?" I asked. "She seems to think that Peter and Mr. Feng got in a fight about something. That's why I'm asking."

Nancy stared at the floor. "I don't know what they would fight about . . ."

The bells above the door jingled, and in walked Esther, a vision of floral glory. Despite the bright outfit she had on that included a teal blouse covered in cherry blossoms, her expression was grim. She approached the hostess podium and assessed me and Nancy. "Lana, stand up straight. You will grow up crooked old woman."

I rolled my eyes and straightened my back. Esther had been guiding me on these particular odds and ends since I was a little kid. Once when I was five she gave me an entire lecture on the importance of crossing your legs and being a lady. I considered her the "strict aunt."

She turned to Nancy. "Ai-ya, why did you come to work today?"

Nancy replied to her in Cantonese, of which I knew none. My mastery of Hokkien, the Taiwanese dialect my family spoke, was shaky from lack of use and my Mandarin was starting to fizzle out of my brain. I swear my mother and her friends spoke Cantonese just to keep secrets from me and my sister.

The two women exchanged a look I couldn't interpret, and then Esther turned to me. "Where is Mommy?"

"She's in the back room."

Esther looked at the kitchen door, and then turned to

us. "I talked to Donna this morning, there is no funeral for everyone."

Nancy gasped. "Why not?"

"Donna did not say," Esther answered. "She will have a dinner next weekend."

"A dinner?" I asked.

She nodded. "Yes, the whole plaza will have dinner together and some people will say nice things about Thomas. Everyone must go."

"Like a memorial?"

"Yah, yah, yah," she replied, nodding vigorously. "We have dinner together as family." Esther gestured to the back room and headed in search of my mother.

Nancy and I stood together, speechless. Despite this surprising news of Donna's decision, I felt okay about it. Funerals always made me uncomfortable. I never knew where to stand, who to look at, or if I should smile. You want to be polite, but at the same time, it's not like you're there for a good time. Best just to avoid the whole thing. But it was the Feng family, nonetheless, and the rest of us Asia Villagers were used to their pomp and circumstance.

"Why would Donna choose to do this?" Nancy asked, her eyes welling up again. "Thomas was very important to the community. Many people will want to pay their respects."

I shrugged. "I don't know. Maybe she was worried that it would become a circus or something."

Nancy cocked her head at me. "A circus?"

"Yeah, you know, too many people would come and make it crazy." Sometimes I forgot when talking to my mother's friends that they wouldn't always catch collo-quialisms. "Like newspeople or things like that."

She seemed to think on it a minute and then slowly started to nod. "Oh, okay, I see now." She shifted her weight. "Can you wait a few minutes for your lunch break, so I can talk with Esther and your mother?"

"Sure, go ahead. I'm in no rush."

To keep my mind off my growling stomach, I checked on the few patrons who were finishing up their lunch and cashed out a couple of tables. It had been a decent morning and there was a nice chunk of change in my apron pocket. Since Lou was in the back cooking, I decided to take my freshly made tip money and splurge on lunch elsewhere.

When I got up front to the podium, I noticed Kimmy walking past the restaurant staring through the window. I waved, but she just kept walking. After a few seconds, she walked by again, still staring, but going in the opposite direction.

What the heck was that girl doing?

I came around from behind the podium and walked to the door, peeking out in the direction she'd gone. Just as I was about to open the door to get a better view, she popped up in front of me and we both jumped, yelling at the same time.

"Kimmy!" I held my palm over my heart. "What are you doing?"

Looking just as startled and irritated as I was, she asked, "Have you read the *Plain Dealer* today?"

I had given up on the news long ago. There are only so many terrible stories of crime and death that you can read before you finally have to throw in the towel. I shook my head, stepping away from the door to let her in.

She handed over the rolled-up newspaper she'd been carrying under her arm. "It's in the Metro section."

My eyes went to the place she pointed to with her index finger, and the headline read: LOCAL ASIA VILLAGE PROPRIETOR FOUND DEAD IN OFFICE: MURDER INVESTIGATION ONGOING

I felt light-headed.

"Well . . ." Kimmy nudged. "Read it."

Thomas Feng, property owner and Asian community innovator, was found unresponsive in his office located within Asia Village this past Tuesday, shortly after noon. The Fairview Park Police Department is investigating the death as there appear to be suspicious circumstances. Officers are pursuing potential leads, but little information has been released.

I cringed at the mention of "potential leads" and wondered if that was a reference to Peter and myself.

The article went on from there to talk about the good deeds that Mr. Feng had done for the Asian community since way back when and the people he had befriended throughout the city during that time. There was even a picture of him shaking hands with the mayor of Cleveland.

"Great." I folded the paper back up and handed it over to Kimmy. "So now the whole city knows that his death is being investigated." I sighed.

"I thought you should know, so you can be prepared." She took the paper, hugging it to her chest. "This is going to turn into a media circus, you watch."

I thought about how I'd just mentioned the same thing

to Nancy in the wake of Esther's news. "I wonder if that's why Donna decided to have a private funeral," I said out loud.

Kimmy sneered. "So you heard that too, huh?"

"Yeah, Esther just came and told us a few minutes ago. At least she's having some type of memorial service, I suppose." Even though it seemed like an odd choice for their family, I was still more comfortable with the idea of a dinner. No urns, no caskets . . .

"I guess it makes sense, it's just that . . ." Kimmy paused. A blank look washed over her face.

"It's just what?" I encouraged her to continue.

She shook her head. "I don't know, but leave it to Donna Feng to throw a party when her own husband dies."

At five o'clock, Vanessa Wen traipsed through the door, her apron slung over her shoulder. Sixteen going on twelve, Vanessa had been forced by her parents to get a part-time job to learn responsibility. Of course, wanting a car—and that being her only real motivation—Vanessa agreed. My mom was a sucker for teaching life lessons, so she'd readily agreed to let Vanessa work at the restaurant.

Meanwhile, my hair was graying.

Her long, pin-straight hair—pulled back in a high ponytail—bounced as she shimmied behind the hostess station. "Hey Lana," she said, smacking her gum. "Is it true that you guys poisoned old man Feng?"

I gasped. "What did you just say to me?"

After she stuffed her purse in the cabinet, she turned

to face me. At sixteen, she was already my height. "Everybody in the plaza is talking about it. They're all talking about how Peter left with the cops the other day."

"First, you might want to show some respect for the dead," I lectured. "And second, don't run around talking like that." My eyes slid toward the back of the restaurant. "His mother is in the kitchen and is on the verge of a nervous breakdown."

She held up her hands. "Geez, sorry."

I closed my eyes and took a deep breath, reminding myself I wouldn't look good in prison orange. "Just try and stay out of the drama, okay? We don't need anything to make this worse."

She threw up her hands. "Fine, whatever. I just thought you should know that literally everybody is talking about it. It's turning into a spectacle out there. There's like . . . a team Peter . . . and then . . ." She stopped. "Well . . . you know . . . the others."

"What do you mean?"

"Well, you know. There's some people who think Peter is totally innocent. And then there's some that think Peter is super guilty. And then there's some . . ."

"Some what?" I asked, folding my arms over my chest.

She looked away. "Some that think you were in on it."

I groaned. Hearing this only gave me more reason to get involved. I couldn't let this whole situation tarnish my reputation or that of the restaurant.

"But you weren't, right?" She looked at me from the corner of her eye. "It's not like you're an accomplice or something, right?

"Vanessa!"

She cringed. "Sorry, I'm just asking."

"Of course I had nothing to do with it. And neither did Peter." My stomach clenched. I could only imagine what types of rumors were flying through the plaza among the other shop owners. "Like I said, do *not* say those things to anyone. It's better if you stay out of the whole thing altogether."

"Okay, okay. Sorry, just thought you should know." Her high-shine, glossed lips formed a pout as she turned from me and walked away.

I thought back to my encounter with Ms. Yi from that morning. Was that why she had snubbed me in the parking lot? Did people really believe that I had something to do with Mr. Feng's death? How could people who'd known us for so long believe something like that?

CHAPTER
8

After work, I walked down a few storefronts to Asian Accents, the best nail and beauty parlor in town. It was also a great place to get information. Next to the Mahjong Matrons, the salon heard the most plaza gossip and I needed to find out the scoop from my stylist.

Jasmine's great. She gets me. And she gets my hair. Hair's important to me. It's a statement. Hair and shoes. If you have those two things going on, you're pretty much solid.

I can't tell you the number of bad haircuts I'd gotten before coming to Asian Accents. The whole "being mixed" thing left me with less-than-manageable hair. After I blow-dry my hair, it looks similar to what would happen if you stuck your finger in a socket. Thank God for flatirons and superhold hairspray.

I pulled open the door and a symphony of Chinese pop music mixed with blow-dryers came rushing at me.

The receptionist, Yuna, smiled at me. "Lana! So good to see you, girl!" She beamed at me over her podium. "Jasmine's finishing up with a client . . . it'll be about five minutes. You want anything to drink?"

"Nope, I'm good." I sat down in one of the plastic chairs that lined the wall.

She rested her elbows on the podium and cupped her chin with her palms. "Sucks about Mr. Feng, huh? I feel like . . . I don't know; it always happens to good people like that."

I sucked in a breath, thinking about what Vanessa had said to me earlier, and wondered which story Yuna was siding with and what information she might have already heard.

Without skipping a beat, she asked, "Have you seen Donna at all? She must feel awful. She and Thomas were fighting like cats and dogs a few days before he died." She whispered the last bit.

"You saw them fighting?" I sat a little straighter in my chair.

She shook her head, her enormous hoop earrings swinging with the motion. "No, I overheard them when I was passing by the office. She was crying her eyes out."

That was peculiar. Mrs. Feng wasn't an overly emotional person. Even seeing her at her house the day after everything happened, she was so well put together. But before I could point that out, Jasmine came floating up front with a client in tow.

Obnoxiously beautiful, she is the type of girl you see and know that she must be into cosmetology. "Lana Lee! Give me a freaking hug, girlfriend!" She giggled as she held her arms out and wiggled her fingers.

She wrapped me in a tight hug, my face buried in her reddish-brown locks.

"I'm so glad you kept your appointment," she said with relief. She ran her fingers through the sides of my hair. "You're completely overgrown."

"Why wouldn't I?" I asked her.

"Well, you know." She winked a smoky shadowed eye and nodded in the direction of Mr. Feng's office. "All the talk that's been going on . . ."

The client and Yuna stood watching us, waiting for my response.

Jasmine noticed and grabbed my hand. "Come on, let's get you shampooed." And she dragged me away. "I love Yuna," she whispered. "But she is always gossiping about everything and I can't talk about this stuff in front of her or the whole plaza will know. I shouldn't have even brought it up, but honestly I didn't think they were paying attention."

"Oh, it's okay. I don't know that it matters anymore," I said, defeat dripping in my voice.

She turned to me and frowned. "Why would you say that?"

I sat down in the shampoo chair and let Jasmine cover me in a cutting cape. "When Vanessa came into work today, she told me how everyone in the plaza thinks that Ho-Lee Noodle House is involved with Mr. Feng's death somehow." I didn't feel comfortable coming out and saying specifically myself or Peter. Just on the off chance that Jasmine hadn't heard these theories. No need to put ideas in her head that weren't there yet.

"Lean back . . ." She pushed on my shoulder and I scooted my butt in the chair to stick my head in the sink. "First of all," she said, "don't listen to that girl. She is just as bad as Yuna. The only allowance I give her is that she's still a teenager. They live for this stuff."

"True," I said, considering that fact.

"Second, not *everyone* in the plaza believes those rumors."

"Really?" I asked, hope trying to break through my cloudy disposition.

"Really. I mean, there are a few . . ."

I groaned, closing my eyes.

Jasmine shampooed my hair, rinsed and repeated, adding extra conditioner to help with my hair's coarseness, my lifelong burden. Before I knew it, I was in the styling chair and looking at my reflection. I could see the general sadness all over me. My shoulders were slumped forward and the look on my face spoke of discontent.

She grabbed a plastic comb from her drawer and stared off as she pulled it carefully through my wet hair. "You know what the problem is?"

"Hm?"

"It's that detective. Detective Truman . . . he's your problem."

"Trudeau."

"Oh right, well, whatever his name is, he's your problem right there. He was all over the plaza asking people to come down to the station if they saw or knew anything. It definitely sparked everyone to start talking . . . just not to him."

"Did you talk to him?" I gulped.

She shook her head. "No. I haven't gone yet, but I don't know that I really need to. I mean . . . I don't legitimately know anything."

"So you don't believe the stuff you've been hearing around the plaza?" I asked a little too eagerly.

She grinned in the mirror. "Relax, like I could ever believe for a minute that you're capable of murdering someone. Please. I can't even bring myself to think that way about Peter."

I let out a sigh of relief. "I'm so glad to hear you say that. I don't know why Mrs. Feng would accuse Peter like this." I looked down at my shoes as if they would hold the answer to everything. They didn't.

"There has to be something we don't know."

"The detective asked me if I knew anything about a fight between Peter and Mr. Feng, but honestly, even if they did fight, I can't see Peter killing him over it. Have you heard anything like that?"

"Not that I can remember. I can try and ask around though. It's all anybody's talking about."

I sighed, watching her reflection in the mirror.

Jasmine pursed her lips. "Something doesn't add up." She focused on my hair, sectioning off portions with little jaw clips. "Where the heck was Mr. Feng's EpiPen? Didn't he carry one around with him? You know, just in case something like that should happen?"

I nodded. "He did carry one on him, and I could swear I saw one in his pocket when I brought him his lunch that day. But Detective Trudeau said they didn't find one on him."

"That's kind of weird, don't you think?"

"It was to me."

"And you know what's terrible?" She pointed her tiny comb at my reflection. "Poor Cindy Kwan was the one to find him. What if no one had had a meeting with him that day? How long would he have been there like that?"

I cringed at the thought. "I don't even want to think about that."

Jasmine finished trimming my hair and took a step back to inspect her work. "I wonder how Donna is holding up. From what I heard, they were having problems. I hope they didn't leave things on bad terms."

"Where did you hear that?"

"Yuna, of course."

We were silent while she had the dryer on and it gave me time to think about the things she'd said. I began to wonder if there was more to this than I originally thought. Donna was an expert at pretending that things didn't bother her, so if she and Mr. Feng were having problems, she wouldn't necessarily be a dead giveaway. But what Yuna had said to me about hearing Donna crying still didn't track with her personality. However, that didn't change the fact that she'd heard a woman crying in his office. Something must have made her think it was Mrs. Feng who was in there. I would have to make it a point to talk to Yuna about it before I left.

Jasmine finished drying my hair and started rummaging through her styling products. She appeared thoughtful as she went through cans and tubes of hair goop. "You know, Lana, I bet this whole thing is going to blow over, and once that detective finally gets his head on straight, he's going to see that this has nothing to do with you . . . and hopefully Peter."

I sighed. "I really hope you're right about that."

"It's just too bad about the dumplings being from

your restaurant. In a way, that kind of keeps you in the mix until this whole thing is sorted out."

Yeah, those dumplings. They really did ruin every-thing.

Yuna was at the reception podium finishing up with a customer. After the woman left, Yuna gave me a once-over, nodding with approval. "Looking great, Lana. No purple yet, I see."

I laughed. "No, maybe next time." I pulled my wal-let out of my purse and waited while she rang up my sale. "I have a question for you," I said, handing over my credit card. "Do you have a minute?"

"Sure, what's up?" She slid my card swiftly through the card reader and punched in a few numbers.

"I wanted to talk to you about the . . . situation with Mr. Feng."

Her eyes widened. "Yeah?"

"I was wondering how you knew it was Mrs. Feng that he was arguing with in his office that day."

She shrugged. "I don't know, I guess just because it sounded personal. It didn't seem like you'd have a con-versation like that with someone you barely knew, you know?"

"Could you hear what they were saying?" I asked.

She thought a minute, and then shook her head. "No, mostly I heard the crying, that's what stopped me." She stared at me. "What does it matter anyway?"

"But you never actually saw Mrs. Feng?" I prodded.

"Who else would he be fighting with?" She handed me a receipt and pen.

"Kimmy Tran, maybe?" I suggested.

"The voice sounded older, but I have seen Kimmy in and out of his office a couple of times looking not too happy. One time I saw her and that Mr. An guy come out of Mr. Feng's office and they were both red in the face."

"When did that happen?"

"About a month ago?" she answered, sounding unsure. "They talked with each other for a few minutes outside the office and then went their separate ways. Whatever they were talking about looked pretty intense." She stopped, eyeing me suspiciously. "Is the reason you're asking me all this stuff because of the rumors going around the plaza?"

I sighed, signing the receipt. "It might be."

She shook her head. "I don't believe any of it for a minute. I've known you, like, forever! And Peter is just too much of a pussycat to do anything that awful." She paused. "If you want to know what I think . . ."

"Yeah . . ."

A throat cleared behind me. "Sorry to interrupt, ladies, but I'd like to check in for my appointment."

When I turned around, a tall, well-dressed Asian man with short, spiky hair was standing behind me. He was wearing a burgundy dress shirt, black tie, and an Italian-cut suit jacket. His dark denim jeans probably cost more than anything I owned and his dress shoes looked just as expensive. His face was narrow and his lips were thin, making him look a little sinister as he smiled at us.

"Mr. Sung, so good to see you!" Yuna said from behind me.

Ian Sung, the other property owner, was a young thirty-something who'd landed the partnership based on his father's relationship with Thomas Feng. Prior to his joining Mr. Feng in his business endeavors, he had been some big-shot executive in Chicago. At least that's what I'd heard from the Mahjong Matrons.

"I'm sorry, miss, were you through checking in?" he asked politely.

It snapped me from my trance and I nodded.

He smiled to himself and stepped around me.

"I'll let you get back to work, Yuna," I said over Ian's shoulder.

"No problem, Lana, stop by and see me sometime next week. Maybe we can get tea or something."

"Lana?" Ian repeated, turning around to face me.

"Yes?"

"Lana Lee? From Ho-Lee Noodle House?"

"The one and only."

He extended his hand. "Ian Sung. I'm so glad to finally meet you. I don't believe we've been formally introduced."

I shook his hand. "I don't think so either," I responded. I didn't know Ian aside from the few times I'd passed him in the plaza.

"Do you happen to have some free time during lunch on Monday? I'd like to talk with you if that's possible."

"Sure, would you like to come by for lunch at the noodle house?"

He grinned. "Actually I was thinking we could meet at the Bamboo Lounge, maybe have a drink or two. Around noon?"

I blushcd, feeling Yuna's eyes boring into the back

of my head. "Um, I don't think they open until late afternoon . . ."

"I'm sure they'll make an exception for me." He seemed to relish that for a minute. "See you Monday then?"

"Sure, is this about the restaurant? Should I bring my mother with me?"

He shook his head. "No, that's not necessary. Just your presence is required." He winked at me.

"Okay, see you then." I gave a final wave to Yuna who gave me the thumbs-up. I tried for a sincere smile, but I have a feeling it didn't pan out.

When I got to my car, I sat there collecting myself, staring out the front windshield at the plaza entrance. What could Ian Sung possibly want to talk to *me* about?

CHAPTER
9

- - - - - - - - - -

I'd overthought the entire scenario with Ian Sung on my way home. I was stopping to walk Kikko and grab a quick change of clothes. Tonight, I was heading out to the Zodiac. Megan insisted it was necessary for me to get out of the house and spend some time socializing with someone other than my dog. Maybe she was right. Of course, I wasn't going to tell *her* that. So, I gave in without much of an argument. It was Friday night, after all, and I had just gotten my hair cut. How could I not? Plus, I wanted to tell her about the conversations I'd had and get her opinion.

It was still too early for a crowd when I arrived at 9 P.M. and there weren't very many cars in the parking lot. Most nights, business at the Zodiac didn't pick up until after midnight.

The Zodiac, a rock bar, themed in—you guessed it— astrology, prided itself on its black-and-white décor, its wall space dedicated to depictions of zodiac symbols and stories that portrayed the twelve signs. To boot, they had a great menu and one of the largest cocktail selections in the city. Megan had started bartending there shortly after college ended and I still hadn't tried all the drinks they had to offer.

I sat down at the bar, picking a stool closest to the door, and threw my purse on the bar top.

Megan saw me and waved. She walked over and leaned across the bar to give me a hug. "I'm so glad you came."

I hugged her back. "Well, you made me feel guilty for sitting at home another night. Plus, I know I'll just sit there and think until 3 A.M.; might as well do it here instead."

"That's the spirit!" She slapped the bar. "Your first drink is on me." She walked away without asking me what I wanted, and busied herself with picking liquor bottles from the shelf behind the bar.

While I waited, my eyes roamed around the bar, looking at the small crowd that was beginning to form. A group of college-aged guys started to congregate around the pool tables and dart boards while a group of girls sat close to the bathrooms in the back, giggling and talking loudly, fighting to hear each other over the volume of the music.

Megan came back with my drink, placing the glass on a napkin with the bar's name on it. The liquid was purple and almost looked glittery. I gave her a cautionary glance. She pursed her lips at me. "It's a Purple Virgo. Just try it."

In general, I was leery of drinks that were blue or purple. They usually meant trouble. I took a tiny sip and shrugged my shoulders. "It's not bad."

She gave me a once-over. "Your hair looks nice."

"Thanks," I said, fluffing the hair on the sides of my head. "I feel ten pounds lighter."

"I'm surprised they haven't convinced you to dye your hair purple yet. I know you said that one girl goes on about it every time you're there."

I took another sip of my drink, this time a bigger one. "Surprisingly, no. She mentioned it, but everyone was more interested in talking about what happened to Mr. Feng."

"Oh?" Megan leaned in, propping her chin in the palm of her hand.

"Yeah . . . both of them had some interesting things to say and it got me wondering." I twirled my straw around the ice cubes in the glass.

"Like what?" she asked.

"I'm beginning to wonder if something more complicated is going on." I paused. "And then I had a run-in with Ian Sung . . ."

"Ian Sung? Mr. Feng's partner?" Megan shook her head. "I'm so confused right now."

I recounted my visit to the salon as best I could, adding my own commentary as I went along. Megan had to walk away a couple times to serve drinks to people coming in, but after about three or four trips, she finally had the full story.

She stood in front of me with her arms crossed over her chest, eyebrows scrunched together. "I wonder why he would want to meet with you. I mean, it can't be business related. You only work there; it's not like you own the place. Wouldn't you think he'd want to meet with your mom instead?"

"I know, right? I can't think of what he'd possibly want to talk to me about."

"Unless it's not business related." She waggled her brows.

I rolled my eyes. "I doubt it's anything more than business. If it were, wouldn't he just talk to me about it right then?"

"Unless he felt embarrassed about it?" Megan suggested. "Either way, I can't wait to find out what it's about."

"That makes two of us."

"And this whole thing with the EpiPen . . ." she started, thankfully moving away from the Ian bit. "It is kind of strange that that day of all days Mr. Feng wouldn't have it. You swear you saw it, right?"

"I don't know," I said, starting to doubt myself. "But that's not all that's bothering me. It's this thing with Peter. I mean, I feel like it came out of nowhere. Since when did Peter and Mr. Feng have bad blood between them?"

"Peter can be kind of weird at times, I'll admit, but I don't think he's a violent person."

"I agree. And I can hardly remember them having any interaction other than Peter delivering his food every week."

As she was about to respond, something from behind me caught her attention. "Ugh, him again." She groaned, folding her arms.

I turned around to see who she was looking at. It was Detective Adam Trudeau. "You know him?" I asked, turning back around.

She rolled her eyes. "I don't know him other than he's kind of a jerk and always comes in every Friday."

He didn't see me sitting there, so I was able to watch him unnoticed. He came in every Friday? I wondered why I had never seen him before. He scanned the bar just as he'd scanned the restaurant the first day I'd met him, cataloging everything in sight. He appeared satisfied with whatever he saw and proceeded to move toward the back near the gaggle of girls. "That's him," I said, following him with my eyes.

"Who?"

"That's the detective." I nodded in his general direction.

Megan gawked at me. "Are you kidding me? That's him? Nice Eyes Guy?"

I pursed my lips. "Can you drop that already?"

"No."

We stared at each other for a solid thirty seconds before she turned around and went to greet the detective. I watched her grab a bottle from the beer cooler and set it in front of him. They barely exchanged two words as she took his money.

She came back over and rolled her eyes again. "What a peach."

"He really comes in here every week?"

"Every Friday night without fail," she replied. "He'll sit there, in that same seat, until closing and not talk to anyone. I've seen some women go up to him every now and again, but he barely looks their way. They eventually give up and move on to the next available guy."

I watched as he sipped his beer, keeping his eyes focused straight ahead. "I wonder what his story is . . ."

She scowled at me. "Oh no, don't even think about it."

"About what?" I asked, my face the picture of innocence.

"I've seen that look before, Lana Lee." She put her hands on her hips. "He intrigues you. It's all downhill from here."

"Oh, please don't be so dramatic." I batted a hand at her. "He thinks I'm a potential suspect. How can I even consider being attracted to him?"

"You tell me. You're the one who's a sucker for nice eyes and rough exteriors."

Before I could come back with a snarky remark, she walked away and started making her rounds down the bar, checking on people's drinks. My eyes couldn't help but travel back over to Detective Trudeau. Even if he was a jerk, I had to give credit where credit was due, and he definitely got points in the handsome department. His black button-down shirt had most likely been what he'd worn for work, but he looked more casual with the top button undone and his sleeves rolled up. Except for a rather expensive-looking watch on his wrist, he was free of what I referred to as "man jewelry." And that included no wedding ring. Okay . . . so I looked. Sue me.

The look on his face wasn't pleasant, but it wasn't cruel either. He seemed to be somewhere else, and had yet to notice me.

As I watched him, I wondered, had the circumstances of our meeting been different, would I be romantically interested in him? The answer to that was most likely yes, but I wasn't ready to fully come to terms with that thought. After all, he was a police detective in a murder investigation . . . and one of his fingers was partially pointed in my direction.

I thought back to the conversation with Jasmine. According to her, Detective Trudeau was my problem. But was he really? Wasn't he just doing his job? He didn't know me from Eve, so why should he believe that I was innocent? Even with Peter, he had no way of knowing.

The instigator on my shoulder told me that he should at least believe I was innocent because I *was* innocent and I should stop making excuses for him.

While my brain was having this argument with itself, I'd gotten off my barstool and was heading over to his end of the bar before I realized what I was doing. That must have been thanks to the instigator on my other shoulder. The same one that usually told me things were a good idea when, in fact, they were not.

And since I felt like everyone, including Megan, was watching me, there was no sense in turning back around. I plopped my purse down and sat next to him on the empty stool. "Hi."

He barely moved his head, but instead slid his eyes in my direction. He turned to look at me when he realized who I was. "Miss Lee?" he asked, sounding puzzled.

"Are you always this formal?" I smirked at him, hoping to lighten the tension that had already wedged its way between us. "Maybe just call me Lana."

"What are you doing here?" he asked.

"Having a drink, much like yourself." I nodded toward his beer bottle.

He glanced at it as if he'd forgotten it was there. "Right."

"My roommate works here." I pointed to Megan who

was pretending she hadn't been spying on me the entire time. "I come up here quite a bit to visit her. I'm surprised I've never noticed you before."

"I suppose you never had a reason to," he said, looking away.

I tapped the side of my glass, not sure how to respond to his comment. "So, how's the case coming?" I tried my best to sound nonchalant, but I could hear the eagerness in my voice. Sometimes my lack of suave really irked me.

Without turning to me, he said, "When I'm off the clock, I don't like to talk about work. And I can't talk about that with you anyway."

"Fair enough." I stared ahead too, looking at the bottles lining the wall, trying to think of something else to say. "So, how long have you been a cop?"

He turned to frown at me.

I held up my hands in defense. "Hey, that's not technically a work question."

He thought about that a minute. "Fair enough," he responded, mimicking me. He took a sip of beer before saying, "Nine years total . . . I just became a detective a little over a year ago."

"Did you always want to be a cop?" I asked.

He set the bottle down. "Look, maybe we don't talk about this right now, okay? I had a hard day and I just came here to unwind." He didn't look at me as he said it, and I couldn't gauge his reaction, nor figure out why his time as a cop would be a sensitive subject.

"Okay, sorry," I murmured.

He seemed to regret his tone and sighed. "Why did you come over here anyway?"

I shrugged. "I thought it might be good to get to know each other. You know, outside of the whole case thing. Maybe if you knew me . . ."

He smirked. "Buttering me up isn't going to help you or your friend." He turned to face me fully, his eyes burning into mine. "Knowing you isn't going to change anything. I have a job to do and that's exactly what I'm going to do. Nothing you say is going to change anything, so if that's why you came over to talk to me, then don't bother."

My face reddened a little bit, partially from embarrassment and partially from anger. I couldn't believe he'd managed to turn my act of civility into a ploy to butter him up. I suddenly felt silly for coming to his defense, even if it was just in my own head.

I picked up my purse and drink, scooting my butt off the stool. Turning to him, I said in the coldest tone I could conjure, "I'm sorry I bothered you, Detective Trudeau." My chin rose a little as I said his name and I could feel the liquid courage of my Purple Virgo setting in. "I'm also sorry that you think so little of me without even knowing anything about my character. Good luck with your investigation."

He started to say something, but I didn't give him the satisfaction of staying to hear him out. If he was going to blow me off, then he would get the same treatment.

Saturday morning I woke up with a small chip on my shoulder and more motivation to get my investigation under way. After my encounter with Trudeau, I decided there was no room to doubt myself or what I wanted to accomplish. His attitude was making me grumpy about the entire situation, and I was left with an added desire to prove him wrong. But in order to do that, I needed to stay as clearheaded as possible. And clearheadedness involved coffee.

I stumbled into the kitchen with Kikko dancing around my feet. "Just let me get the coffeemaker started and we'll go out, okay?" I said this half expecting her to protest. The pee-pee dance was serious business in this household. For all parties.

To my surprise, the coffeemaker was already on and a fresh, full pot awaited me. I stood there staring at it, amazed that the smell of brewing coffee had escaped my sleeping nostrils.

"I couldn't sleep anymore," a groggy voice said from behind me. I turned around to find Megan sunk into the couch with a coffee in one hand and a bagel in the other.

"Did you even get any sleep?" I asked, walking over to the couch. I fumbled around for the dog leash and found it sticking out of the couch cushion next to her.

She shrugged. "Sorta. It's actually sunny out today and I wanted to take advantage of that. Who knows how many more days like this we'll have?"

"True." I noticed that she'd opened all the blinds in the living room, letting the sun fill the room. The winters in Cleveland could drag on and the sun would soon become a stranger.

I took Kikko around the complex to her favorite tinkle spots. She sniffed the grass leisurely, soaking up the sun, and I stared off into space planning the details of my mission.

I had learned a couple of tidbits along the way, like

the woman crying in Mr. Feng's office, Peter and Mr. Feng allegedly arguing, and Kimmy's thoughts on Mr. An and reasons to murder someone.

The plaza would be as good a place as any to dig into the information I'd already learned. Maybe someone saw something and didn't realize it. I could check if anyone else had heard or seen Mrs. Feng in the plaza within the past two weeks. She didn't usually come by, and when she did, she made sure to stop by and say hello to everyone. I was still having a hard time believing that Donna Feng would allow herself to be heard arguing with her husband like that. I wasn't even sure she was capable of that much emotion.

But I had seen Kimmy Tran fall apart in public. Kimmy's strange behavior and extreme dislike for our recently deceased landlord had been niggling at my brain since the day we had our visit with Donna Feng.

And that day outside his office, she had said that Mr. Feng had needed to learn a lesson. That just so happened to be the same day he died.

After Kikko had exhausted all of her possibilities, we headed inside, my mind now focusing on the coffee that was waiting for me in the kitchen. Megan was still sitting on the couch and the only difference was that her bagel was gone.

I dug in the cupboard for a mug and filled it up, leaving room for cream and sugar. While I made my coffee, Megan padded into the kitchen to refill her own cup.

"What do you have planned for today?" she asked. "I need new jeans, everything I have is getting so worn out. Want to come shopping with me?"

"I can't today. I have to run a few errands at the plaza."

"What errands?" she asked, eyeballing me. "Maybe I can come with you? Then we can go to the mall afterward."

I looked up from my coffee cup. "Nothing important. It's actually pretty boring stuff, you wouldn't want to go."

She pursed her lips. "I feel like I've hardly seen you at all this week."

"I shouldn't be gone too long. Maybe we can get lunch later," I suggested.

"Fine." She pouted. "Text me when you're done."

After absorbing enough caffeine, I found a sweater and jeans to throw on and was out the door before Megan could ask any more questions about my errands. I don't know why I felt the need to lie to her, but I wasn't ready to tell anybody what I was up to yet, even her.

It was about ten o'clock when I got to the plaza. While I was pulling in to the parking lot, I noticed a couple of news vans parked on the street right outside the gates. There were a reporter and cameraman standing outside the van, filming. The plaza and its lot were considered private property, and reserved for customers unless otherwise invited. Donna had made sure of that, and signs were posted right outside the gate warning that trespassers would be prosecuted. When she'd had them installed, I thought it was a little overboard because nothing exciting ever happened around here. Who would have thought it'd come in handy?

A few cars sprinkled the lot, but it looked as if the

holiday shoppers hadn't begun their day yet. I was thankful for small favors. That meant the shop owners wouldn't be too busy to talk to me and maybe I could learn something helpful before the stores got too busy.

As I got out of the car, I heard a sharp whistle, and followed the sound over to the news van. The cameraman I'd seen on my way in was signaling me to come over. I simply waved, and gave my biggest smile. I shouted, "No English!" and walked inside.

CHAPTER
10

My first stop would be Esther's place. She was pretty forthcoming with me most of the time, so I saw it as a good place to get information.

On my way to Esther's shop, I passed Mr. An's store. I stood in front of it for a minute and stared at the large windows displaying giant pieces of art. The GOING OUT OF BUSINESS signs were gone. When did that happen?

I decided to stop in and inquire. I had never been inside the Painted Pearl before, and I took my time admiring the walls that were covered from ceiling to floor with beautiful paintings. In the middle of the room stood four wooden shelving units that held carefully painted porcelain dishes, clay pots, and figurines. A small sign sat on each unit and proclaimed HAND-PAINTED. The back of the store had a long wooden counter that displayed handcrafted jewelry and small trinkets.

Mr. An stood behind the counter with his hands behind his back. He smiled at me. "Hello, Miss Lee. It is so nice to see you again."

I smiled back. "You have a lovely store," I said, gesturing to the paintings on the walls.

"Thank you." He looked thoughtfully at his collection. "I have been collecting art for most of my life."

"You have some fascinating pieces." My eyes continued to skim the room, taking in all the stunning artwork. "I can't believe I've never stopped in before." I stopped by a painting portraying a sad woman dressed in traditional Hanfu clothing. She sat under a cherry blossom tree with her head tilted down, her face thoughtful but sad.

"Are you interested in a new piece of art?" Mr. An asked, noticing the painting I was looking at. He came out from behind the counter, his hands still behind his back, and walked up to it, nodding at the woman in the painting. "That is a beautiful one. It is called *Lost Love*."

Fancy that, I thought. I knew a thing or two about lost love; maybe that's why I was so drawn to that one. "Actually, no," I said, breaking my attention away from the painting and turning to him. "I was just stopping by because I noticed the GOING OUT OF BUSINESS signs are gone."

He nodded, his face brightening. "Yes, I was able to sell enough paintings that I no longer have to close. I think business will be much better from now on."

"That's wonderful news!" I exclaimed. "It's too bad that Mr. Feng wasn't able to see it happen. He would be happy to know that the threat of an empty store was gone."

His eyes dimmed and he looked past me, staring off into the plaza. "Yes . . . that is unfortunate."

"So unexpected . . ."

He continued to stare off in the distance and I began to wonder if he'd heard me. I was about to speak again, but his eyes slid toward me. "Often death is unexpected, even when we are waiting for it." He clenched his jaw, but the rest of his face remained still as he watched me.

"It won't be the same without him," I replied. "Did you know him well?"

"I knew everything I needed to know."

His lack of expression unnerved me and I felt a chill trickle down my spine. I shook it off and focused on the trinkets sprinkling the counter and decided to change the subject to something more cheerful. "I was thinking to myself that I'll have to stop by after I get my paycheck to pick up a few things. There are so many to choose from."

"Yes, please do so." He bowed his head a fraction of an inch. "Thank you for stopping by."

I waved a hurried good-bye and made a beeline for Esther's shop. It might have been paranoia but I could feel his eyes following me the whole way there.

Chin's Gifts was one of those places where clumsy people shouldn't go. All of the shelving, showcases, and most of the merchandise are made of glass. This is where you learned the best lesson of keeping your arms in and your hands to yourself. I should know, I had spent a lot of time there.

The entrance to Esther's shop was kept wide open during business hours and I rushed inside to escape the eyes of Mr. An.

I found her sitting behind a long row of glass showcases, her eyes glued to a small television screen. I swear, she and my mother could be the same person. "Whatcha watching?" I asked, trying to peek over the counter.

Esther looked up at me from over her reading glasses. "Chinese movie," she said, turning the volume down. "What are you doing here today? You do not work on Saturdays."

Instead of answering her question, I jerked a finger toward the entrance and asked, "Did you know that Mr. An is staying in business?"

She sneered. "Yah, he took down his sign the other day."

"You're not happy about it?" I asked, somewhat surprised by her response.

She shrugged. "Mr. An is not very nice. And his store is too expensive."

I looked around at Esther's things and realized that he sold a lot of similar knickknacks. Probably Esther was concerned now that Mr. An was staying and getting a little more business, that he would take business away from her. I decided to stay away from that apparent sore subject. After all, that wasn't what I had come to ask Esther about. "How did things go at the police station for you the other day?"

"So-so." Her eyes slipped back to the TV screen. "I do not understand where the shrimp dumplings came from. I know this was not from you and Peter. I told the police they are making a mistake."

"Speaking of Peter, did you happen to hear him and Mr. Feng fighting a few weeks ago?"

She narrowed her eyes. "Why?"

Trying to appear casual, I leaned against the counter. "Just wondering. The detective brought it up and I've heard people talking about it. I thought it was strange. What would they have to fight about?"

"Stand up straight," she said, wagging her finger at me. "You will become crooked in old age. I tell you all the time."

I couldn't help but feel she was trying to dodge the subject. But she wouldn't stop giving me the stink eye. I stood up with a sigh, straightening my shoulders. Not even my own mother lectured me this much about my posture. "So, why would they be fighting? Did you see anything?"

"You stop worrying about these things," Esther lectured. "You have to worry about you."

"Now you sound like my mother," I said bitterly.

She looked at me sympathetically. "You are going through hard times. We worry about you."

"I'm fine, really," I said, holding up my head. "Things are getting better." Okay, that was partially true. I'd stopped crying over sappy commercials, most of the time. And I didn't hate happy couples when I saw them anymore. That's progress. Right?

Esther gave me a look that told me she wasn't convinced.

"Okay, fine, I'm going," I said, throwing up my hands. "I'll see you on Monday."

"It's Saturday, Lana," Esther said, as I walked out the door. "Go find a boyfriend to make your mommy happy."

CHAPTER
11

Instead of finding a boyfriend, like Esther had instructed, I decided I would hit up the next best thing. The bookstore. I needed books to add to my "to be read" pile, and while I was there, I could question Cindy about the day she found Mr. Feng's body. Hopefully she would prove to be more informative than Esther.

As I stepped inside, I stopped and took a deep breath, closing my eyes and taking in the intoxicating smell that is the Modern Scroll. This was my favorite store of all. It was a small slice of heaven, and I came in any chance I got just to be around the books. Books were my solace, my escape.

There was nothing like that feeling of holding a book in your hand and traveling to another place, another time . . . another life. I was called a nerd a lot because of it, but I didn't care. I wear that hat with pride.

I stopped at a display in front and browsed through Cindy's selections of the month. She had placed a few

Amy Tan and Lisa See books together on one side, and on the other were books on meditation, and the *Tao Te Ching*.

Cindy stood behind the counter, flipping through a magazine, her stringy black hair hanging in her face. When she noticed me approaching her, she looked up, pushing her thick-framed glasses farther up her nose. Smiling, she said, "Lana Lee, back for some more books already?" She slid her magazine to the side and leaned on the counter space next to the register.

The cash register was centered in the back of the store and in front of it was a grouping of mismatched velvet couches and a coffee table for people to lounge while looking through potential purchases.

I laughed. "Since I was in the neighborhood, I figured why not. How are you?"

She shrugged. "Can't complain really. Business is starting to pick up for the holidays. I'm hoping this year treats me good."

"I saw that Mr. An is staying in business." I gestured to the wall she shared with the Painted Pearl. "So, that's got to be a good sign, right?"

She snickered. "I was shocked to see that happen and just a pinch disappointed."

"Really?" This piqued my curiosity. "Why is that?" I asked, noting that much like Esther, she wasn't thrilled.

"That man is a pain . . ." she answered, rolling her eyes. "And don't let his quiet demeanor fool you. He can get pretty loud sometimes, more often than not lately, it seems."

"You can hear him through the walls?"

"Oh yeah," she said, and pointed to the door directly behind her counter. "This back here is my office . . . and it's fairly quiet in there. You may not realize it because you work in a restaurant, but these walls are pretty thin. And his office is on the opposite side of this wall." She pointed to her right. "I can hear pretty much everything going on in his office and in the service hallway."

"Wow," I replied. I didn't think too much about the service hallway since I barely went back there. Its main use was to take out garbage and receive deliveries, which Peter or my mother usually took care of.

"Wow is right. I've never heard someone so angry before."

"Could you hear what he was yelling about?" I looked at the wall, half expecting to hear something right then.

She shook her head. "No, not really . . . it was muffled most of the time. You could just hear the anger in his voice."

A customer walked up behind me holding a stack of paperbacks. I stepped to the side and Cindy rang him up, thanking him for his purchase and wishing him a great day.

She repositioned herself against the counter. "Now that I think about it more, I did hear a few things, but I don't know who he was talking to, or about. There was something about a woman, and money. He was constantly talking about money."

A woman . . . and money. Now that was interesting. "Are the two connected?" I asked, hoping for more information than just that.

"Not sure," she said.

"Do you know who he was arguing with?"

"Sometimes with Thomas . . ." She looked down as she said his name. "Sometimes with Ian . . . and other times, I have no idea. But there was definitely a lot of commotion there lately."

"Did he argue with Mr. Feng recently?"

"Since the day he moved in is more like it." She leaned in closer. "As far as I could tell, the two of them hated each other. Thomas stopped in about once a week, and they'd always end up arguing about something."

"Could you hear anything between the two of them?"

She shook her head. "A lot of times they would speak in Cantonese, and my Cantonese is not very good. I could pick up a few words, but nothing worth mentioning."

"Do you think it's strange that they spoke in Cantonese? I rarely hear anyone around here use it."

She shrugged. "Maybe Mr. An is better with Cantonese than Mandarin? I don't know much about him to tell you the truth. Just that he lived in California for a number of years. Can't imagine why he'd come back to Ohio. I mean . . . these winters."

"So, he's from here originally?" I asked. I couldn't remember my mother ever telling me about him.

Cindy nodded. "I think he lived here through his college years and then left for California shortly after. When he first opened his store, I think I heard someone say that he'd had a falling-out with someone, but I have no idea with who."

"Do you remember who you heard that from?"

"It was so long ago . . ." she said, adjusting her glasses. "I have a hard time remembering last month."

If Mr. An had lived here before, maybe my mother had known him when she was younger. I'd have to ask her about it. She might know more of the story. "By the way, I hope you don't mind me asking, but how are you?" I asked, shifting the subject. "It must have been hard to find Mr. Feng that way."

She looked away from me, her eyes squinting as if she were blinking back tears. "It's not how I expected my day to go, I can tell you that." When she looked at me again, her eyes were bloodshot. "But I'm better. I imagine it'll be something I'll think about for a while, but I just try to take everything one day at a time."

I nodded, trying to imagine what it would have been like for her. She wasn't much older than me, and I have no idea how something like that would affect me. I wasn't looking to find out any time soon either. "Were you close with Mr. Feng? You were meeting him for lunch, right?"

"No, it was a business meeting." Cindy hesitated. "My experiences with Mr. Feng are not as . . . cheerful as some of the other shop owners. I only talked to him when I had to."

"How so?" I asked.

She shifted her weight. "I'm a people watcher. Mostly, I keep to myself and observe my surroundings. You can learn a lot that way." She paused, looking around to see if anyone was nearby. "Mr. Feng was not the pleasant, happy-go-lucky guy that everybody knew and loved."

"He wasn't?"

"No. He was a troubled man, with a heavy burden on his shoulders. I don't know what that burden was, but I gathered he didn't like his life very much and that's why he spent so much time here." She stared at me pointedly. "Away from home if you get my drift."

I did get her drift.

"A lot of times, I'd be here late, after closing, and I'd keep an eye out on the plaza." She looked past me, out into the plaza, as if he were there now. "I'd see him walking around the pond in circles with the strangest look on his face, almost like he was constantly worried about something. A lot of times he'd stop and stand in front of Mr. An's shop and just stare at it. Then he'd circle around and he'd stare at Ho-Lee Noodle House for a while."

"He did?" What reason would he have to be staring at our restaurant? Or Mr. An's store, for that matter?

"When I stand at the front door, I can see right over the pond across the footbridge, and there he'd be, just staring. I don't think he ever noticed me."

"What do you think he was doing?"

"I have no idea. But he did it almost every night that I was here late."

"And how often is that?"

"Two or three times a week."

I wondered to myself if he followed that routine every night and if anyone else had seen him doing this. Was he looking for something? What did the Painted Pearl and Ho-Lee Noodle House have in common?

"Aside from that, he seemed to be in a lot of confrontations with people," Cindy added as an afterthought.

"Like who?"

She thought for a minute. "Well, Kimmy Tran was over there a bunch, and of course, his encounters with Mr. An. And your cook a couple of times too."

"Peter?" I perked up. I had almost forgotten I wanted to ask about that.

"Yeah, one time in particular, a few weeks before . . . you know, I saw the two of them arguing in front of the property office. I was just coming in for the day, and the two of them were going back and forth; Peter had his back to me, and all I could see were his arms waving around. Thomas saw me coming and must have told Peter because he got quiet real fast. After that, they went into the property office and shut the door."

So, Peter and Mr. Feng *had* gotten into an argument with at least one witness. It made me curious as to who else had seen it and if anyone heard something in particular. I still couldn't imagine what they'd have to fight about. "Did you tell this to Detective Trudeau?" I asked.

She nodded. "Yeah, he was actually the one who asked me about their argument. After that, he asked if I knew anything about the relationship between all of you, and if I thought anything suspicious was going on."

I exhaled. "And?"

She laughed. "Don't worry, I'd never do that to you. Plus, if you ask me, this place is riddled with enough motives to keep the detective busy without looking at you or Peter twice."

"Well, I appreciate your faith in me and Peter." I looked out into the plaza. "There are a few people here who think otherwise."

Cindy gazed out toward the plaza. "I'm telling you,

Lana, if everyone around here just stopped and watched for a little bit, they'd see a whole lot more than what's on the surface."

After my talk with Cindy, I hung around and riffled through the bookstore for a little while, browsing shelves and clearing my head. I left with a few new paperbacks and a whole lot of questions. On my way out, I tried to stop at a few other stores, but by the time I'd left the bookstore, the plaza had started to fill with shoppers, and everyone was too busy for small talk.

I replayed the conversations I'd had on my drive home and felt even more stumped than when I'd left the house that morning.

There was something peculiar about the relationship between Mr. An and Thomas Feng, but what was it? If there was bad blood between the two men and somehow a woman was involved, could that woman be Mrs. Feng? Assuming, of course, that all the references to a woman were the same person.

And the falling-out that Cindy had mentioned happening before Mr. An moved to California, was that a hyped-up story from the gossip mill, or had something actually prompted Mr. An to leave Ohio?

On top of all that, now knowing that the fight with Peter and Mr. Feng had occurred, I had to wonder who had originally told the detective.

When I got home, Kikko waddled to the door, snorting at me in excited spurts. I couldn't help but smile as I knelt down to give her back a good scratch. "I wish I knew what I was doing . . ." I said to Kikko.

"Doing with what?"

I looked up. Megan was standing in the hallway, scrutinizing me. "I didn't realize you were home," I said, straightening up.

"I was just about to text you and see if you were ready to have lunch yet. I was thinking we could head over to Effie's Diner. I'm starving!"

My stomach lurched at the thought of food. I didn't realize until she mentioned it that I'd forgotten to eat all morning.

While we drove to our destination, she filled me in on her shopping adventures and the plans she wanted to make for the rest of the day that now included a trip to Home Depot. More paint shopping. Joy. I stayed quiet as she talked, still lost in thought over my morning conversations.

The parking lot at Effie's was practically empty and there was no wait for a table once we got inside. We followed the hostess to a booth by the front window. I scooted in and sighed as I watched traffic go by. Everyone out there was probably having a normal day Christmas shopping or doing something fun with their friends. Meanwhile, I was thinking about motives for murder.

Megan slapped the table with her palms, startling me. "Okay, spill it," she said with resolution in her voice.

"Spill what?"

She shook her head. "Oh, don't give me that." She pointed an accusatory finger at me. "I know you're up to something. You've been acting weird since yesterday, so tell me what's going on."

"Okay, okay," I said, giving in. "Can we order first, though? I'm famished."

"Fine," Megan said with a clenched jaw. "We'll order first. But then you're going to tell me what's going on with you."

After the server had come back with our drinks and we ordered, I told Megan about my trip to Asia Village and the people that I'd talked with that morning. I'd never gotten the chance to tell her about the conversation I'd had with Detective Trudeau the night before, so I threw that in for good measure too. By the time we got our food, she had the whole story from start to finish.

She stared at her chicken sandwich, chewing on her lip.

"Well?" I asked. "Aren't you going to say anything?"

"I'm trying to figure out why you wouldn't just tell me that you were looking into things."

I shrugged, looking down at my own plate of food. "I thought you'd think I was silly."

"Silly?" Megan snorted and unrolled her wrapped silverware. "Lana, are you kidding?"

I looked up at her, a little embarrassed. "No . . ."

"Lana Lee," she said, staring me square in the eye. "As your best friend, I am totally and completely insulted."

My jaw dropped. "You are?"

"Yes!" she squealed. "I would totally help you! Besides, you can't do this by yourself."

"I can't?"

"No, duh. Think about it. Cagney and Lacey . . . Rizzoli and Isles . . . and . . ."

"Laverne and Shirley?"

She pursed her lips at me. "Whatever. We'll figure this out together. Lana and Megan are on the case!" she declared, holding up her butter knife.

"You really don't have to get involved," I told her.

"Nonsense, what are best friends for?"

"Well, if you're sure."

"Yeah, I'm sure. Plus, I'm way sneakier than you are." She smiled wickedly as she bit into her sandwich.

CHAPTER
12

The rest of the weekend I did regular-people things. Megan and I trampled around Home Depot conversing over paint swatches, which we never decided on. Eighteen different swatch cards followed us home.

On Sundays, my family normally meets for dim sum, but this week my mother cancelled, wanting to spend the day by herself, so Megan and I spent a lazy day around the house watching movies and entertaining ourselves with Kikko and her toys.

It was nice to have some time to do nothing and relax my mind, but I still found myself staring down the long face of Monday morning all too soon.

The November morning was crisp and frost had finally made its appearance. I was thankful there had yet to be any sightings of snow.

I went through my morning routine on autopilot, anxious for my meeting with Ian. As I moved effortlessly around the restaurant, straightening up table settings and adjusting chair placements, I chuckled to myself. It was odd how easily I had transitioned from office life to the service industry. At times, I felt like I'd never lived that life of business casual and two-hour meetings about nothing in particular. My time as a reporting analyst was kind of like a dream.

I thought back to that fateful meeting and it played out in my head like a montage for a new prime-time drama series. There I was sitting at an oak table among my colleagues. My boss was sitting across from me reviewing the reports I had just handed her with pride. Then, confusion and agitation appear on her face. Within seconds, the papers are in the air, sprinkling down like large confetti as she pounces up from her chair with her finger inches away from my nose. "What is this!" she shouts. "This isn't what I asked you for at all!"

In this part of the montage, there's no music or background noise, just a close-up of my face for added drama. Then I'm up from my padded office chair and speed-walking back to my cubicle where I start throwing personal items into my bag. I'm done. I've checked out. A girl can only take so much. While I'm packing up my desk, I imagine a hurried instrumental piece that synchronizes with my arm movements.

End with a flash-forward of me surrounded by a pile of bills. Maybe I blow a chunk of hair out my face as I read the "past due" stamp on the front of an envelope.

I've had much time to perfect the details of this persistent montage.

Since that time, I've thought about how things could have turned out differently if I hadn't lost my cool. I mulled over this scenario along with a few others with

Megan about eleven ways from Sunday, but who can really say? I couldn't change the outcome and it was too late to go back. Really, I didn't think I even wanted to. I was happy here. Sort of. Minus the whole alleged-murder thing and smelling like teriyaki every night. But what job didn't have its ups and downs?

Lou rapped on the door and it broke my train of thought. Probably for the best. I let him in and he returned the favor with a cheesy smile.

"What's that face for?" I asked.

"Nothing, you look different today." He gave me a once-over and continued to grin. "You look nice."

Okay, unintentionally, I had dressed up a bit for my meeting with Ian. Instead of throwing my hair up in a ponytail like I normally did for work, I had spent extra time on it and pinned it up with jade combs that my mother had gotten me for my last birthday. I also might have worn better shoes and thrown on a skirt for good measure. And some extra makeup might have accidentally gotten applied. Couldn't a girl get a little dolled up for work now and then?

"So I don't look nice otherwise?" I asked, a scowl forming on my face.

He chuckled and held up his hands. "I'm not getting caught in that trap," he said as he hurried to the kitchen.

For a Monday morning we were pretty busy and I was starting to regret my choice of footwear. Platform wedges might have been a bit overboard considering I spent most of the day standing. It was only 11 A.M., and my feet were already killing me. I could kick myself for forgetting to bring an extra pair of shoes to work.

At eleven forty-five, minutes away from my meeting, the door chimes jingled and in walked Detective Trudeau. What perfect timing, I thought.

"Good morning, Miss . . . Lana," he said. His voice was husky and I liked the way my name sounded when there weren't accusations in the midst.

I kept my cool. "Detective Trudeau . . . to what do I owe this pleasure?"

"I thought I should stop by and apologize for the way I acted the other night." He looked away from me, glancing around the dining room. "It was uncalled-for. I realize now that you were just trying to be friendly."

I folded my arms over my chest. "I accept your apology."

His eyes slid back to me. "I also thought I'd have lunch while I'm here."

"Are you sure you're not worried we'll try to poison you too?" My hand flew up to my mouth.

His eyes widened. "Really? I just came here to apologize and — "

"Lana!" my mother bellowed from behind me.

I jumped. "Mom! What?"

"It's time to go. Do not be late and keep Ian waiting."

I turned to face her and she stood there with her hands on her hips.

"Meeting with Ian?" Detective Trudeau looked from my mother and then back to me. "As in Ian Sung, the other property owner?"

"Yes, that Ian Sung," I said.

"Interesting . . ." he said, sounding taken aback.

My mother looked at the detective, taking a minute

to register who he was. As recognition dawned, she widened her smile and stepped in front of me, pushing me out of the way. "Detective, how can I help you?"

"I came to speak with your daughter and possibly have some lunch," he said, straightening his back. He eyed me warily over my mother's head.

My mother clapped her hands together. "I can help you with lunch. Let me take you to our best table." She took a menu from the podium and grabbed the detective by his bicep.

I watched Detective Trudeau's face fill with surprise. He looked at me and I shrugged. My mother was his problem now.

She started to pull him into the dining room. As they walked away, she glanced over her shoulder and nodded toward the door. That was my cue.

The Bamboo Lounge, the newest addition to Asia Village, was a hit from the day it opened its doors. Who didn't love Chinese karaoke? Okay . . . I didn't. But that's beside the point. Everyone else did, which brought a lot of new business to the plaza.

As I reached for the bamboo-handled door, my eyes drifted toward the property office two storefronts over. Someone had died there, but we were conducting business as if nothing had happened. The only indication that something was amiss had been the crime scene tape guarding the door. They must have removed it sometime over the weekend, since now everything looked back to normal.

I shook the thought away and pulled on the door

handle, realizing how heavy it was. Was it locked? Nope. I guess this was a good reminder to start working out with Megan.

The restaurant was empty except for the few employees who had come in early to prep for their late-lunch menu.

Ian sat at a two-seater booth near the window, staring out into the parking lot, deep in thought. His head turned as I neared the table. He was dressed as impeccably as he'd been the day I saw him at the salon, and I was relieved I'd decided to make myself a bit snazzy. Nothing worse than feeling like a hobo in front of an attractive male.

He stood up as I approached, and said, "Please, have a seat."

I slid into the booth, thankful to be off my feet.

"I hope this is okay," he said as I sat down. He looked around the empty restaurant. "The office is still a mess and the community center has people coming in and out. Hardly a chance to have any privacy. It's all I could come up with until I have the office just the way I like it."

"I'm guessing the police took everything they need?" I asked.

"Yes," he said, shaking his head. "Although I don't know how they made sense out of anything in that mess. Thomas wasn't exactly a neat freak. Would you like something to drink?" Ian gestured to the teapot on the table. "I can get something stronger if you want. Or maybe you'd like to eat while we're here?"

"Tea is fine."

He flipped over the unused teacup in front of him and filled it up. As he eased the cup closer to my side, he studied me from across the table. A slight smile played on his lips. "I'm sorry to have been so elusive with you the other day about meeting with me. I know that salon is a hot spot for gossip."

I laughed. "Well, I'm sure they've told the entire plaza you wanted to meet with me in private."

He rested his elbows on the table, his fingers steepled under his chin. "Perhaps it's better to let their imaginations wander."

I shimmied in my seat and focused on the teacup. "So, why exactly am I here?" I asked.

"I had a business proposition I wanted to discuss with you." His tone was less playful and he straightened in his seat. "I'm planning on creating a board of directors to put together events for Asia Village and handle large community projects."

"Does this mean you're taking over the responsibilities of the plaza?"

He chuckled, more to himself than to me. "Sorry. I tend to get ahead of myself." He nodded and leaned forward. "Mrs. Feng doesn't feel that she's the right person for the job. She'll act as more of a silent partner . . . she'd still like to keep her hands in the jar, so to speak."

"When was this announced?" I asked, confused at the fact that no one seemed to have mentioned something this important.

"It hasn't been," he replied. "Mrs. Feng would like to announce it during the memorial ceremony. There's still some paperwork for her to fill out and she's had a lot on her plate arranging all of the services. I don't intend to rush her."

"Ian . . ." I shifted in the booth. "I'm not sure why you're telling me this."

"This committee that I'm creating . . . I'd like for you to be a board member. I think having another fresh, young voice, like myself, who knows this plaza would benefit all of us."

"Me? But I only started working at the restaurant full-time a few months ago. I'm sure someone like Kimmy Tran would be much better to help you . . ."

"No," he responded firmly. "I'd like for it to be you. Besides, your parents have been with the plaza since the beginning. I have a feeling you know more about this plaza than you're letting on."

I sat in silence thinking over his proposal. "I'm not sure what to say . . ."

He laughed. "That's easy—say yes. It would be a great opportunity for you. And, who knows, you may end up rubbing elbows with someone who could benefit you in the future."

I glanced out the window. "But I'm not sure it's something I could manage while working at my parents' restaurant and they really need me right now."

"It'll be no problem. A majority of the time, our meetings would be in the evenings or on weekends," he said matter-of-factly. "You have to remember, most of the people who will be on the board are already active members of the plaza. They'll have the same time availability as you."

"That's true . . ." I murmured. I tried to think of another excuse to get out of this, but nothing came to mind except a flat-out "no" and I had a feeling he wasn't going to take that as an answer.

"Lana, I have big plans for this place, and I'd like for you to be a part of them. I think we could work well together."

"But you just met me," I pointed out.

"Call it a hunch." He folded his arms on the edge of the table and leaned toward me. "Trust me, we'll get all the details worked out later. My goal right now is to get you on board with this."

"I have to think about it . . . can I have some time?"

"Take all the time you need . . . well, for now anyway. Nothing is going to be set in motion until after the memorial service. Once Mrs. Feng puts me in charge, I'll start setting everything up. I just wanted to give you a chance to be first on board."

"Well, I appreciate that," I said, giving him a lopsided grin. "I'll let you know as soon as I decide."

"Like I said, take your time."

"So, no one else knows about this board of directors you're putting together?" I asked, to clarify the point.

He leaned in. "Not even Mrs. Feng. I want all of this to be a surprise. With everything she has going on, I don't want to bog her down with a lot of the particulars I have in mind. I think she will be pleasantly surprised to find out later how much thought I've put into this. I've been thinking about these ideas for a while now. It'll be exciting to finally put them in motion."

How long could he have been thinking about all these supposedly wonderful ideas? Mr. Feng had only passed away last week. "I feel odd keeping this from people," I admitted. "Especially my mother. She'll ask me why you wanted to see me and I don't know what to tell her."

He smiled. "I've already thought of that."

"You have?"

"Yes, and you can tell her it was the second reason why I asked you to see me."

"The second reason?"

He leaned in even farther over the table, his eyes sparkling with amusement. "Have dinner with me."

I blanched. The list of things I didn't see coming was getting longer and longer.

It was close to one o'clock by the time I got back to the restaurant. I had stopped in the bathroom to collect myself and investigate just how red my face was . . . it was pretty red.

Ian had caught me off guard on both counts and I hadn't been able to give him a definite answer to either question. He'd assured me that he could be patient. He struck me as the type of man who was confident he would get what he wanted.

I was most certainly *not* a patient person. And now the pit in my stomach left me with an inkling of suspicion. Ian was moving pretty fast with this whole "taking over the plaza" thing. I thought it was strange that he was coming up with all of these plans that Mrs. Feng didn't even know about yet. What purpose could hiding that information from her serve? Wouldn't it work more to his benefit to tell her about all the ideas he had?

I was lost in la-la land when I entered the restaurant and didn't realize that both my mother and father were standing at the hostess booth staring at me expectantly.

"Dad . . ." I said, puzzled to see him. "What are you doing here?"

"Is that any way to greet your old man?" he replied, coming out from behind the booth with his arms spread out. "Give me a hug, you little goober."

He bear-hugged me and the air popped out of my lungs. "Dad, don't call me that . . . it's embarrassing."

"Nonsense. You'll always be my little goober." He kept his hands on my shoulders and held me away from him, looking at me with a silly grin on his face. He tweaked my nose and winked.

I rolled my eyes. "Dad . . ."

"So . . . what happened?" my mother asked, wringing her hands. "What did he want?"

I shrugged, avoiding eye contact. My parents usually knew when I was lying. Especially my dad. "He just wanted to introduce himself."

"What do you mean, that's it?" My mother put her hands on her hips and frowned. "You have been gone since twelve o'clock."

Before I could answer, Detective Trudeau walked up behind my parents. He looked relieved to see me. "Oh good, you're back."

"Lana, answer me," my mother said, interrupting the detective. "What did he say?"

I huffed. "It's nothing, Mom. He asked me out to dinner."

"What?" all three asked in unison.

"It's no big deal, don't make it a thing." I could feel the redness spreading in my cheeks.

"Oh, Lana." My mother beamed, clapping her hands together. "This is good for you. You need a boyfriend so you're not lonely anymore. Ian Sung is perfect for you."

Detective Trudeau scoffed in the background.

"I thought you said you didn't like—"

She waved her hand at me. "Forget about that. He will be an important man now. Maybe he will ask you to marry him and then you will own the plaza one day too."

"Mom, that's a little . . ."

My father laughed. "Now, now, Betty, don't embarrass her in front of the nice detective."

She clucked her tongue. "I am going to tell Esther right away. She will be so happy for you." And she ran off toward the back room.

I sighed in frustration. "Dad . . ."

"Don't worry, I'll handle your mother." He laughed and ran after her.

Detective Trudeau looked at me and raised an eyebrow, amusement dancing in his eyes. "So, Ian Sung asked you out on a date, huh?"

I returned his question with a flat stare.

"If you ask me, the guy's kind of a—"

"Ugh, let it go." I moved behind the counter. "It's not a big deal, and I'm probably going to say no anyway."

"Why?" he asked with a smirk.

"Why do you care?" I folded my arms over my chest.

He shrugged. "I don't know. Just curious, I guess."

"How was your lunch?" I asked, changing the subject.

"It was good. I had hoped to talk with you more . . . but . . ." He looked at his watch. "I really have to be going."

"Well, thanks for stopping by," I said sarcastically.

"I just have one last question before I go."

"Oh yeah, what's that?" I asked.

"Did I hear your dad call you 'little goober'?"

By three o'clock, I started to crash and my feet were throbbing. I could feel my shoes getting smaller with each step. The excitement from earlier that day had drained me and I was ready to go home. The lunch rush was over and only a few stragglers meandered in, a table at a time. I sat at one of the front booths so I could keep an eye on the door. I tried to zone out and roll silverware into cloth napkins. It must have worked because when I looked up, Megan was staring down at me with her arms crossed.

"Do you not check your cell phone these days or what?" she asked.

"Ugh, I'm sorry, today has been a hell of a day."

She sat down across from me, resting her hands on the table. "I have been coming up with a plan for our . . . investigation. And really, I think we should call it an operation, don't you? Like, Operation Dumpling . . . or Operation Save Peter . . ."

I let out an exaggerated sigh. "Okay, you are way too into this. We're not calling it that."

"Why not?" She pouted. "Do you want to name it?"

"Can we talk about this at home?" I glanced over at the customers to see how they were faring. I'd probably have to get up in a few minutes and I didn't have the mental capacity to have this conversation.

"What happened today that is so horrible?" she asked.

I gave her a quick rundown of the story, promising I would fill in the blanks later.

"Wow, you're right. That is one hell of a day." She leaned forward in her seat. "Also, what did I tell you? I knew he was going to ask you out."

I grunted.

"So, are you going to go out with him?"

"Ian?" I asked.

"Yeah, I mean . . . why not? It wouldn't hurt to just go on a date with this guy. It doesn't have to be anything serious."

I threw up my hands. "Why is everyone trying to set me up with someone?"

"You like that detective guy, don't you? You wish he would ask you out, don't you?"

"Really?" I stopped rolling the napkin in my hand and looked at her. "What is it with you today? How much coffee have you had?"

She leaned back in the booth and shrugged. "I barely had any coffee. And nothing is with me today. I'm being observant, is all."

"Shouldn't you be getting to work?"

She checked the time on her cell phone. "In a few minutes . . . and don't change the subject."

"Megan . . ." I whined.

"Okay, fine," she said, slumping in her seat. "Do you at least want to hear why I stopped by?"

"Do I have a choice?"

She chose to ignore me and continued. "I've been coming up with a list of suspects and I think we need to get organized. You know, write everything down. I don't know how you've been keeping everything straight in your head."

I wasn't about to tell her that the inside of my head

looked like a table at a flea market. "Okay, so who is on your suspect list?"

"Kimmy Tran is at the top of my list. So far everything you've told me about that girl makes me believe she wanted to get rid of Mr. Feng before something happened with her parents' store."

I nodded, thinking it over. Kimmy was definitely on my list, but I wouldn't give her the number one spot.

Megan went on. "Second on my list is Mrs. Feng. The spouse is always a suspect in these types of things. You know? Plus, that Yuna girl said she heard them fighting."

"We still don't know that it was actually Mrs. Feng." I reminded her.

"True," she said, sitting back in the booth. "So, who is your number one?"

"Right now I'm going back and forth between Mr. An and Ian."

"Ian?"

I grabbed another napkin to roll. "He seems a little too eager to take over the plaza, almost as if he's been waiting for his chance." I thought about what he'd said during our little meeting in regard to having these plans for a while. It made me cringe.

"And this Mr. An guy?" she asked. "That's the one who was going to close his store but is now staying in business, right?"

"Yeah. The timing of it is just too weird for me. And, that conversation I had with him at the store . . . he definitely has some hard feelings toward Mr. Feng."

"And you said that Cindy mentioned talk of a woman. That woman and the crying woman could be the same person."

"I've thought that too. But who could it be?"

The bells tinkled above the door and I looked up, Nancy was back and walking toward us.

Megan turned to face the front door. "I suppose we'll continue this conversation at home."

"Yeah, probably a good idea." I smiled up at Nancy as she came to stand at the edge of our booth. "Have a nice lunch?" I asked her.

"Yes, very nice," she answered. "Hello, Megan, it is always so nice to see you."

"You too, Ms. Huang," Megan replied.

Nancy looked at my pile of wrapped silverware. "Let me help you."

Megan stood so Nancy could take her place. "We'll talk when you get home tonight." And off she flounced.

Nancy watched Megan leave. "I hope she is not leaving because of me." A small hint of sadness appeared on her face. "I feel that a lot of people are avoiding me because they think that Peter is guilty."

"Oh no!" I assured her. "She was just about to leave for work before you came. Believe me. She knows Peter better than that."

We sat in silence, folding napkins and occasionally getting up to tend to the customers. I was happy to say that the rest of the afternoon passed without incident. When the bells tinkled near five o'clock, I was surprised to see my sister walk in with her work clothes on.

Anna May smiled. "Hey there, little sis. I've come to relieve you of your duties."

"What happened to Vanessa? I thought she was working tonight?"

"She has an algebra test tomorrow, and of course did not study for it. So she's cramming tonight and asked if I could cover for her."

I rolled my eyes. "Figures."

Anna May clucked her tongue. "Don't be so hard on her. You remember what it's like to freak out over exams in high school."

"Yeah, yeah."

Anna May crouched down and removed my purse from the cabinet, shoving hers in its place. She thrust it at me. "Now you go home and do whatever it is that you do," she said, shooing me away.

I clutched my purse against my chest like a teddy bear. "I do stuff."

"Oh yeah? Like what?"

I contemplated for a minute, thinking about what exactly I did with my time after work besides watch random movies and make Kikko dance for treats. "I do stuff . . . and things . . . lots of things."

She snorted. "Lana, you don't do anything anymore. Ever since what's-his-name broke up with you, you've been a mess and you need to get yourself together. It's time to move on."

"I have moved on. And for your information, *I* was the one that broke up with him." I clutched my purse tighter. "Plus, I do a lot of things."

"Yeah, you said that 'things' part already. Still wasn't convincing the second time."

"Whatever." I couldn't think of a cleverer comeback.

"I'm telling you, a guy like Ian Sung is not going to go for a girl who doesn't have something going on in her life."

"What?" I asked through clenched teeth.

"Yeah," Anna May said with satisfaction. "Mom called me today and told me all about your little lunch date with Ian."

"Oh my God, I can't believe her," I grumbled.

"It's a step up from the trash you were dating before . . . and if you ask me, you could do a lot worse." She patted my shoulder. "Trust me on this, Lana, you don't say no to a man like him."

"Then why don't you go out with him?" I asked. *Yeah, take that,* I thought.

She shrugged. "He hasn't asked me out. But if he did, I wouldn't waste time thinking about it."

CHAPTER
13

"Uh-oh," Megan said, freezing in the open doorway to our apartment. Her hand was holding the key that was still in the lock. She observed me from my position on the couch. "What happened after I left?"

My eyes slid toward her. "Anna May." I crossed my arms over my chest.

Megan rolled her eyes and shut the door behind her. "Lana, what did I tell you about listening to your sister?"

I huffed in response.

She dropped her purse on the floor and headed for the kitchen. "Let me get situated and we'll talk this out."

I listened to her rummage around the kitchen, and she returned to the couch with a bag of chips and two bottles of beer.

Megan plopped down next to me, on top of my mound of blankets. Kikko sat on my other side. Her head stuck out of the blankets and she eyed the bag of chips. "So, tell me exactly what happened."

I gave her a full recap.

"She's just jealous you're getting the attention. I think it might also be the added stress of the recent . . . passing of Mr. Feng that is getting to both of you."

I turned to face her. "I do stuff though, right? I mean, Anna May's not right about that."

"Uh-huh," Megan mumbled.

"What?" I asked, setting my untouched beer on the table.

Megan looked away. "Well, you know, you have been kind of moping around the house lately."

"You said it yourself," I reminded her. "Mr. Feng just passed away."

"Even before that."

"Oh, so you're going to just take Anna May's side like that?" I folded my arms back up. "This is ridiculous." Kikko hopped off the couch, disappearing down the hallway.

"I'm not taking anyone's side. There are no sides to take. I'm only saying that it's true you've been on the inactive side lately."

Kikko came back with a stuffed duck and jumped up on the couch, plopping her toy on my lap. She looked at me expectantly. "You're the only one who understands me," I said to my flat-nosed friend.

Megan snorted. "Oh please."

I threw the stuffed duck across the room and Kikko happily raced after it. She gave it a good shake in her mouth and then pranced off.

"Do you want to hear the rest of my plan?" Megan asked, trying to change the subject.

I sank farther into the couch. "I guess."

"Oh, don't be like that." Megan repositioned herself on the couch to face me. "Okay, so my plan . . . first, we have to make a list of all the people and potential scenarios like we started to earlier today. And I mean everything, even the silly ideas." She gestured with her hands. "Then we cross out the completely ridiculous ones. Whatever's left is what we investigate, and we can split that list in half, you look into your people and I'll investigate mine."

I thought about the list that had been forming in my head.

She watched me, waiting for me to agree with her. "There have to be things that stick out more than others. There's no one that's liked by everyone. He had to have enemies somewhere and I think if we split it up like this, we can cover more possibilities."

Her idea wasn't bad. It couldn't hurt to map everything out. The only problem was those darn dumplings. "What about the fact that the dumplings came from Ho-Lee Noodle House?"

"I've been thinking about that," she replied, bouncing on the couch. "Which is one of the things I wanted to tell you earlier today when I stopped by, but we ran out of time." She sat forward, leaning toward me. "What if the dumplings were switched?"

"How? I'm the one who delivered them."

"Yeah, but what if someone came to see him after you? Maybe he was having lunch with someone."

"Or maybe it really was Peter," I concluded. Even as I said it, I wasn't convinced. "Maybe there's something we don't know about the two of them. I feel like Nancy has been acting strange ever since it happened. As if she's upset about more than just Peter."

"What has she said about the whole thing? Anything interesting?"

"Not a whole lot. All she told me is that Peter refuses to talk to anyone, including her. And she seems devastated about Thomas, more so than everyone else. She started to cry when I brought it up."

"Okay, let's try this instead," she said, tapping her chin. "First, gut instinct, who do you think did it?"

I looked at her blankly. "Well . . . Kimmy Tran."

She cocked her head at me. "Okay, that's different than your answer earlier today. What makes you pick her above Mr. An and Ian?"

"Well, you said first instinct. And she was pretty mad at him. When I think about who had the mental space to do it, it's her. Plus, she mentioned that someone should make him pay. That's been bugging me this whole time. I've never seen her that angry before." I let the thought develop for a minute. "But, at the same time, she isn't killer material."

"Okay . . . that's a good start." She stood up from the couch and started pacing in front of the coffee table. "Now go back to the Ian angle. How do you feel about that?"

"Well, it was that conversation we had that got me thinking. Listening to how anxious he was to get started with his ideas, I realized how much he has to gain. Also, he didn't seem too upset with the fact that Mr. Feng is out of the picture."

"And then Mr. An goes on our list too."

"My talk with him at the Painted Pearl gave me the heebies and that's what put up the initial red flag. Something about the way he looked when I mentioned Mr. Feng's name. Plus, he stopped by the restaurant to ask what was going on the day that Peter left with Detective Trudeau."

"He did?" Megan asked. "You didn't tell me that."

"It must have slipped my mind with everything else going on. At the time, I didn't think anything of it."

"Okay, and then let's circle back to Peter since he seems to be at the front of this. What do you think about him?"

I looked at her with apprehension. "I really don't think . . ."

She held up her hands. "Okay, I know. I don't think he did it either. But that's part of our problem. We know these people too well and we're not looking at this objectively. We said we would talk about all of the possibilities even if they were ridiculous, so let's just say he did it for the sake of this argument. What reason would he have?" she asked.

I sat thinking, twirling a piece of my hair. "I can't come up with anything really . . . except . . ."

She stopped pacing and sat down next to me. "Except what?"

"Well, he seemed pretty worried about what would happen to the plaza now that Mr. Feng is gone. He was the only one that thought to bring it up and it was one of the first questions he asked after we found out. The rest of us were more upset about the death. That part didn't seem to bother him all that much."

"Do you think there's any reason why he wouldn't want Mr. Feng in charge anymore?"

I shook my head. "Nothing I can think of."

"What about this whole rent-increase thing that's going on?"

"I'm not sure that Peter knew about it. Plus, the restaurant isn't in trouble, so there should be absolutely no reason for him to worry about that."

She tapped her chin. "We need to find out more about these people and their relationships with Mr. Feng. And . . . Mrs. Feng."

"Right . . . Mrs. Feng."

"I know you like her, but there are oddities there that I don't think we should ignore."

"I know, you're right. If we're going to include Peter in this, then we should include Mrs. Feng too." I felt slimy even saying it out loud, but I couldn't dismiss the fact that Megan had a point. Mrs. Feng had been so quick to give Peter's name to the police; that could have been a way of diverting attention away from herself. Nor could I dismiss the fact that even for a well put-together woman, she was holding up a little too well for a widow.

"We might have to find some other ways to get information too. Maybe some less direct ways."

Another good point. Whether I liked it or not, all the people we'd discussed had potential motives.

It was still hard to think of these people that I'd known for so long being capable of anything like murder. It was one thing to hate someone or even sabotage them, but it was something else entirely to end their life.

After talking with Megan, I felt a million times better, and I'd almost forgotten the awful things that Anna May had said. Almost. Right now, I had bigger things to worry about.

The following day, I showed up at the plaza in a black peacoat and sunglasses. Detective Lee was on the case. At least, that's what I told myself when I was getting dressed that morning. I was getting in the zone.

Mr. Zhang, the owner of Wild Sage herbal shop, noticed me when I walked in. I had a feeling my detective ensemble wasn't doing the trick.

As I approached his store, he waddled over to me, with his hands behind his back, his glasses on the tip of his nose. He tilted his head to look up at me.

"Lana Lee, you look like a movie star," he said with a big smile.

I took my sunglasses off, feeling silly. "I thought it was supposed to be sunny today," I lied.

He shook his head. "No, no. Today is a dark sky." He looked up at the skylights and sighed. "But it matches my heart."

I cocked my head at him. "What do you mean?"

"My heart is heavy and sad like the clouds." He pointed with a crooked finger at the skylight.

I looked up and noticed the storm clouds passing by. It was threatening to snow any minute now. "Why are you so sad today, Mr. Zhang?" I asked, even though I had a feeling I knew the answer already.

"I am sad for my friend Thomas. He was too young to die . . ." He bowed his head. "I watch many people die."

I didn't have a hard time believing he'd seen a lot of loss in his life. Mr. Zhang was so old that no one had any clue exactly how old he was. No one dared ask. My guess was that he was at least one hundred. I liked to believe it was all his herbs that kept him young.

"Mr. Zhang, do you believe the stories that people are telling about us?"

To this, he gave a hearty laugh. "No, these stories are nonsense. You are a rabbit; rabbits do not like to fight."

I looked at him, baffled. I was surprised he took my Chinese zodiac sign into consideration. "Who do you think could do such a thing?" I asked. "It's hard to believe that anyone here would want to kill him." I looked accusingly at all the storefronts in the plaza.

His nod was slow and thoughtful. "A man with many secrets will have many enemies. Enemies will always find you, even when you think you are free."

"Did Mr. Feng have a lot of secrets?" If that were true, then it could be a number of people. People we hadn't even considered yet.

Mr. Zhang chuckled. "When you look at the ocean, do you see what is underneath?"

I scrunched my eyebrows. "No . . ."

"Many people are like the ocean . . ." he replied. "Now, you go, and do not worry about things that are past. You are young and life is waiting for you." Without another word, he turned around and shuffled back into his store.

The morning was busy enough to keep my mind occupied. Despite the cold weather, the holiday shoppers had decided to pick up the pace. Many of them stopped in for warm bowls of wonton soup and hot cups of tea.

At noon, Mr. An walked in, scanning the restaurant. His eyes settled on Nancy and his expression softened.

I greeted him at the hostess booth. "Would you like to dine in today or carry out?" I asked.

He turned to look at me as if he hadn't realized I was standing there. "I would like to dine in."

"Follow me." I grabbed a menu and led him into the dining area.

As he sat down in the booth, he looked up at me curiously. "Are you not normally on lunch now?"

"Yes, but it's been so busy, there's no time." I gestured to the packed tables.

His glance traveled around the room, and he nodded.

"Nancy will be right over." I had purposely seated him at one of her tables so I wouldn't have to deal with him.

This seemed to please him. Before I could walk away, he asked. "Is Peter back to work yet? I have not seen him since the day that he left with those men."

A warning bell went off in my head. "He had some vacation time he wanted to use and figured now was as good a time as any."

Nancy came up behind us and rested a hand on my shoulder. "I can take over now, thank you, Lana."

I stepped out of the way and moved to my side of the restaurant, far away from Mr. An and his creepy vibe. Asking about Peter . . . again. I would have to add that to my list.

About an hour later, my mother popped out of the back office with a bowl of udon noodles, my favorite, and waved me over to a booth in the back. I signaled to Nancy who was waiting on a table that just walked in. She gave a nod and turned back to her customers.

"You eat," my mom said, handing me the bowl and a pair of chopsticks.

I gladly took the bowl and sat down across from her. I'd gone too long without eating and I could hear my own stomach grumbling. I took a bite of the noodles, burning my tongue in the process.

"You be careful. It's hot," my mother scolded me. "You are too impatient."

I ignored the jab about my patience. "Mom . . ." I twirled my noodles around the bowl, waiting for them to cool down before taking another bite. "You've known Mr. Feng since you first came to the U.S., right?"

"Yeah. I have known Mr. Feng a long time."

"Did he have a lot of secrets?" I asked.

She scrunched her face at me. "Why do you ask this question?"

I shrugged. "Just wondering, I guess. I was thinking about him today and I realized I didn't know him that well."

"Mr. Feng was a nice man. He always liked to take care of people. But he had many problems when he was a young man. He was very handsome when he was young, and a handsome man always has trouble."

"What do you mean?"

"Too handsome . . . too many women come to find you."

I looked at her with surprise. "Did you feel that way about him too?"

"No, I liked your father right away. He was very handsome too." She laughed.

"So, Mr. Feng had lots of girlfriends when he was younger?" It was hard to picture him as a ladies' man.

"Too many, I forget how many." She looked into the distance. "But Donna was his favorite. When he saw her, he did not want to be so crazy anymore. Donna was good for him. She made him be a good man."

Despite my mother's confidence in Donna's ability to make Mr. Feng an honest man, it didn't mean there weren't things they didn't know. Maybe he was just more careful these days. That could explain the unknown woman crying in his office.

"Why did you not say yes to Ian Sung?" my mother asked out of the blue.

I shuffled my noodles around in the bowl. "I'm just not sure I want to go out with him. That's all."

"He can take care of you."

My body tensed at the subject. "Mom . . . I don't need a man to take care of me. I can take care of myself."

"You always say this."

"Because it's true." I stuffed my mouth with noodles, not wanting to continue this conversation.

"Anna May is jealous," my mom threw in.

"Well, tell her to go out with him then."

"Ian Sung does not like your sister this way."

"That's her problem, then, isn't it?"

"Why can't you be nice?" my mother asked.

"I am nice. She's the mean one." I stabbed the bowl with my chopsticks. "Wait a minute . . . we were talking about Mr. Feng."

My mom leaned back in her chair. "Okay, okay. What do you want to know?"

I decided to try the blunt approach. "Did anybody hate Mr. Feng?"

She seemed to think about it for a minute. I didn't know whether she was rehearsing her answer or if she was coming up with a list. "Mr. Feng had a hard life. He did make many mistakes when he was young. But later, he was better. If someone did not like him, it is from a long time ago." She looked away.

"What about the rent being raised?" I'd almost forgotten that we hadn't discussed this yet. "Did you know about that?"

"Who did you hear this from?" my mother wanted to know.

"Kimmy Tran."

"Ai-ya." She slapped the table. "That girl has a big mouth."

"So, you knew about it then?" I pointed my chopsticks at her in accusation.

"Yes, I know about this," my mother admitted. "But it was not true. He would say this all the time when people were not making good money in their store."

My eyes widened. "He did?"

She nodded in reply. "Yes, but he would never do this. He was too nice."

"Mom! That's terrible. People believed him. Sue Tran believed him," I reminded her. "And Mr. An was going to move his store to a mall because of it. And what about the people who've left?" I thought about the empty stores scattered around the plaza.

"You are too young to understand. Business is business. Mr. Feng would say this so people will try harder. Sometimes people get too comfortable."

"So he's never raised the rent on anyone before?" I asked, confused.

"No, not because of this reason. Mr. Feng always tried to help people stay."

"What about Mr. An? He wasn't planning to help him stay . . ." I set my chopsticks down. "I heard he lived here before he moved to California. Did they have some kind of problem with each other?"

She looked away, her eyes shifting toward the entrance. "No matter what anybody says, he was a good man." My mom patted the table and got up, disappearing back into the kitchen.

Guess that conversation was over.

That evening as I drove home, I could hardly believe what my mother had told me. I felt she was being a little naïve about the whole situation. In my eyes, Thomas Feng was scaring people into leaving the plaza. How many people had he told and how many people had left over the years because of his made-up claims? If he was so helpful, why hadn't he tried to stop Charles An from putting the GOING OUT OF BUSINESS signs in his windows?

Clearly, Mr. An had actually planned on leaving. If Thomas hadn't died when he did, would Mr. An still have gone ahead with closing his store? Would Mr. Feng have tried to stop him?

With the threat of Mr. Feng raising the rent no longer looming, Mr. An didn't have to worry about coming up with extra money. I began to wonder if he'd really sold enough art to keep himself in business or if he was still scraping by.

And then of course there was Kimmy's mother, who had obviously heard the news; both she and her husband had gotten second jobs because of it. But why wasn't Sue Tran familiar with this tactic like my mother was?

I did a quick assessment in my head of how the stores at Asia Village were doing financially. It seemed like Mr. Zhang was holding on surprisingly well even though he had very few customers. The salon always did well, and the Chinese grocery was holding its own, so no worries there. Even the Bamboo Lounge had a packed house every night of the week.

So who were the weak links?

Without question, it circled back to Kimmy Tran and her struggling family. But what was Kimmy doing to help? She hadn't said. Unless she had started to work without pay, which would lighten a little bit of the financial load on her parents. That didn't seem likely though.

I made a mental note to find time to stop and see her.

I also needed to find out once and for all who the woman was in Mr. Feng's office that Yuna heard crying that day. With what I'd found out from my mom, it was entirely possible that he'd kept some of his old habits. Maybe a situation with a lady friend had gotten out of hand.

Pulling into the parking lot of my apartment complex,

I gave myself a minute to collect my thoughts and form a list of things to remember. Megan was right, we needed to write this stuff down. I needed a notebook to keep it all straight.

While sitting there, I decided I would accept Ian's offer to join the committee he was putting together. It might make it easier for me to find out information about Mr. Feng. After all, they were partners. Surely he would have talked to him about things like rent increases or other Asia Village decisions. Regardless, I would find a way to make it work to my benefit.

As for his other question, well, the jury was still out on whether or not I'd accept his dinner invitation. Right now, he was on my suspect list.

CHAPTER
14
- - - - - - - - - - - - - - -

When Nancy came in at noon the next day, I asked her if she'd mind covering for me while I did some running around. Being Nancy, she was more than happy to help. With each day, she was looking a little better, and I had a feeling that being needed by someone, even if it was just me, was helping that along.

My plan was to meet with Ian and tell him I'd take the offered slot on the board of directors committee. Then I would make a quick stop to see Kimmy Tran and find out what she'd been up to lately.

As I was about to leave, my mother came out of the back room, her hands on her hips as she watched us.

"Lana, where are you going?" my mother asked as she walked up behind us.

"I have some errands to run today, so Nancy is going to cover the dining room by herself until I get back."

She eyed me with suspicion. "Where are you going?"

"I have some stuff to do," I said, flinging my purse on my shoulder.

"Where?" my mom asked again.

I huffed. "If you really need to know, I'm going to see Ian and then I have to make a couple of stops." I looked away as I said the last bit.

My mom beamed and clasped her hands. "Are you going to tell Ian that you will be his girlfriend?!"

Nancy chuckled and mumbled something in Mandarin.

"No," I said with an exaggerated sigh. "I'm just stopping by to see him . . ."

The luster left my mother's eyes. She stared at me stone-faced. "Pretty soon Ian will find somebody else. Do not play games and waste time."

"I'm not playing games." I inched toward the door. "Why are you always giving me the third degree?"

"I worry about you," my mother said. "I want you to be happy again."

"Okay, well, I'm happy." I faked a smile. "See? Happy."

My mother pursed her lips.

"I have to go. See you later!" I waved as I slid out the door.

I stood in front of the vacant shop between our restaurant and the Trans' store where my mother couldn't see me. China Cinema and Song was only one shop away from Ho-Lee Noodle House. Right now, the property between us was vacant, and had been for a while.

I checked the time and saw that it was just a little past twelve. I had some time to kill before I met with Ian, so I decided to stop and see Kimmy first. Might as well get it out of the way.

The Trans' store was a top five on my list of favorite places to go in the plaza. Kimmy's mom had the best stuff imported from China and Taiwan and was one of the only places in the area where you could find these types of videos and CDs.

Kimmy stood behind the counter, filing her nails. I looked around the store and not one customer was in sight. Kimmy didn't even notice that I walked in. She looked tired, and even from the entrance, I could see that she had bags under her eyes.

I walked past racks filled with DVD sets and movies, making my way around a group of organized bins of music CDs. Next to the sales counter sat a new selection of movie posters.

"Hey there, Kimmy," I said cheerily as I walked up to the register.

She stopped in mid-file and looked up. A look of relief washed over her face. "Oh, Lana . . . it's just you."

"Are you avoiding someone?" I asked.

She shook her head. "No one in particular, just don't feel like being Sally Shopkeeper today."

I took another glance around the store. No danger of that. "How's business?" I asked, leaning against the counter.

Kimmy shrugged and focused on her nails. They were cherry red, which surprised me. Normally Kimmy went for more understated stuff. Right now she wore a baggy black T-shirt and jeans. Her hair was up in a sloppy ponytail. She wasn't exactly a fashionista. "It's still slow," she replied. "I told my mom to go out for a bit and get some lunch or something. Did she stop by the restaurant?"

I shook my head. "I didn't see her."

"She's been meaning to talk to your mom for days. Don't know what about though."

"How's her other job going?" I asked, shifting the conversation toward my prepared line of questioning. I'd practiced on the drive into work that morning so I wouldn't get off track.

"She hates it. She gets up at about four in the morning to deliver those damn newspapers. I don't even think it's worth it."

"Why doesn't she find something else?"

"The hours fit. Since she spends most of her time here, she doesn't have a lot of options."

I nodded in understanding. "What about your dad?"

She stopped filing her nails long enough to sneer. "He's working at some factory making lamp shades. He takes shifts whenever he can. I guess the manager is an old friend of his and lets him fill in for people when they need a day off." She eyed her handiwork on her left hand and then moved on to her right. "If you ask me, they should just close up shop and forget about it. Or move like Mr. An was planning. I've heard the plaza on the east side has cheaper rents."

"Speaking of, do you know Mr. An well?"

She shrugged. "He's cool. We talk about art stuff, and he'll buy a lot of CDs to play in his store." She looked up from her nails. "Why do you ask?"

I looked away. "Just wondering, I suppose. I was surprised to see that he didn't have to close his store after all. Talk about a lucky break."

Her eyes shifted back to her nails. "Yeah, well, at least someone around here got lucky."

"Who knows, maybe with the holidays, you guys will pick up extra business."

"I'm not holding my breath."

"By the way, what did you tell me your second job was? I know you told me, but I can't remember what you said." I looked at her innocently.

Her file stopped mid-stroke and she looked up at me, her eyes narrowing. "When did I say anything about a second job?"

"Oh, didn't you?" Maybe I wasn't as smooth as I thought.

"No, I hadn't mentioned it." She leaned forward. "What have you heard?"

I shook my head. "Nothing, I haven't heard anything."

"Why are you asking all these questions?" she asked with a growl. "What are you up to, Lana?"

"Nothing . . . I just stopped by to see how you were. I had some time to kill before—" I looked down at my hands.

"Time to kill before what?"

My cell phone rang and I answered it a little too eagerly. "Hello?"

"Hey."

It was Megan. "Oh hey, is everything okay?" I asked, feigning concern.

"Uh, yeah. I just called—"

"Oh no, I'm sorry to hear that. Just give me a second."

"Lana, what the heck are you talking about?" Megan asked.

I looked up at Kimmy and gestured to the phone. "I'm sorry, I have to take this . . . I'll talk to you later."

She shrugged. "Okay, whatever."

When I was out of range, I put the phone back to my ear. "Hey . . . you still there?" I asked.

"Um, yes, what the hell is going on over there?" Megan asked. "Who was that in the background?"

"Kimmy Tran."

"Oh?"

"Yeah, and she got real defensive about having a second job," I told her.

"What do you think that means?" she asked.

"I'm not sure, but whatever it is, she doesn't want anyone to know."

"Well, I just called to tell you that I got you something. I left it on your bed."

"Is it doughnuts?" I asked.

She sighed. "No, it's not doughnuts."

"So, what is it?"

"It's supposed to be a surprise."

"Then why did you call me?"

"I don't know, but aren't you glad I did?"

I groaned. "I have to go; I'm meeting with Ian in a few minutes," I said, looking toward the property office.

"Okay, good luck. I'll see you tonight."

I put my phone back in my purse and squared my shoulders. It would be the first time I went back into the property office after Mr. Feng's death.

Ian was sitting at his desk against the far wall with his back to the door. He had stacks of papers lined up on his desk. As I walked in, he was shaking his head, mumbling to himself.

I cleared my throat. "Hi, Ian."

He whipped around, looking at me as if he hadn't been expecting me. "Oh, Lana, come in!" He rolled away from his desk and stood to greet me.

"I hope this isn't a bad time," I said, gesturing to the stacks of papers.

He reached for my hand. "No, no, not at all. I didn't realize how late it was already. I was attempting to sort through some of the documents that Thomas had saved in these filing cabinets. I've been trying to make sense of it all morning." He looked over his shoulder at the stack. "I think he kept just about everything he's ever gotten."

I looked at Mr. Feng's desk, now covered in boxes. It had been the last place I'd talked to him. My heart sank a little and I remembered our conversation. "Well, I won't keep you long, I just came by to tell you—"

"That you'll have dinner with me," he said, a confident smile forming on his face.

"No . . . I came to tell you that I'll take the position on the board of directors."

"Oh." His shoulders slumped.

"If it still applies . . . ?"

He shook his head as if to clear his thoughts. "Yes, of course, I just thought . . ."

I looked down at my feet. "I still haven't made a decision about that. I'm not sure if it's the best idea right now."

He turned away from me. "It came through the grapevine that you wanted to meet with me to accept my dinner invitation."

"It did?" I had only told my mother less than half an hour ago. How could it have gotten back to him that fast?

"You know how this place is . . ." He turned again, smiling sheepishly.

"Unfortunately, I do."

"But, still, no pressure. The offer is open whenever you decide to accept it."

I made a mental note of his ability to be positive, *whenever I decided to accept.*

"I'm assuming your mother doesn't know about the board of directors part then?"

"No, and I feel terrible not telling her, but it would have made it all over the plaza by now."

He nodded. "Exactly. That's why I'd like to keep this under wraps until Donna makes her announcement."

"What will be your next step after the announcement?"

"Well, once I put together my excellent board of directors, we're going to amp up this plaza with some fresh tactics, get the younger generation involved. A lot of these stores have been struggling and we need to give them a second chance. Breathe life into this old place." Ian spoke with the air of a political candidate.

"I agree with that. But how are you planning on doing that? Isn't it up to each store owner to handle their business?"

He smirked. "They need guidance, and we're going to be the ones to give it to them. We're going to be a real community." He paused. "And this nonsense about raising the rent. That's completely out of the question."

My ears perked. "So Mr. Feng talked about this with you?"

He nodded. "Thomas and I didn't agree on this subject at all. They're already paying enough and we can't compete with the other plaza. Before you know it, everyone will be out on the east side."

So Ian hadn't known that Mr. Feng wasn't really planning to raise the rent either. I filed that away in my brain. "How did Donna feel about the rent increase?" I asked, hoping that Ian might have some insight on that.

"Don't get me wrong. She's a smart woman, but she doesn't know a lot about business as it pertains to this day and age. Most of the time, she went along with whatever Thomas said." He tilted his head back and the same sinister grin he'd had the day I met him reappeared. "I think she's making a wise choice letting someone like myself handle this property."

I managed a curt smile. "Well, I look forward to seeing how things play out."

"As well you should," he said. "Things are going to get really interesting around here."

CHAPTER
15

- - - - - - - - - - - - - - -

On my way home from the plaza, I picked up a notebook to jot down all of my ideas. Everything was starting to jumble together, and Megan's idea of writing everything down had won me over.

By the time I'd gotten home and taken care of Kikko's tinkle needs, I had forgotten about the surprise that Megan had left on my bed. I found it waiting for me on my pillow. "You have got to be kidding me," I said to Kikko.

A black book with white lettering sat staring back at me, *How Regular People Become Private Detectives*. A Post-it note was attached to the front cover: *To help with Operation Dumpling.*

I sat on the edge of my bed and held the book. This was absurd. Kikko put her paws on the edge of the bed and sniffed the book in my hands. "You like this book, huh?" I asked her.

She snorted in return.

"Well, that makes one of us."

I flopped back on the bed and stared at the ceiling. Lying around me were my stack of mystery novels, a book on private investigation, and my blank notebook. I sat and thought on how I'd gotten here, and my mind momentarily drifted back to the day that I had quit my job. The montage cycled through my brain. None of this would be happening right now if I hadn't quit my job.

Instead of taking myself any further down that winding road, I sat up and grabbed a pen off my desk. I opened to the first page of my fresh notebook and stared at the blank paper. After a minute of contemplation, I wrote: *Who killed Thomas Feng?*

Looking at it written on paper made it all the more real. In the back of my mind, I knew that Peter was innocent, which meant that the killer, whoever it was, was probably walking around the plaza positive they were going to get away with what they'd done.

With that thought in mind, I jotted down notes on the people who kept coming up in relation to Mr. Feng. At the top was Ian, who was gaining quite a bit from Mr. Feng's death. After him, I wrote down Mr. An's name because he had potentially gained something as well. I couldn't shake the feeling that something was off about the timing of his suddenly being able to keep his store. After him came Kimmy because of her outburst the day Mr. Feng died, and her odd behavior since. I added the fact that she had gotten defensive over having a second job. Regrettably, I added both Mrs. Feng and Peter to my list like Megan and I had discussed.

In a careless scribble, I added things that Cindy had told me about her observations of Mr. Feng. Then

I added the information that I had learned from Yuna and Jasmine at the salon.

By the time I was done, I'd filled up two pages with gibberish. So far, none of it was coming together for me. Frustrated, I stared at the information I'd written. If anything, it presented me with more questions.

Disgusted with the whole thing, I lifted up my mattress and stuck the notebook underneath for safekeeping. No need to have that lying around. If someone were to stop over and accidentally peek inside they might think I had lost my mind. And honestly, I kind of felt like I had.

That instigator on my shoulder reappeared and asked me what business I had trying to solve a murder case. I was a server in my family's Chinese restaurant. I wasn't supposed to be spending my time trying to figure out "whodunit."

I told the instigator to shut up, my neck was on the line too. Plus, I wanted things to go back to normal. I've always been taught that if you want something, you have to work for it. So, with reservations, I gave in and opened the private investigation book that Megan had gotten me. Maybe I could learn a thing or two.

CHAPTER
16

- - - - - - - - - - - - - - - -

The last person I expected to see first thing in the morning was Donna Feng standing right in front of Ho-Lee Noodle House. In a well-fitted black pantsuit, Donna stood holding her matching Prada handbag with both hands firmly wrapped around the handles. Her facial expression was contemplative, and as I approached her, I watched her gaze travel over the length of the plaza, her eyes moving over the skylights and finally stopping on the property office.

Without turning to me, she said, "Do you know, I haven't been in that office since before Thomas died?"

"No, I had no idea." A lightbulb went off in my head, reminding me that this information was important. "How long has it been since you've visited?"

"A month, at least," she replied.

If I remembered correctly, Yuna had said the argument she overheard was just days before the incident. If Mrs. Feng was telling the truth, then it couldn't have been her in that office and my suspicions were right. There was another woman lurking around somewhere.

She turned to face me, her lips curving up in a brilliant red smile. "I hope you don't mind that I'm here so early. I have much to do today and I'd love to chat with you for a minute about the upcoming memorial."

"Sure thing," I said as I unlocked the door. "Come on in."

She followed me in and waited for me to turn on the lights. As sections of the room lit up, she seemed to give the restaurant a thoughtful glance just as she had out in the plaza.

"Can I offer you any tea or coffee?" I asked.

She nodded. "A cup of oolong would be nice, thank you." She moved forward to the nearest table and sat delicately on the edge of the booth, her back as straight as a board.

I went back into the kitchen and set my things on the counter. I pulled out a teapot and started prepping our drinks. In a few minutes, I had everything ready and headed back out to where she was seated, setting everything down on the table between us. I took the seat opposite her.

As I poured the tea, I said, "I'm sorry if you had hoped to talk with my mother, she usually doesn't come in until around eleven or noon."

She smiled. "This is the great pleasure of being the boss. You can sleep in."

I laughed, sliding the hot cup to her side of the table.

She brought the cup up to her nose and inhaled. "I love the smell of oolong, don't you?"

"It's my favorite."

"Lana . . ." She placed her cup gently on the table and looked me square in the eye. "I understand there has been some upset in the plaza recently."

I looked away. "Has there been?" I hoped that my questioning around the plaza hadn't gotten me into any trouble.

"I do have eyes and ears around here, and a few things have gotten back to me."

I thought about the investigation notebook under my mattress. "Oh?"

"As I mentioned to you when you stopped by my house, I don't blame you or your family for anything that happened that day."

I glanced up at her. "I know . . ."

"Now Peter on the other hand . . . well, I don't want to bore you with my thoughts on him." She pursed her lips. "But regardless, I like to imagine myself a fair woman. And Peter has not been proven to have done anything . . . yet."

"Mrs. Feng, I don't think Peter would do anything like that, he just doesn't have it in him."

She held up a hand. "Please, Lana, you are no longer a little girl, there is no need to call me Mrs. Feng anymore. I would very much like you to call me Donna."

"Okay . . . Donna," I said, testing it out.

"Now, as I was saying, Peter has not been charged with anything yet, and as much as I have my reservations about that young man, I feel it is only fair that he be found guilty the old-fashioned way. Even if it means I have to wait a little longer."

I nodded, unsure of where she was taking this.

"The general unrest in the plaza has made things

quite uncomfortable for some. There has been a lot of bickering and gossiping. I can't imagine that this attitude will help business for anyone."

"I agree."

"And from what I've heard, Peter has taken some time off work?"

"He's been off since he was questioned by the police," I admitted.

"I see." She paused. "As you know, the memorial for Thomas will be held this weekend. As an act of good faith, I would like for your family as well as Peter and his mother to sit with me at the head banquet table. This will show everyone that I have no hard feelings and hopefully life can go back to normal around here." She took a sip of her tea, and waited for my reaction.

"I would be honored to sit with you at the banquet. But will there be enough room for everyone? I'm assuming that your children and mother will sit with you as well."

She waved her hand. "My mother has taken Jill and Jessica to California until after the New Year."

I raised my eyebrows. "Oh?"

"She felt all the commotion was upsetting them unnecessarily and asked to take them on a winter vacation of sorts. I'm sure the girls are soaking up the California sunshine as we speak."

I thought it an odd time to be separated from their mother, but what did I know? "I'm sure they're appreciating the time away," I offered.

"Ian Sung will be joining us as well. I've heard that you've recently met."

I blushed. "Yes, I've met Ian."

The smile on her face was devilish. "He is quite handsome for his age."

I looked away. "He's okay."

She laughed. "I suspect that his interest in you is more than professional . . ."

Embarrassed, I looked up at her, but before I could reply, Lou tapped on the glass, causing me to jump a few inches out of my chair.

Donna turned around to face the door. "I had better get going; it's almost time for you to open and I'm sure you have work to do."

We both stood and made our way to the door.

"Please let your mother know that I stopped by and fill her in on the details of the memorial. Although I'm sure she's received the official invitation in the mail."

"I will," I promised, unlocking the door. "Thank you for stopping by personally."

She smiled at me. "It was my pleasure, Lana."

As she turned to face the door, Lou opened it, holding it in place for her. He bowed his head. "Mrs. Feng," he said, his voice barely above a whisper.

"Hello, Lou," she replied curtly, and then moved past him without another glance.

I noticed how she didn't correct his formality and thought that was strange.

Lou stepped into the restaurant, but kept his gaze on Donna as she walked away. After she had exited through the main plaza doors, he turned to me and jerked a thumb over his shoulder. "What the heck was that about?"

I shrugged. "I guess we're sitting at the main table for the memorial."

"Thirteen pairs of chopsticks are missing," my mother said to me, her hands on her hips.

We had just finished the lunch rush and my mother and I were having a standoff in the kitchen. Lou stood behind her watching us bicker.

"I don't know what you want me to do about it," I responded. "It's not like I can help that people steal stuff."

"This always happens. If this keeps going, I am going to buy cheap wooden chopsticks."

Lou nodded in the background. "Wooden chopsticks would be more cost-effective."

I rolled my eyes. "It's not that big of a deal."

"You want to pay for thirteen new pairs of chopsticks every week? This happens all the time now."

The answer to that was no. NO, I did not want to pay for chopsticks on a weekly basis, today or ever.

She shuffled away from me and into her office, returning with a twenty-dollar bill. "Go to the grocery and buy new chopsticks." She handed me the twenty.

I groaned. "Fine."

My mother followed me out into the dining area. I left her standing at the hostess podium as I hightailed it across the plaza to Far East Foods, our Asian grocery store.

Because it was the largest in northeastern Ohio, and the main market at Asia Village, it was forever busy. I made my way through the shopping carts and packs of people shuffling through the aisles.

In the back of the store, there was a small section dedicated to Asian cooking utensils and dinnerware. Colorful plates with Oriental designs lined the walls amid rice cookers and cast-iron woks.

A neat shelf of chopsticks sat at eye level and I perused the options. There were so many styles and colors. I inspected a set of black chopsticks with a cherry blossom design at the top. I knew my mother wouldn't want anything like these, even though they were more exciting than the vanilla-colored plastic ones she chose for the restaurant. They were your standard, find-them-anywhere chopsticks with the green and red engraving.

I picked up two packages and turned to leave. Because I wasn't paying attention to where I was going, I ran straight into the chest of a man who clearly spent time at the gym. When I looked up I saw that it was Detective Trudeau.

He grabbed my shoulders to steady me. "Careful where you're going."

The heat from his hands seeped through my shirt and I blushed. "What are you doing here?"

"Is that any way to greet someone?" he asked, letting go of my arms.

I closed my eyes, taking a deep breath. "I'm sorry, how are you, Detective?"

"I'm fine. Your mother told me that I could find you here." He looked down at my hands. "Got what you need?"

I nodded and held up the packages of chopsticks. "Chopstick run."

"Good, let's get those back to your mother, then I'd like for you to come with me down to the station."

My eyes widened and I felt panic settle in my stomach like a greasy burger. "What? Why?"

I thought I caught a hint of humor in his eyes, but his expression remained flat. "I need to discuss something with you and I think it would be best if we talked about it there."

"What is this about?" I started to make a beeline for the register, Trudeau on my heels.

"I think you know."

"I don't know what you're talking about . . ." I avoided eye contact, keeping my focus on the woman standing in front of me. "Besides, I'm working."

"It's about the case," he said firmly.

"Well, I figured that much."

"I already cleared it with your mother. She said it would be fine for you to leave."

"Why do I have to go now? Can't we do this later?"

"It's about Thomas Feng's murder," he said, a little too loud.

The woman standing in front of me turned around and stared.

I could feel the heat rise in my cheeks. "And . . . ?"

"Like I said, it's best discussed at the station."

"Fine." I paid for the chopsticks and left the plaza in a daze.

CHAPTER
17

"Would you like anything to drink?" Detective Trudeau asked, as if we were out to lunch. "We have a pop machine in the break room."

"I'd rather just get to the point, Detective." I was back in the same interrogation room as before, only it felt stuffier this time. I was in no mood for a Coke. I looked behind him at the two-way mirror and wondered if anyone was looking back at me. I squirmed in my seat.

He shrugged, unaffected by my discomfort. "Suit yourself."

This was the moment I had been dreading. The one that had been playing over and over in my head. My new montage where they had found some type of incriminating evidence that was misunderstood and somehow led to me. They were going to pin it on the wrong guy. And that "guy" was yours truly.

Trudeau straightened the stack of papers he had

pulled out of a manila folder. He took care with straightening the corners of each page so they lined up exactly.

I could have smacked him. "Detective . . ."

He stopped shuffling the papers and looked me in the eye. "I finally had the chance to sit down and go through all the takeout receipts from the day of Thomas Feng's death."

Okay, not exactly what I had expected him to start with, but it was better than what I'd originally thought. "And . . . ?"

He pushed himself back in his chair and stood up. He leaned against the two-way mirror and folded his arms over his broad chest, taking his time to answer me. "I think that Peter set you up."

I stared at the table, trying to make sense of the words that were coming out of his mouth. "Why would you think that?"

"Because there were no other takeout orders around the time that you delivered Thomas Feng's food. What Peter told you was a lie."

My lower lip trembled and I kept my eyes plastered on the table. "I don't believe it."

He sat back down and leaned forward, folding his hands on the table right where I was staring. "I'm afraid you're going to have to consider the possibility. I know this is tough . . ."

"Do you, Detective?" I asked, looking up at him. "Do you have any idea how long I've known Peter? And you're just going to sit here like it's any other day and tell me that *my friend* set me up for a murder he committed?"

He sighed. "Just because you've known someone for a long time doesn't mean that you know everything about them." He leaned back in his chair. "How well do you know Peter exactly?"

"Pretty well," I spat.

"Have you ever been . . . in a relationship with him?"

My face scrunched up at the thought. "No, of course not, he's a family friend."

"Okay," he said, sounding relieved. "Well, then why don't you explain to me why he asked you to deliver the food that killed Thomas Feng?"

My mind started to race. Why would Peter ask me to deliver the food? I tried to remember how and when he asked me to take it. He said that he was swamped with a rush order and that he didn't want to leave the food or it would burn. I was so preoccupied with hurrying to deliver the order before my own lunch, I hadn't noticed whether he was preparing anything else.

I could see the bag in my mind, sitting up on the metal counter, the receipt stapled firmly in place. Normally, I would pack the bag, but I didn't think anything of that either because Peter delivered the orders more than I did. If I had packed the bag myself, I might have noticed that the dumplings were wrong.

"Lana!"

I jumped. "Sorry . . ."

The rough lines around his mouth softened. "I was asking you . . . can you think of any reason why Peter would try to pin this on you?"

I shook my head. "No, we've always gotten along."

"Your mother mentioned to me that he's taken some time off."

I nodded. "I haven't seen him since the day he left with you and your partner."

"Good," Trudeau replied. "I'd like for you to stay away from him as much as possible until this whole thing has been straightened out."

"Detective . . . there's one thing I don't understand."

"What's that?"

"Why would he implicate himself? I mean, if this is true, he made the food that killed Mr. Feng. Wouldn't he think this would come back to him?"

Trudeau tilted his head. "You were the last one to touch the food, and you left the premises with it so that gives a lot of leeway for things to happen."

I gulped. "So you still think I'm a suspect?"

He shifted in his seat. "Do I personally think so?" He shook his head. "No . . ."

"But . . ." I added for him.

"But it's my job . . . like I said the other day. I have to look into every possibility."

I nodded. "I understand."

"I'm very good at reading people, and from what I can tell so far, you don't seem like the type of person to poison someone and then go about your day."

"That's probably because I'm not."

"The reason I brought you down here was to let you know what was going on and to tell you to be careful. Peter could be unstable."

"So, can I go?"

He nodded. "Yes." He started to rise from his chair. "Oh, and another thing, try not to air this information all over the place. If Peter thinks we're still looking into other possibilities, he's less likely to do something stupid."

I got up from my chair, feeling heavy and suddenly exhausted. This was a lot to take in. I couldn't imagine going back to work after this.

Trudeau opened the door and a cool breeze entered the room. "In the meantime, I'd like you to do me a favor."

"What's that?"

"Keep your eyes and ears open. I want you to call me if anything bizarre happens."

In the car, on the way home from the station, I called my mom and let her know that I wouldn't be coming back to work and that I'd see her tomorrow. She questioned me about my trip to the police station, but I maneuvered around the parts that included Peter potentially framing me for murder. She was going to find out about the takeout orders anyway, if she didn't already realize it, and I didn't know how to tell her without her completely freaking out. Keeping secrets from your family isn't quite as amusing in your late twenties as it is when you're a teenager. Especially when the secrets revolved around something as serious as murder and frame jobs.

When I got home, I found Megan lounging around before her shift, so we decided that I needed some retail therapy. We headed to Crocker Park and were walking around the Nordstrom outlet, half paying attention to the racks, and half contemplating my current situation.

"I don't get it," she said, eyeing a black cocktail dress. "Why would Peter want to frame you? You've been friends for so long."

I followed behind her, a midnight-blue Calvin Klein dress catching my attention. "I don't get it either. I've been asking myself the same thing since I left the police station. I can't see Peter doing something so malicious."

She looked up from the black dress in her hands. "Besides, wouldn't that implicate him too?" She shook her head. "I mean, he made the stupid dumplings to begin with."

I checked the price tag on the dress and my eyes widened. "That's what I said to Trudeau. But he insists that Peter might not have been looking at it that way."

"Well, gee, if we could just get inside Peter's head, all of our problems would be solved." Megan moved over to the next rack of dresses, picking up a strapless red dress with a ruffled bottom and holding it up to herself. "What do you think about this?"

I shook my head. "Can't wear red."

She put the dress back down and moved on to the next rack. "You know what else I don't get?"

"Hm?"

"This whole thing with Donna and the seating arrangements at the memorial."

"I know!"

"She's so adamant that Peter is guilty. But then she wants him and his mother to sit at the memorial with her? Like everyone is just one big happy family?"

I thought about it for a minute while I looked at a few more dresses on the rack. Megan had a point, and I couldn't argue that Donna's request wasn't odd. What purpose did having Peter sit at the same table serve? "I didn't understand that either. She said it was for business reasons—the plaza's in upheaval—but wouldn't she worry this would discredit her accusations?"

Megan snorted. "And does she really think that Peter is just going to go along with it? I mean, she's accusing him of murdering her husband, not of being a bad chef or something petty like that. Does she honestly think he wants to sit and have dinner with his accuser?"

"I wonder if anyone's told him anything yet."

"He still hasn't come back to work, huh?" Megan asked, holding up a purple spaghetti strap dress.

"No," I replied. "To both." I nodded at the dress.

"I don't know if that makes it look worse or not. He's in hiding . . . that's the way I see it. And I think it makes him look guiltier."

"Maybe." I was getting frustrated with the dress selection. Our conversation wasn't helping.

"I wonder if there's something about Peter and Donna's relationship that we don't know."

"What do you mean?" I stopped and gawked at her. "A relationship?"

Megan pursed her lips. "Not *that* kind of relationship. I mean, if they have some kind of history where he made her mad or something like that."

I sighed. "Maybe we should take a look at the relationships between all the people who're on my list at home. If there are connections, it might explain some things."

"Agreed. We can go over it when we leave here. I'll go in to work late tonight. Robin's there. They should be fine without me."

Huffing, I backtracked to the original rack I had been looking at with the blue dress. "I'm going to try this one on, and if it fits we're leaving. I can't shop anymore." Calvin Klein was winning the dress competition. As for the murder-suspect competition, there were too many people in the running.

CHAPTER
18

- - - - - - - - - - - - - - - -

We left with the Calvin Klein and rushed home to go over the list in my notebook and add the new information about the takeout orders from the detective. Until Megan left for work, we talked over the things I knew about each person's relationship with the other and came up nearly empty-handed. As far as I knew, none of the suspects on my list had a connection other than the plaza. But after the "people are oceans" speech from Mr. Zhang, I wondered if there was more to each of their connections than I knew.

The clock on the kitchen wall told me it was only six o'clock and Megan had only been gone for a half hour. I felt restless. And when I feel restless, I tend to get into trouble, which is actually what I was scolding myself about as I pulled up in front of Peter's apartment thirty minutes later. This was probably not the best idea I've ever had.

I don't know what made me do it. Maybe it was the

detective's warning to stay away, or maybe it was the sudden desire to look Peter in the eye and see if I knew him at all. Either way, here I was.

I looked up at the shabby brick building and read the address over again. I had only been here once in the past to pick up and drop Peter off for work when his car had broken down a few months ago. He hadn't even invited me in.

When he answered the door, he looked taken aback. "Lana." He studied my face. "What are you doing here?" He held open the door and stepped to the side to let me in.

I took a careful step into his apartment, looking around. It was an average apartment with the same brown carpet as mine. He'd kept the walls white but covered them with martial arts posters. A worn black leather couch sat in front of a giant flat-screen TV. The screen was paused on what looked like a war video game. The coffee table in front of the couch was littered with beer cans and snack wrappers.

He shut the door behind me, and folded his arms over his chest. He wore a white undershirt and black sweatpants. "Lana? Is everything okay?"

"I wanted to stop by and see how you're doing." It was harder to look him in the eye than I thought it'd be. "I haven't seen you since the day you left with the police."

"Oh." His arms dropped to his sides and he returned to the couch, sitting in a spot that looked worn from the weight of his body. "Yeah, man, it's been a rough time. I don't really want to talk about it."

I stepped farther into the apartment, not quite wanting to sit on the couch. There was no other furniture, so I just stood. Besides, he hadn't offered me a seat anyway. "Have you talked to Mrs. Feng recently?" I asked.

He snorted. "Why would I?"

"She stopped by the restaurant the other day," I told him. "She wants all of us to sit at the main table at the memorial . . ."

Peter laughed and it came out bitter and hard. The sound unnerved me.

"So, she hasn't mentioned it to you then?"

He laughed again. "No, and there's no way in hell I'll sit at the same table as that woman." His face dropped. "I'm not going to the memorial anyway."

"What? Why not?"

His face was still, but I could see the tension rising in his shoulders as he straightened up. "I don't want to deal with people looking at me like I did something wrong." He glanced away. "I don't do well at those things anyway."

"Have you talked to your mother? She's very worried about you."

He snorted. "Yeah . . . so worried about me."

"Peter, what's going on with you?" I took a step closer. "This . . . whatever this is . . . it's not like you. You don't even sound like yourself."

He glared at me. "Do you even know who I am?"

My heart skipped. "What do you mean?"

"You think I did it too, don't you?" he spat.

"No, actually, I don't."

He turned away from me. "Look, I appreciate you stopping by, but I don't need your pity or your concern . . . I'll be fine once this whole thing is over with."

I didn't know what to say. I had never seen Peter act like this and I didn't know how to deal with it. Maybe he was right, maybe I didn't know him at all. Despite all that, I had a hard time giving up on people. "Is there a reason that Donna wouldn't like you? That she would assume that you killed her husband?"

He stared at the paused TV screen. "I didn't make those dumplings."

"I know you didn't. That's not what I'm asking you."

"Why don't you ask her that question?"

"Because I want you to tell me."

He didn't say anything. He just kept staring at the screen.

"Peter, I want to help, I've been looking into some things, and it would help me a lot if I could fill in some of the holes. But I can't do that if you're not honest with me."

He finally looked at me, and for the first time since I walked in the door, I saw the old Peter that I knew. He seemed fragile somehow, like a little boy who'd just lost his first dog.

He started to speak, but before he could start, there was a knock at the door.

We both looked at each other in surprise.

"Expecting anybody?" I asked, glancing over my shoulder at the door.

"No, dude . . ." He got up from the couch and put his eye up to the peephole. He groaned and opened the door.

"I need to talk to you," an agitated female voice barked.

"Now's not a good time," Peter replied.

I knew that voice. Who was it? I tried to peek around Peter to see who it was.

No need. Kimmy Tran came barreling through the door. She froze when she saw me. "Lana . . . what are you doing here?"

I gripped the handle of my purse. "I came to check on Peter. What are you doing here?"

"I need to talk to Peter." She crossed her arms over her chest. "In private."

I looked at Peter and he shrugged.

"Okay, well, I guess I'll let you guys talk then." I started to move to the door. Peter stood in front of it awkwardly. He gave me a pointed look, but I didn't understand why. "I hope that you change your mind about Saturday."

Kimmy snorted.

After Peter shut the door behind me, I stood there for a few minutes trying to hear what they were talking about. I couldn't make out anything except for Kimmy talking in an agitated tone. Almost as if she were scolding him. I didn't know what business Kimmy Tran would have to come to Peter's apartment and demand to speak to him. Or what she could possibly scold him about. But you better believe I'd find out one way or another.

I sat anxiously on a bar stool at the Zodiac, watching Megan work her way down the bar. Occasionally she'd stop to pop the top off a beer bottle or grab an empty glass and put it under the counter.

The Rolling Stones blared through the speakers and laughter and chatter flowed through the bar.

Megan set a glass in front of me; the contents were bright red. "It's an Aries Flame Thrower," she said. "Tastes like cherries."

I took the glass from her. "Thanks . . ."

"So . . . Kimmy Tran at Peter's house, huh? That's not weird or anything." She leaned against the bar.

"I know he was about to tell me something," I said. "And she ruined it."

"Well, you'll have to try again," Megan replied. "Maybe he'll show on Saturday, after all."

I stabbed the ice cubes with my straw. "If he'll even confide in me . . ."

"Don't be so hard on yourself, it's not like we've investigated a murder before or anything. That's why I got you that book. Did you even look at it?" she asked.

I sighed. "I skimmed through it, but I didn't read it thoroughly or anything."

"Well, maybe you need to. It might help."

"I just don't know if we should even be doing this. I mean, we're not professionals, we don't know how to look into things. We're just a couple of girls."

"People don't have to be professionals to solve mysteries. You should know that from all the books you read."

"I don't know, maybe . . ."

"What don't you know?" a voice said from behind me.

When I turned to see who it was, Trudeau sat down on the stool next to me and folded his hands on the bar. He looked between the two of us.

Megan turned around, walked over to the cooler and grabbed a bottle of beer.

"Let me guess," Trudeau started, "you're getting into some kind of trouble, aren't you?"

"Why do you assume I'm up to something?" I asked.

"Because you look guilty," he said with a crooked smile.

"Well, you're wrong. I'm just sitting here minding my own business."

Megan came back with his beer and set it down in front of him. "Did you want any food tonight?"

He shook his head. "Not right now, thanks."

Megan slid a look at me, and turned around, leaving me and Trudeau to talk.

"So," he said, taking a sip of his beer, "here again, huh? That's two weeks in a row I've run into you."

"Rough day." I sipped my drink. "I thought I'd come in, have a drink, and visit with Megan."

"You want to talk about it?" he asked.

"Not really."

We sat in silence for a few minutes as I contemplated whether to tell Trudeau that I had stopped to see Peter and that Kimmy had showed up. But I didn't know what it meant yet. More importantly, I didn't want to get reprimanded.

"Whatever's wrong with you, it's written all over your face."

With a sigh, I admitted, "It's this whole thing with the dumplings . . ."

He leaned back. "Are you upset because of what I told you about Peter earlier today?"

I nodded. "It's hard a thing to swallow."

"I wish there was something I could say to make you feel better, but these are the facts." He spun his beer bottle on the bar top.

"What if there's something else?"

He stared at me for a minute. "Like what?"

"I don't know. What if there's something we don't know about . . . like a checkered past."

He sipped his beer. "Generally, these things aren't like the movies."

"I'm not saying that, I'm just saying . . . what if Peter is the one who was meant to be framed, and I got caught in the middle?"

"I've considered that," he replied. "But there's nothing to indicate there was another party involved."

"What if I could find you something?"

He turned on the stool to face me. "No, don't even think about it. You stay out of this."

"But what if I could help you? I have a lot of people that I could talk to at the plaza. They'd probably be more willing to talk with me anyway." Judging by his initial reaction, I figured it was best not to tell him that I had already started questioning people.

"That may be true," he said. "However, you shouldn't, and I don't suggest that you do. Leave this to me and my team."

"Are you even looking into anyone else?" I asked.

"We're looking into a few leads, yes."

"Who?"

"So, this is what's on your mind?" he asked, ignoring my question.

"Yes, isn't that enough?"

"Nothing about a certain suitor?" He looked away from me, focusing on the other end of the bar.

"What?"

"Never mind . . ." he said.

A butterfly fumbled around in my stomach. "Why would you ask me that?"

"Ian Sung is a suspect of ours. I thought you should know . . ."

"Oh." My shoulders slumped.

He scrunched his eyebrows. "Disappointed?"

I was. But not for the reasons he thought. "No, I haven't given him an answer yet . . ."

"What are you waiting for?" He slid his beer bottle away from him, and signaled Megan for another.

"I don't know."

Megan came over, popped the top off a beer bottle, and slid it toward Trudeau. She glanced at my drink and took the glass out of my hand, refilling it. She left without saying anything to either of us.

I sipped my drink and cringed. Megan had made this one extra strong. "I had a bad breakup and I'm not sure that I'm ready to date again."

"How long ago?" he asked.

"It's almost been a year . . . it was right before Christmas."

Trudeau winced. "Ouch, that's a rough time of year."

"Yeah, tell me about it." I leaned an elbow on the bar. "I was Christmas shopping for that jerk, and I ran into him shopping . . . with his other girlfriend."

Trudeau was silent.

I glanced at him. "Sorry, didn't mean to start a sob story. I'm fine really, just a tad bitter."

He took a deep breath. "I can see why."

"So, yeah, I'm just a little wary of going out with anybody right now."

He tilted his beer bottle. "Well, we're not all bad guys." He turned to me. "Who knows, maybe the right guy will come along and convince you otherwise."

His words hung between us, and for a brief moment there was nothing else. No music, no people, nothing. His hand, so close to my leg, rested on his knee and I could feel the space that separated us.

"How about you?" I asked, breaking the silence. "Are you—"

"No, it's just me," Trudeau responded. He kept his focus on the bar top in front of him. "I've found the people I care about tend to go away."

"Maybe we have something in common after all."

He smirked to himself. "I should leave you to the rest of your night . . . you've had a long day." He stood up from his seat and tipped his beer bottle. "In the meantime, try to stay out of trouble."

CHAPTER
19

The memorial for Thomas was scheduled to start at 5 P.M. and I was running late. I checked my cell phone, 5:13 P.M. Great, I'd never hear the end of it from my mother.

The memorial was being held at Li Wah's, which was part of the plaza located on the east side of Cleveland. Donna had told my mother she'd picked Li Wah's so Asia Village could close for the day. Signs had been posted at the entrances that we were CLOSED IN HONOR OF THOMAS FENG. Everyone from Asia Village was expected to attend.

I parked my car in the lot right outside the restaurant and scurried into the building, my heels clacking against the pavement.

At the entrance to the restaurant, a hostess stood on either side in white button-up shirts and black vests. They wore pleasant smiles and passed out pamphlets to the guests walking in. I took one as I crossed the threshold, giving it a quick glance. It was a program of the speakers for that evening. On the front cover, a regal photograph of Thomas stared back at you. Underneath the photo it read in both Chinese and English, *In Loving Memory*. The back of the pamphlet listed a menu that was split into four courses.

The place was packed as I stepped in and surveyed the area. Li-Wah's had a floating wall that they removed for large events and it opened up the restaurant to twice its regular size. Everyone who was anyone in the Asian community was in attendance. I saw the directors of the Asian community relations boards, everyone from Asia Village, and even the mayor of Cleveland.

I spotted my family sitting at our special reserved table toward the back of the room. My mother made eye contact and waved me over. "Lanaaaa!!" she yelled from across the room. A few people stopped and looked at me. The eye roll that followed was out of my control.

She continued to wave at me until I was about three feet from the table. She was seated on the side farthest from me next to my dad. She came around and looked at me, giving me a once-over. With my heels on—I'd gone with a classic black patent leather—I was towering over her. "You look too skinny," she said, scrutinizing me. "Are you eating at home?"

"Yes, I'm eating, Mom."

"Why did you take so long? We are all waiting for you. Ian is over there talking to his father." She pointed across the room near the entrance to where the two men were talking. Ian was an exact replica of his father except twenty-five years younger. They wore matching black suits and crisp white shirts. Both wore plain black ties and polished dress shoes.

"Where is Donna?" I asked, looking at the half-empty table.

"Talking, talking, so many people to talk to," my mother said. She shimmied back around the table and sat down.

My father stood up to hug me. "Hey goober, you look nice tonight."

"Thanks, Dad," I said, hugging him back. "So do you." Suits were his second skin. I got so used to seeing him in them that when he didn't wear one, he looked out of place. "Where's Anna May?" I asked, skimming the room for my sister.

"I don't know . . . somewhere," my mom said absently.

"You better get yourself a drink and get situated." My dad tapped his watch. "The first speech is going to start any minute now."

I glanced at the bar and the line forming in front of it. I headed straight over and prayed the line moved fast.

"At least there's an open bar," a voice said from behind me.

"Peter . . ." I turned to face him. "You came after all."

He looked down at his shoes. It was the first time I'd seen him without Chuck Taylors or combat boots on. In their place were shiny dress shoes that were clearly new. "Yeah, well, my mom begged me."

"I'm glad you came," I said, giving his arm a supportive squeeze.

To a casual observer, we looked like we had matched our outfits on purpose. He was dressed in a midnight-blue dress shirt that almost matched my dress and a blue and purple striped tie. His dress pants were black, and by the stiffness of the material, I had a feeling they were new too. "Hey, dude, I'm really sorry about the way I acted yesterday. I know you were only trying to help."

The line moved up and we moved with it.

"I can understand why you feel the way you do. I feel it too, you know."

He ran a hand through his hair. "If I would have just delivered the food, you wouldn't be in this mess. I'm sorry about that too."

"Why didn't you deliver the food that day?"

He tugged on his tie. "It's kind of a long story."

"Maybe if you talked about it, it would make you feel better. You know I'm always here for you."

Peter looked around, scanning the people in line and the tables near us. "This isn't the place, man."

I glanced at the people surrounding us, and I wasn't sure if he meant that specific place or the memorial itself. I decided not to press the subject too hard. "You know where to find me. We can talk whenever you're ready."

He gave me a half smile. "Thanks, Lana."

"Hey guys!" Jasmine said, sidestepping a couple walking in front of her. Yuna stood behind her, waving.

"Hi," Peter and I said in unison.

"Lana." Jasmine flashed a smile, grabbing my shoulders. "Your hair is looking fantastic!"

"Thanks! It helps to have the best stylist in the city."

She cocked her head to the side. "Although I think you need to come in for a trim. Your ends are looking kind of dead . . ."

I grabbed at the ends of my hair. "What? But I just—"

Jasmine squeezed my shoulders and winked. "A quick trim should do it, maybe stop in tomorrow, if you've got the day off?" She winked again.

"Okay . . . yeah, I'm off . . ."

"Can't have my clients running around with split ends." She patted me on the shoulder. "Well, we're off to find our seats. We'll talk to you both later!"

By the time they walked away, it was our turn in line. We ordered our drinks and hurried back to the table.

Nancy and my mother were sitting next to each other and whispered excitedly to one another, no doubt gossiping about something or someone. My dad sat on the other side of my mother, people-watching. My sister was still nowhere to be found.

I shimmied in between our table and the next, my drink threatening to spill over the sides.

Nancy looked up at us. "Peter, come sit next to me." She pointed at the empty chair next to hers.

He shrugged and moved to the seat next to his mother.

The lights flickered, signaling everyone to their seats. Ian and Donna, smiling and talking as they walked, headed in our direction. Donna whispered something to Ian and he nodded in return, taking the lead in their path to the table. His eyes fell on me and he grinned, a little too eagerly for my taste.

Behind them was my sister, her long ponytail bobbing side to side as she made her way over. They all arrived at the table at once and greetings were exchanged. Donna set her purse down next to me and was ushering Ian to sit on the opposite side of me. Before he could make it over, my sister shimmied her way past Ian and sat down between me and my father. Ian frowned at my sister.

Anna May wrapped her arm around my shoulder as if she were going to hug me. As she leaned in, she whispered, "You owe me."

Ian took the only seat available, next to Peter. The look on his face told me he was not amused. He leaned forward, grinning at me. "You look lovely this evening."

"Yes," Donna added with a smile. "Quite a beautiful young lady, isn't she?"

My sister snorted next to me.

"Thank you," I said, keeping my eyes focused on Donna. She was dressed in an elegant cream pantsuit that probably cost three times more than my discounted Calvin Klein. Her signature hairstyle, the classic French twist, was flawless. A dainty pearl hair stick peeked out from the side. "You look rather stunning yourself."

Across the room, the mayor of Cleveland stood behind a podium in a dark blue pin-striped suit. He shuffled through some note cards and then cleared his throat into the microphone. A hush fell over the room, and everyone turned in their seats to face him.

He smiled and scanned the room, his eyes stopping on every table. "It is both an honor and a privilege to be the guest speaker tonight. Thomas Feng was a very good friend of mine, and he'll be greatly missed, not just by the Asian community, but by everyone's lives he touched." He paused. "I remember when I first met Thomas . . ."

All of a sudden I had that sensation that someone was staring at me. Without being too obvious, I glanced around the room. Mostly everyone around the room was looking at the mayor. He had a captive audience and I watched as the crowd nodded in unison.

I spotted Kimmy, sitting diagonally across from me some tables over, in a strapless purple dress that clashed with her skin tone. She was seated next to her parents and didn't even try pretending she wasn't bored. Her head was down and my guess was that she had her cell phone out underneath the table.

Her hair, which was usually thrown together in a sloppy bun, out of carelessness, now looked intentionally styled that way. A few sparkles shimmered from her hair, and it reminded me of a girl going to the prom.

At her table were a few people from the plaza. The Yi sisters sat next to Daniel Tran, and opposite them was Mr. An. Our eyes met and when he noticed me looking back at him he turned away.

My sister shoved my leg with hers under the table. When I looked at her, she nodded toward my mother, who was giving me the stink eye. She nodded toward the podium.

I turned my attention back to the mayor.

". . . and they said, 'Don't give him any more rice then!'"

Everyone laughed and a few people clapped.

"But seriously, folks, I don't know how I would have come this far without the support of the Feng family." He held his hand out, palm up, toward Donna. "Thank you for giving me this opportunity to speak for such a great man. Things won't be the same without him."

The room applauded animatedly while the mayor

gave a final wave to the audience. He returned to his seat and the other people at his table all leaned in with what was sure to be eager praise.

One of the owners of Li Wah's stood at the podium and alerted the crowd that appetizers would be served before the next speaker, which, according to my program, was Donna herself.

While the mayor had been talking, it'd been enough to keep our table occupied. But now that his speech was over and there was nothing for our table to focus on, the tension among the eight of us became tangible.

The waitress came by with rice in small bowls, passing one to each of us. As if all of us had the same thought, we acted a little too interested in our rice bowls. Other servers came over and filled our lazy Susan with dumplings, spring rolls, and Japanese-style tofu.

I stared nervously at the dumplings.

My dad broke the silence. "Well, look at all this food." He spun the lazy Susan, picking something off each dish. The rest of us followed suit.

After the guests had had time to fill themselves on appetizers and replenish their drinks, the room lights dimmed again, and Donna dabbed at her mouth with a cloth napkin. She placed it over her plate and made her way up to the podium. She stood with her chin up and her back straight, her hands placed firmly on the sides of the stand. She put on a pleasant smile for the crowd as she scanned the room, validating that all eyes were on her.

"I want to thank everyone for coming tonight. I know a lot of you were disappointed with my decision to not have a public ceremony, but with the media lurking about, I felt it was necessary for the privacy of my family."

A few people in the crowd nodded in understanding.

She continued, "I always thought that Thomas and I would grow old together. And to take this unexpected road in life is a difficult adjustment to make." She paused. "Since Thomas has been gone, I've thought much about where my life is headed and what roles I need to play in the community. And I have come to the conclusion that running Asia Village is not where I am needed."

There were a few gasps in the crowd.

Donna chuckled. "No need to be alarmed by this news, it doesn't mean what you think it does."

The crowd quieted again and, surely now, all eyes were on her.

"Ian Sung," she said, pointing to our table. "He will be taking over all responsibilities regarding Asia Village."

A murmur filled the room as people whispered among themselves, the looks on their faces reflecting surprise and general upset at the news. It didn't appear to be going over well with everyone. Was it Ian himself? Or the fact that Donna was stepping out of the way?

She raised her voice to be heard over the clamor. "Even though Ian will be in charge, I will act as a silent business partner to ensure that, according to Thomas's wishes, the plaza stays within our family."

This did not seem to relieve the crowd, and Donna held up her hands, signaling the crowd to quiet down.

"Now, I know some of you may be concerned about the changes that will be taking place during this transition. But I can assure you that I have the utmost confidence in Ian as a business partner, and I can see Asia Village growing under his care. I promise, good things are coming."

The room was silent again. Perhaps people were contemplating the news and letting it settle with them. Donna continued on with her speech as if the interruption hadn't taken place. She wrapped up by talking about Mr. Feng's love for the plaza and how she was excited for the coming changes.

After she was done speaking, we were given another short intermission to freshen our drinks and use the restrooms. The next person to speak was Ian, and I was anxious to hear what he was going to say for himself. I don't know what everyone thought. Had they really assumed Donna would be running the show? She was hardly around to begin with.

Kimmy cornered me at the bar. I had a hard time making eye contact with her, but mostly because of what she was wearing. It was very revealing, to say the least.

"Just so you know," she said through clenched teeth, "I saw you and Peter talking earlier. I know that he told you everything."

She had caught me off guard, and I stood there staring at her like she'd sprouted horns. "I don't know what—"

"Don't lie to me, Lana Lee. I've had enough of people lying around here." She looked over her shoulder to see if anyone was there.

"No, really, I swear, Peter didn't—"

"I'll do whatever it takes to keep you quiet, do you understand me?" Her eyes narrowed into slits. "No one can find out . . ."

"Okay . . ." I said, my hands beginning to sweat. There was no mistake that Kimmy was threatening me, I just didn't know about what.

She glared at me for a few more minutes, let out a large groan and stomped off.

I wasn't sure what she meant, but I had a feeling that it couldn't be anything good. Her recent arguments with Mr. Feng before his death, and her strange interactions with Peter made me think that maybe I should be looking at her more closely.

I'd left my cell phone behind and I hurried back to the table. I needed to tell Megan about this. When I got back, a small crowd of people hovered around Donna, no doubt talking to her about the announcement she'd just made.

Mr. An stood next to her with his hands behind his back. But, instead of listening to her as everyone else was, he was watching me as I neared the table. I smiled at him as our eyes met, but he looked away, turning his attention back to Donna.

I tried to shimmy around the opposite side of the table, but that was blocked too. The only way to get back to my seat was to go through the crowd gathered around Donna. There was a small opening between her and Mr. An that I could sneak through.

As I passed her, Donna reached out and grabbed my wrist. "Lana, dear, let's switch seats," she said, ignoring the people talking around her. "I would like a few minutes to talk with Anna May." Her smile was sly as she said it, and I knew that wasn't the truth.

I looked at the empty seat next to Ian's chair and sighed. If she thought she was fooling anyone, she was wrong. Begrudgingly, I nodded in acceptance.

Mr. An was blocking the seat I agreed to sit in. I gave him a light tap on the shoulder. "Excuse me, Mr. An, would you mind if I snuck past you." I pointed at the chair.

"Of course, Lana," he said, stepping to the side. "The space is so tight between these tables."

I sat down in my new seat and exchanged a glance with my sister.

The lights flickered and the people that had encircled Donna said their good-byes and moved back to their tables.

I pulled out my phone and was about to text Megan when the lights dimmed. Crap. It was time for Ian's speech.

Anna May hissed at me. "Hey, put away your phone . . . your boyfriend is about to speak."

My nostrils flared. "You're lucky I'm sitting over here," I said, glaring at her from the other side of Donna.

My mother snapped her fingers at us. "Be quiet."

I straightened up in my chair and faced the podium where Ian had positioned himself.

He fiddled with his tie, loosening it at the neck and straightening it under his jacket. I had never seen him this uncomfortable. If I didn't know any better, I'd say he was nervous.

The microphone crackled as he said, "Good evening," and the sound made him step back. He tried again, keeping his mouth farther away from the microphone. "Good evening, ladies and gentlemen. I am so happy to be here." He stopped, a look of horror on his face. "No, I don't mean that . . . not happy. What I mean is, it's my pleasure to be . . . given this honor."

The crowd remained silent, their faces expression-less, minus a few who looked annoyed. His father was one of them. I watched him as he looked down at the table and shook his head, disappointed.

Ian seemed to refocus himself, taking a deep breath and flipping through note cards he had in his hands. He looked back out into the crowd, his eyes shifting back and forth. "It is a sad time for all of us at Asia Village, for we have lost a great friend. But, as Thomas loved this plaza, so do I. And he would have wanted us to soldier on—"

Donna smacked her hand on the table, rattling the plates, and rocked back and forth in her chair. Her hand went up to her throat and she held it there, with her mouth hanging open as she gasped for air.

Everyone turned to face us.

Donna looked straight at me before her eyes rolled back in her head and she collapsed face forward onto the table. The room was a united gasp and people stood to get a better look at what was happening.

Everything after that was confusion. The last thing I heard was someone say, "Call 911," and I'm pretty sure that was me.

CHAPTER
20

The paramedics had just wheeled Donna out on a gurney. She was unresponsive, but to our relief, she was still breathing. The memorial attendees lumped together in groups around the room, chattering in speculation. I sat in my chair, taking deep breaths, while Detective Trudeau hovered over me. He'd heard the news come over the radio, and rushed over to see what was going on.

"So, you said that she grabbed her throat, looked at you, and then hit the table?" he asked me for the third time.

I nodded, demonstrating for him this time. "First she slapped the table, like she was trying to get someone's attention."

"I see." Trudeau scribbled in his trusty notebook. "But she didn't actually say anything to you?"

I shook my head.

A few chairs over, my mother wrung her hands. Esther, who had been sitting two tables over, sat beside my mom talking softly to her in Mandarin. My father stood over my mother and rubbed her shoulders supportively. Lou hovered in the background. He'd been seated at the table next to us and came over after Donna had been taken away. Anna May sat beside me, staring blankly at the table.

Peter and his mother had stepped outside. Apparently the commotion was too much for Nancy and she felt faint. That made two of us. I had no desire to be sitting here right now, feeling cornered against a wall. The room didn't feel as big as it had an hour ago.

He looked at me with a pained expression on his face. "I think we better step outside."

My mother's head jerked up. "What? Where are you going with my daughter?"

"I think maybe it would be best if your daughter and I took a walk outside. She could use the fresh air." He looked at the crowded room of onlookers.

"Excuse me for saying so," Anna May said with lead in her voice, "but I don't see why it would be necessary for you to take my sister anywhere. I'd be more than happy to take her for a walk."

Trudeau pursed his lips, clicking his pen methodically. "I can assure you that your sister is safe with me. You're still needed to answer questions." He skimmed the room for the other officers who were taking statements. "Someone should be over shortly."

My sister huffed. "This whole thing is ridiculous to begin with. I don't understand why you're questioning everyone when it's clear that Donna was choking on something. It's hardly anything to interrogate the whole room over."

Through a clenched jaw, Detective Trudeau said, "I find it a little odd that Mrs. Feng would have an episode like this after what happened to her husband. We need to take every precaution."

I grabbed his arm. "Wait, are you saying that she—" I couldn't bring myself to say the words.

In a gentle tone, he turned to me and said, "She was experiencing the exact same symptoms as someone would with an allergic reaction. This wasn't just a choking fit." He looked down at the table, his eyes studying the contents. His eyes narrowed and he crouched down near Donna's teacup. "Whose teacup is this?" he asked, looking directly at me.

"It's Donna's."

He looked back at the cup, and at me. "And where is your cup?" he asked.

I pointed to the cup on my right. "This is mine."

He picked up the kettle and opened the lid, sniffing the contents. "What is all this stuff floating around in here?"

"Chrysanthemums."

He put the lid back down and investigated the cups again.

"Who was sitting here?" He pointed to the empty seat next to me.

"Ian Sung."

"And you were sitting here?" He pointed to my chair.

"Well, originally yes, but Donna and I switched seats."

He studied the table. "No one touch anything," he said to the group. He looked over his shoulder, signaling a police officer to come over.

A young guy with a blond buzz cut came to stand at the edge of our table. "Yes, sir?"

"We need something to contain this evidence." Trudeau pointed to the table. "Do you have something?" Trudeau asked.

"Yes, of course, sir," the young man replied.

"I want to mark all of these cups and who they belonged to. We're taking everything with us. Tea, food . . . all of it. I'm having it tested."

"Yes, sir." The young man nodded and hurried off to get whatever it was they planned to put everything in.

My mother looked up at my dad. "Bill, what's going on?"

"It's okay, Betty, don't worry," my father said, squeezing her shoulders. "The police will handle it."

Detective Trudeau looked at my parents. "I think that Mrs. Feng was poisoned. It could be anything on this table, but since she was the only one affected, I think it was in her tea."

Everyone at the table, except me, gasped. I was too busy thinking about how Donna and I had switched seats.

Trudeau and I stood outside of the plaza, staring out onto Payne Avenue. "I appreciate you getting me out of there so fast," I said. "I don't think I could have taken it much longer."

"You're welcome." He stuck his hands in his pockets. "It was getting stuffy in there . . . even for me."

I kept my eyes focused on the street in front of us. It

was easier than looking at him while I said what I had to say. "Do you think that tea was meant for me?"

The detective remained still. "Why would you say that?"

"Because we switched seats, and if I wasn't paying attention, I might have grabbed the wrong cup." My eyes began to well up and I could feel the temperature dropping. I shivered.

"We won't know until all of the tea has been tested," he replied. His voice was calm, and it helped soothe my nerves. "Don't get worked up over anything just yet. No one else seemed to have any reaction to their drinks."

I sniffed back my tears. I didn't want the detective to see me cry.

"I need to ask you something," he said gently.

I chanced a glimpse at him. "What do you want to know?"

"Did you notice anything out of the ordinary tonight?"

"No," I said, thinking back. There hadn't been anything strange. Just my little encounter with Kimmy. "Except . . ."

"Except what?" he prodded.

I shifted my weight, my heels tightening around my toes. If I told him about my run-in with Kimmy, then I'd have to explain how I'd gone to Peter's house the day before. "Kimmy Tran . . . she approached me . . ."

"Okay," he said, looking confused. "She approached you . . . and?"

"She said that she'd do anything to make sure that no one found out."

"That no one found out about what?" he asked with caution.

"That's the thing. I have no idea."

"Why would she say this to you to begin with?"

There was no way around it. I'd have to tell him the truth. "I stopped at Peter's yesterday to talk to him about the memorial. Donna wanted all of us to sit together at dinner, and I didn't know if anyone had told him." I sucked in a breath. "While I was there, Kimmy showed up and practically threw me out of his apartment because she needed to talk to him in private." I paused to let him absorb the story. "Then tonight, when she approached me, she assumed that he had told me whatever they talked about. Only he didn't."

His hands went up to his face and he covered his eyes with his palms. "You went over there?"

"It was only for a minute."

He turned to me, his face red where his hands had been. "Only for a minute?" he repeated.

"It was—"

"Lana, what did I say? I said to stay away from him, and then you go over there?" Trudeau started to pace. "Did you go straight there from the station, or did you at least stop at home and give it some thought?"

I watched him as he paced back and forth in front of me. "I went shopping with Megan . . ."

He laughed. "Oh, well, at least you went shopping."

"I had to see him for myself. Besides, I can handle myself."

He stopped pacing and stood in front of me. He leaned in, his face inches from mine. "This isn't about whether or not you can handle yourself . . . don't play the tough-girl act with me. Not now, Lana. Not while I'm trying to keep you safe."

I softened a little when I noticed the worry in his voice. The more I saw him, the more human he became. I felt a hint of guilt for upsetting him.

"What can you tell me about Kimmy Tran?" he asked, breaking into my thoughts.

I shrugged. "She used to be a nice girl . . . always kind of grumpy though. I'm not very close with her now so I can't tell you much."

Trudeau looked away, his jaw clenching. "Well, she just became part of my investigation."

About an hour later, I was home and in my pajamas. Kikko and I were snuggled up on the couch under a jumble of thick blankets. Her head poked out from under one, a bone held firmly between her paws. She took out her frustrations on the bone I'd just given her. Sitting Indian style, I had my notebook balancing on my right leg, and the private-investigating book open on my left leg.

I was still worried about the possible poisoning from earlier that night. I jotted down some notes about what I remembered, emphasizing details of Kimmy's strange behavior. I couldn't think of anything that would connect her and Peter. It bugged me. She was so comfortable coming into his apartment, as if she'd been there before. But as far as I knew, they weren't more than acquaintances. And they definitely didn't run in the same social circles.

My phone rang, and I reached for it on the coffee table. The readout said: ANNA MAY.

"Hello?" I grumbled into the phone.

"What happened with you and the cop?" Anna May asked without a greeting.

After I'd come back inside from talking with Trudeau, we didn't have a chance to speak in private. I wasn't planning on telling my sister anything anyway. I knew it'd get straight back to my mother. "Nothing, he asked me if I was okay, and then we went over what happened again."

"Mom just called me, Donna is conscious."

"Is she okay?"

"She didn't give any details, just said that we should go visit tomorrow."

"Okay, do you want to go together?" I suggested.

"I told Mom I would work at the restaurant tomorrow so she and Dad could have the day off together. He's been so busy working they've barely seen each other. I'll find time to go after Nancy comes in or something. You go ahead without me."

"Well, aren't you just the good little daughter," I teased.

"Hey, one of us has to be," Anna May said.

"Whatever."

"Love you too, little sister." She made some kissy noises and hung up.

I tossed my phone back on the table and stared at my notebook. I flipped through the previous pages and snickered to myself about my earlier thoughts of Donna being a potential suspect. Well, that was out. I scribbled over her name.

I made a few more notes to myself before I turned my attention to the private investigating book. Maybe Megan was right and I needed to spend more time looking at it. It might give me some ideas I hadn't thought of.

I flipped open the book and skimmed the table of contents. It had everything from becoming a PI to state requirements. I didn't want to actually become a PI; what I wanted was to figure out what I should do next with all this random information I had. I fanned through the pages. That's when I saw it, "Investigating the Crime Scene" . . . and it hit me—I had to go to the crime scene. I had to get into the office of Feng and Sung.

"This idea is crazy!" Megan screeched from the kitchen. She had just gotten home and was digging around in the fridge, while I told her the new scheme I had been plotting all night while waiting for her come home from work. I watched her mull it over.

"Well, are you in or not? I can't do it by myself."

She stared at me. "Of course I'm in. What do you take me for?" She took a swig of her beer. "How are we going to get in?"

"Leave that all up to me," I said with pride.

Megan plopped down on the couch next to Kikko. "Do you really think someone was trying to kill her? I mean, geez, first her husband, and now her too?"

Kikko, not one to be disturbed while chewing her bone, secured the rawhide in her mouth and jumped to the floor. She repositioned herself on the rug and turned her back to us.

I sat down on the couch next to Megan, sticking my feet under the pile of blankets. "I don't know." I hadn't told her that I thought the tea might actually have been meant for me. "I can't believe that something like this would happen during his memorial."

"I wonder if Peter hadn't showed up, this still would have happened."

"Megan!"

She looked at me sheepishly. "What? I'm just saying . . ."

"Well, don't say."

"Okay, sorry." She leaned back on the couch. "So, what about this Kimmy thing then, what do you think that's about? If she's that worried about him telling you, to react the way she did . . . well . . . then I really want to know what it's about."

"For which, by the way, I'm going to need you to do a little bit of recon."

Megan perked up, sitting straighter with her shoulders back. "You have a job for me? I thought you'd never ask."

"I need you to do some digging on the computer."

She slumped over. "Oh."

I shook the investigation book at her. "This book has a list of Web sites you can use to look up information on people. While I'm at the hospital visiting Donna tomorrow, I need you to do some digging on Peter and Kimmy and see what you can find out about them. Maybe check out their social media too. Peter doesn't really use that kind of stuff much, but I know that Kimmy practically lives on it."

She grabbed the book from me. "It'll be my pleasure

to dig up dirt on Kimmy. She has to be up to no good with that crap attitude of hers."

"She's definitely hiding something," I agreed. "She's been acting too strange lately not to be." I leaned back on the couch and reached for my notebook. I looked at Donna's name scratched out and felt a bit of relief that I could take her off my list. At least that was one less to worry about.

Before I closed it and called it a night, I put a big black star next to Kimmy's name.

CHAPTER
21

- - - - - - - - - - - - - - -

I hate hospitals. In my life, I've only been to about four different hospitals, but I think it's safe to say, the smell is universal. It's antiseptic and stagnant. You can decorate the walls with pleasant photographs or paintings, but it won't change the stale taste that fills the air. Or the apprehensive look on the faces of just about everybody in sight. The most pleasant people are typically the gift shop workers.

I had come armed with balloons that had cheery "Get Well Soon" plastered all over them. Donna had a private room according to my mother, and that made me feel better. I despised the awkwardness that came when visiting someone and knowing that a complete stranger was eavesdropping from the other side of the curtain.

The door to her room was ajar, and all I could see through the small glass window were her feet. The television was on, but I couldn't hear any sound.

I tapped lightly on the door, hoping that she was awake.

"Come in," Donna replied, her voice sounding fragile.

Pushing the door open enough to slip inside, I shimmied in with the balloons until I was in plain view. Donna started to smile as she saw me walking in. "Oh, Lana, you shouldn't have." She waved me over. "Come in, come in." She looked tired and I wondered if she'd slept at all since she became conscious.

"I thought these might help cheer you up." I walked farther into the room and placed the balloons near the window by her bedside table. They were tethered by a weight wrapped in bright purple foil.

She turned her head to look at them. "They're wonderful. Just what I needed."

There was a cushioned chair angled next to the bed, so I sat down, folding my hands in my lap. "How long do you have to stay here?" I asked, giving the room a once-over.

Donna followed my gaze. "Oh, it's not so bad. Maybe just another day or so. They want to make sure that everything is out of my system and that I'm fully hydrated and back to normal."

"What happened exactly? If you don't mind telling me . . ."

She looked up at the ceiling. "Apparently, it was an abundance of yellow jasmine . . . I guess I took too much?"

My eyes widened. "Yellow jasmine? What's that?"

She sighed. "It's an herbal remedy that I take for my migraines. Mr. Zhang promised me that it was safe to take, but I guess it can be quite dangerous. My doctor was pretty upset with me."

My brain was moving faster than I could process the information. "It's something that Mr. Zhang sells in his store?"

"I have been struggling with migraines for quite some time. And I hate taking prescription medicine." She turned back toward me and smiled weakly. "So, when Mr. Zhang suggested yellow jasmine, I thought why not. It couldn't hurt to try something new."

My brain was still moving at warp speed but I forced myself to sit perfectly still and nod in understanding.

"I guess I've been so overwrought since Thomas passed that I haven't been paying attention to what I'm doing. I'm just glad that my mother took Jill and Jessica to California. I'd hate to put them through this too."

Without realizing it, Donna had given me the perfect segue for the plan I had cooked up. "That reminds me," I said cheerfully. "Why don't I stop by your place and make sure everything is okay? You know, water your plants and check your mail."

Donna clasped her hands together. "What a great idea. With everyone gone, there's no one to check on things, I'm afraid. I had thought about asking Ian, but since you're already here . . ." She looked around the room. "Oh, over there, in that drawer, is my purse. Will you get it out for me?"

I went to the drawer on the other side of the bed and opened it, pulling out her purse. She stuck her hand inside and dug around for her keys.

"Now," she said. "There is an alarm that's set. I'll

write down the passcode for you to get in." She dug around in her purse some more and pulled out a little notepad and pen. She jotted down the number and tore the page out. "You have sixty seconds to enter this code."

I took the paper from her and did a jump for joy in my head. That worked out much easier than I thought.

I stayed with her and we talked for another thirty minutes before I made an excuse to leave. "I'll swing by your place after I'm finished helping Anna May at the restaurant. I can have my mother bring back the keys when she comes to see you tomorrow. Do you want me to send anything with her?"

"Not that I can think of," she said. "I don't feel much like reading or doing anything."

I said my good-byes and practically ran out of the hospital all the way to my car.

Once in the driver's seat, I took a minute to collect myself. I looked at the keys in my hand and took a deep breath. My plan was in motion. Now, all I had to do was search the Feng house for a set of keys to get into the property office at Asia Village. Piece of cake. I'm sure there was a spare set somewhere in their house.

But first, I had to get a hold of Detective Trudeau. I needed to talk to him about the yellow jasmine.

I was fortunate enough to be shown to Trudeau's office this time, which was a step up from the interrogation room. When I'd called him, he was just about to leave the office, so I'd had perfect timing. He sat behind his desk, with day-old scruff, and a wrinkled dress shirt.

I had just finished telling him about my conversation

with Donna, minus the taking of the keys, when he held up one hand and put the other on his forehead. "And you're telling me all of this because?"

"If she's taking the stuff already, then she just over-dosed on it. Right? Which means that no one was try-ing to poison her . . . or me."

He reached for the Styrofoam cup sitting in front of him and took a swig. "It's a possibility. The tea is al-ready at the lab so we might as well have it looked at anyway. I'm having the individual cups tested and com-paring it to the pot that was at the table. It might take a couple of days."

"Even if she told me it was her own fault?" I asked.

He nodded. "Absolutely. It might be something dif-ferent than she thinks, and I'm not taking any chances since we still haven't figured out who's responsible for her husband's murder. It won't hurt to find out the re-sults."

"Well, hopefully it's all just a crazy coincidence."

He drummed his fingers on his desk. "Do you re-member anybody being at the table that shouldn't have been there?"

"Not that I can think of. When I came back from the bar, there was a group surrounding Mrs. Feng . . . mostly people from Asia Village." I thought back. "I remem-ber seeing the Yi sisters, Cindy from the bookstore, and Mr. An, but I wasn't there the whole time. I was being accosted by Kimmy Tran at the bar." I shivered at the memory. There was still that whole ordeal to contend with.

"That might have been her plan," Trudeau suggested. "She verbally attacks me while I'm up from the table and then Peter drops poison into the tea?" As I said it, I visualized it. There I am talking to Kimmy and meanwhile, Peter's back at the table sneaking droplets of random poison into a cup.

Trudeau stared at me. "What happened to Peter being innocent?" he asked.

I looked down at my hands. "It's like you said, everyone's a suspect."

He stood up from his chair and came around to sit on the edge of his desk in front of me. "I'm really sorry that you got dragged into this. I know these people are your friends . . ."

He sat inches away from me, and I could feel the exact amount of distance between us just like I had at the bar. His body tensed and he cleared his throat. "Until we find out for sure, nothing changes. You still stay away from Peter . . . and maybe Kimmy too. Hopefully this will be over soon." He got up and walked over to the door, refusing to look at me.

I started to rise. "Should I stay away from Mr. Zhang too?" I asked with a hint of sarcasm.

"Actually, that wouldn't be a bad idea."

When I got in the car, I called Megan. "I'm on my way to the Feng house now," I informed her.

"So, no problems getting the key then?" she asked. I could hear glasses clinking in the background.

"Nope, she was so happy that I was willing to do her a favor."

"Great," Megan replied. "Come by the Zodiac when you're done, I have something to show you."

She clicked off before I could ask what it was.

As I pulled into the Fengs' driveway, I started to doubt that I could go through with my plan. The pit of my stomach was lined with guilt at the thought of going through someone's personal belongings. But I couldn't think of another way to get into that office. I didn't know how to pick a lock and I didn't have the time to learn.

I turned the ignition off and sat staring at their house, giving myself a pep talk. *This will be a piece of cake*, I said to myself, trying to restore the confidence I had when I left the hospital. No one was home and no one would be the wiser. No reason to be nervous. I would be in and out before I knew it. Right? Yeah, right.

As naturally as possible, I got out of the car and walked up to the door, trying hard not to look over my shoulder. *Just act normal, Lana, no one knows you're up to something*, I told myself.

After grabbing the mail from the box attached to their porch wall, I turned the key and rushed inside, spotting the keypad on the wall in the entryway. I tapped in the four-digit code with fingers that vibrated like I'd had ten cups of coffee.

The silence in the house was overbearing and I cleared my throat, listening to the sound resonate in the hall. There was a long table to my right with a giant, ornate mirror above it. I took a peek at myself. One of these days I'd have to work on my poker face.

But for now, the sooner I pulled it together, the sooner I could find what I needed and leave. Reminding myself that my intentions were good helped a smidge.

Since I had it in my hands, I riffled through the mail that I'd taken out of the box. Nothing of significance stood out to me. Just a couple of credit card bills and some junk mail. I set it on the table and went to poke my head in the kitchen.

Everything was immaculate. The marble countertops were spotless and there wasn't a single bit of clutter. The stainless steel appliances sparkled as if they'd just been cleaned that morning.

I opened a few drawers, but found nothing except kitchen utensils. Evidently this family didn't have a junk drawer. Their house—though fabulous—was more like a showroom than a home, and there was nothing cozy or warm about it. Made me wonder how it was to be a teenage girl living in this palace.

I headed up the carpeted staircase from the main hall, and stood at the top staring down the hallway. There were six doors, two on my left and three on my right, and one straight ahead. I started on my left and found that both rooms on that side were Jill's and Jessica's bedrooms. The first one was right out of a Barbie catalog. I'd never seen so much pink. The other was more sophisticated and decorated in neutral tones with a dash of blue here and there, but nothing exciting.

The door at the end of the hall turned out to be the bathroom, and wow, I could have lived in it and been happy for the rest of my life. It was a massive tiled room with a Jacuzzi bathtub, a standing shower, and his and hers vanity sinks. There was even a chaise positioned in the empty space near the tub. I could probably fit five of my apartment's bathrooms in there and still have space left over. I took a minute to contemplate the life of luxury.

After I was done drooling over their magnificent

bathroom, I headed back into the hallway and checked the door on the right nearest the bathroom. It appeared to be a guest bedroom, plain and decorated in neutral tones similar to the one across the hall. An oil painting of a peacock hung above the bed.

Moving on to the next room, I opened the door and when I looked inside, my mouth must have dropped to the floor. Mr. Feng's office was well lived in. The room contained every piece of personal character that existed in the house.

I stood in the doorway and absorbed it in its entirety. On the walls were pictures of his kids, wedding photos, photographs of important ceremonies he'd attended, and pictures of what I assumed to be China. The room was lined with bookshelves—thick hardcovers on boring topics like business, finance, and property ownership. Against the far wall was an L-shaped desk that was covered with papers and more photographs. I would make that my starting point.

Giving the top of the desk a quick scan, I didn't find anything of importance. Bills and letters from local companies littered the desk, and from what I could tell there was no organizing method. I thought about Ian trying to sort through the mess at the property office.

There were a few photographs of his family off to the side, but other than that, there wasn't much to look at.

I opened the first drawer on the right and found more of the same, random papers that didn't mean anything to me. Mainly I was looking for some type of key.

On the left side, the top drawer had a ring of keys in it. I couldn't be entirely sure that these were the right ones because none of them were marked, but I took them anyway, and slipped them into my pocket.

I dug around a little more, and not finding anything of interest, I decided to be thankful that I'd found anything at all. I had a set of keys I could test out. I could go.

I shut the door and raced back downstairs. I froze in the middle of the staircase. At the door, a person stood with their face pressed against the small, frosted-glass window, their hands cupped around their eyes, looking in. They seemed to notice me and started pounding on the door. I made my way down, dragging my feet on the remaining steps. Who the heck could this be? And couldn't they have waited until after I'd left to stop by?

I opened the door a sliver and poked my head out. Staring back at me was a middle-aged woman with big blond hair, and an equally big scowl on her face. "Who the hell are you?" She put her hands on her hips and gave me a stern, disapproving look. "And why are you in Donna's house?"

I opened the door wider, assuming that this must be one of Donna's neighbors. "I'm Lana Lee, a friend of the family. Donna is in the hospital and she asked me to come check on things while she's away."

Skeptically, she looked me up and down. "I see, and why exactly is Donna in the hospital?"

"I'm afraid she got very ill at the memorial for her husband last night. She collapsed and was rushed to the hospital."

She put a well-manicured hand on her chest and shook her head. "That poor woman, she has been through the wringer if ever I've seen it."

I nodded in agreement. "I was just about to get going, she should be home tomorrow or the next day."

"Well, you tell her to rest up and I'll be sure to keep an eye on things around here. The last thing she needs is a break-in."

"Exactly." I walked back into the house and made a show of arming the alarm. Shutting the door behind me, I gave her a confident smile. "I've got it all locked up now."

She looked at the house with approval and followed me down the drive. "You make sure to let Donna know I have her in my prayers."

"I'll do that," I said, scrambling to get into my car.

She stood in the driveway and waved me off as I pulled out with my heart thumping in my chest.

CHAPTER
22

The Zodiac was empty, except for a couple of guys playing pool. Megan was able to give me her full attention for a change.

"So, Donna was taking this stuff regularly?" Megan asked in disbelief. "This stuff is pretty wild. All these Web sites mention taking it as a homeopathic drug," she informed me, pointing at her phone. "But there's warning after warning on it. I even found a few stories where people were murdered with it."

We had just finished Googling information about yellow jasmine and found that it came with a long list of warnings and contraindications because of its toxicity level. It made me wonder why Mr. Zhang would suggest such a poisonous herb.

I nodded, sipping the latest concoction that Megan had brought me, a Pisces Punch. I needed it, after the day I'd had. "I'm not sure why anyone on earth would take it willingly. I'm going to talk to Mr. Zhang tomorrow when I take my lunch break and find out more about it and why he would even let her take it to begin with. He had to have known."

Megan tapped her phone screen. "Wow, did you know that Sir Arthur Conan Doyle experimented on himself with this stuff? He wanted to see how the toxins would react in different doses!"

I gawked at her. "Would you pay attention?"

She put her phone down. "Sorry . . ." Megan traced a line of split wood along the bar top with her finger. "So, it's possible that what happened last night has nothing to do with anything involving Mr. Feng's murder?"

"Adam still wants to check it out, just to be sure," I informed her.

She raised an eyebrow. "You're calling him Adam now?"

"Trudeau . . . I meant Detective Trudeau."

"Uh-huh."

I changed the subject. "What did you have to tell me?"

She threw up her hands. "Oh! Right!" She dug under the bar and pulled out her purse. From it she removed a wad of folded-up papers. "I found this."

Taking the papers from her, I unfolded them and smoothed them out on the bar. "What are these?"

"Random information that I dug up on Peter."

I skimmed over the papers she had printed out from her computer search. The first two pages were screen shots from different social media sites.

She pointed to the page I had stopped on. "This is a screen shot from the day that Mr. Feng died." She tapped the page. "You guys left the plaza that day and went home early, remember?"

Staring back at me was a picture of Peter drinking with a few of his friends and it was marked 4:00 P.M. That was only an hour or two after my mother had sent us home for the day. In the photo, he was eyeing the camera with a beer bottle held up to his mouth while a few of his friends laughed in the background. Didn't look like the Peter I knew, and it certainly didn't match up with the recluse that Peter had become recently either. I nodded. "We left shortly before three."

"Yup, that's what I thought," she said. "And look at this." She flipped to the third page. "I copied this from a police blotter."

"'Asian-American male, thirty, is arrested at local strip club for disorderly conduct,'" I read aloud.

"There are a couple more of these and they're all dated within the past couple of weeks." She looked at me pointedly.

I ignored her and skimmed the pages of screenshots she'd taken.

Megan watched my expression. "Lana, how well do you actually know Peter?"

I avoided the question. "What about the information on Kimmy?" I handed her back the papers.

"Oh, that was a huge bust." She folded the papers back up and stuck them in her purse. "I found zero interesting things on her. Even her Facebook is private, so I couldn't look at anything. But I'm telling you, it's looking more and more like it was Peter."

Again, I found myself at a loss for words. I took a deep breath. "There's no actual proof that the police blotter is talking about Peter; it could be anybody."

"That is true." Megan nodded thoughtfully. "But with everything going on . . ."

"We don't know for sure," I insisted.

She planted her hands on her hips. "Well, you know what that means then, right?"

"What?" I asked, knowing I would regret it later.

"We have to find out for ourselves."

CHAPTER 23

We couldn't agree on what we should do next so we flipped a coin to decide which route to investigate first: the property office or Megan's idea of tailing Peter. The property office won.

In order for us to pull off getting into the property office without being seen, we had to adjust our work schedules so we could both be at the plaza after closing. My mother had argued with me a little bit because it meant she had to open the restaurant, but she caved at the mention of my doctor's appointment. Fake, of course, but she didn't have to know that.

I strolled into the restaurant around noon, and found my mother sitting behind the hostess booth flipping through one of her Chinese newspapers. She barely looked up at me. "I missed my soap opera," she said bitterly.

"Sorry, Mom," I replied as I shuffled behind the counter to store my purse.

She grunted and turned the page of her newspaper. "How was your doctor's appointment today? Are you sick? What is wrong with you?"

"No, I'm okay."

She looked up at me over the top of her newspaper. "Why did you go to the doctor?"

"Oh." I busied myself with stuffing my purse in the drawer while I thought up something . . . why hadn't I thought of this before? "I was having stomachaches . . . thought maybe I had an ulcer, but I'm okay."

My mother shook her head in disapproval. "It is because you eat too many doughnuts." She folded her paper shut. "I am leaving to go see Donna at the hospital. Maybe she will go home today."

"That's great news, Mom." I looked around the dining room and saw Nancy standing at a table chatting with a customer. But other than that, the restaurant was empty, which was unusual for this time of day. "Business is slow today, huh?"

"So-so." She looked down at her watch. "You want noodles before I go?"

I nodded. "If you're cookin'."

My mom gave a firm nod and scooted off the stool, tucking the paper under her arm. "Give me fifteen minutes."

While I waited, I took a quick lap around the dining area and did some spot cleaning. I couldn't sit still or I would worry about the office adventures that were taking place later that night.

The plan was to close out the restaurant like normal. Megan would come roughly fifteen minutes before the main doors closed and then we'd stay until we were sure everyone was gone. Most everyone left within a half hour of closing. The only cameras were outside in the parking lot so we would have total privacy.

When I circled near Nancy, I realized that she was chatting with Mr. An. She seemed worried, and he appeared agitated. As I got closer to them, they both stopped talking and looked at me.

"Hi." I waved awkwardly at them, feeling as if I'd just intruded on a secret meeting.

Mr. An bowed his head. "Good afternoon, Lana. You are here late today."

Nancy replied for me. "She had an early appointment."

Something passed over Mr. An's face, but I couldn't quite describe it. As quickly as I'd seen it, it was gone, and he replaced the look with a smile. "I hope that everything is okay. We have had too much excitement around here in the past few weeks. Do you agree?"

I nodded. "It definitely hasn't been dull, that's for sure."

My mother appeared from the back. "Lana, come eat!" She was standing at a table right outside the kitchen clanking a pair of chopsticks on a soup bowl.

I smiled to Mr. An and Nancy before I turned to leave. I could feel him watching me as I walked away. I didn't turn around until I got to the table where my mother had placed my noodles. I sat in the seat facing Mr. An's table, but when I looked at him, he was occupied with something on his table. Nancy had gone up front to greet some customers that just walked in. Maybe I was being paranoid.

I kept an eye on Mr. An while I slurped my noodles. Fifteen minutes later, he got up and went to pay. Nancy was at the counter waiting for him, and she still seemed worried. After he left, she sat down on the hostess stool and stared out into the plaza.

When I finished my noodles, I abandoned my bowl, and went up front to talk to Nancy. "Is everything okay?" I asked her.

She jumped at the sound of my voice. "Oh, Lana! You are so quiet, like a cat."

I chuckled. "Sorry, I'll make more noise next time."

She put a hand on my shoulder. "I am okay. You should not worry so much."

"Has Peter said anything about coming back to work?" I asked. I hadn't talked to him since the night of the memorial, and I didn't know if anything had changed. I was hoping our talk would have encouraged him to stop hiding out in his apartment.

She shook her head, tears welling in her eyes. "I'm afraid that Peter is still not talking to me. He only talked to me at the memorial. He doesn't answer when I call him."

"Lana!" my mother yelled from across the restaurant.

I whipped around. She was standing at the table where I'd had my lunch, pointing at the bowl I'd left behind.

"Clean up!" she yelled.

I groaned and excused myself to hurry back to the table to collect my bowl.

My mother had her coat on and was digging around in her oversized purse. "Okay, I am going now," my mother said, pulling her keys out. "Vanessa is coming later to help, you be nice to her."

My jaw dropped at the implied accusation. "I am nice to her."

My mother made a face and went on her way.

"Oh, Mom!" I yelled, running toward the front to catch up with her. "Can you take Donna her keys for me? I went to check her mail yesterday."

"Hurry up," my mother lectured. "Esther is waiting for me, she is coming too."

I pulled out my purse from under the hostess stand and dug around for Donna's keys.

My mother snatched them from my hand and left without another word.

Before I forgot again, I took my noodle bowl into the kitchen and rinsed it out in the sink. Lou was preparing pork dumplings for that night's dinner special.

He looked up as I passed him. "That detective guy has a thing for you," he commented, his hands working on the dumplings as he talked.

"What?" I turned from the sink to look at him. "Why would you say that?"

"I could tell by the look on his face at the memorial."

"You're probably reading it wrong," I said, dismissing his theory. "He's just doing his job."

He tilted his head. "I don't know, he seemed more worried about you than anyone else."

"Why is everyone so concerned about my love life?" I asked, feeling annoyed.

Lou chuckled. "One has to wonder why you aren't."

I wasn't going to dignify that with a response. Instead, I headed back out into the dining area without saying anything. Nancy was still sitting at the front of the restaurant, staring out into the plaza.

I headed up to stand with her, but got stopped on the way. A middle-aged woman with curly brown hair signaled me to her table. "Excuse me, miss?" she said in a singsong voice. She was sitting with another woman who turned around to look at me.

"Yes?" I smiled, scanning their table. "Did you need something?"

She looked at her friend with a sparkle in her eye. "We're from out of town and have never been here before . . ." she started to explain.

"Oh! That's wonderful! I hope that you're enjoying yourselves."

She grinned. "Oh, absolutely . . ." She looked back at her friend and then they both looked up at me. "But we just wanted to know something."

"Sure. What would you like to know?"

"Is it true that someone was murdered here?" she whispered, looking around the restaurant.

My eyes bugged out. I had been waiting for this reaction, but since it hadn't happened already, I assumed the coast was clear. Guess not.

The two women looked at me, holding their breath, no doubt wanting a juicy story to share with their friends when they returned from their trip.

I got a hold of my infamous smile and grabbed their teapot. "Would you like some tea?" I asked instead. "Why don't I bring you some more tea?" I scurried back into the kitchen. I couldn't wait for this nightmare to be over.

"I brought you a doughnut," Megan said, handing over a small paper bag. "I figured you'd need it to calm your nerves."

"Shhhhh." I put my finger to my lips. "Vanessa and Anna May are both still here!"

Megan rolled her eyes. "Oh great, both of them?"

"Unfortunately," I replied, opening up the doughnut bag and taking a peek. Boston cream, my favorite. "Thanks for this. You're the best."

She smiled. "I know." She glanced around the restaurant. "When are they leaving? I must have done like a thousand laps around the bar today. I can't wait anymore."

I closed the bag and stuck it under the hostess station. "Vanessa leaves right at nine. Then Anna May will probably be here an extra half hour cleaning the kitchen and prepping a few things for tomorrow."

"Do you think she's going to wonder why we're still here?" Megan looked anxiously at the kitchen door.

I shook my head. "I've already thought of that. It's been a while since I've closed the restaurant so I'll just blame doing the books for why I'm taking so long. And you're here to keep me company and make sure I don't get kidnapped in the parking lot. She has no reason to stay."

Megan gave me a wide smile. "I'm impressed, Miss Lee, you're turning into quite the little fibber."

"Oh, stop it."

Vanessa came stomping out of the kitchen, smacking her gum and humming to herself. She was usually singing some new pop song she'd heard on the radio that I'd never heard of. One time she accused me of being old because I'd rather listen to the Rolling Stones than Lady Gaga. "Okay, I'm going now. Are you going to be able to manage without me?" She giggled as she walked up to us. "Oh hey, Megan, I didn't know you were here."

"Hey, Vanessa," Megan said with zero enthusiasm.

"Yes, I'll manage to live without you, Vanessa," I said, shooing her toward the door.

"Okay, well, don't get accused of any more murders, otherwise I'll have to look for a new job," she joked.

No one laughed.

She shrugged and flung her purse over her shoulder and pranced out the door.

One down, one to go.

Megan and I sat holed up in the office while I counted the day's money and organized the receipts for my mother to look at in the morning. We could hear Anna May out in the kitchen cleaning up and washing dishes.

Megan tapped her foot while she scrolled through her phone. "This is the longest half hour in the universe," she groaned.

I looked at the clock on the wall and watched the seconds tick by. She wasn't kidding. I had never been so anxious in my life. I'd thought sneaking into the Feng house was bad, but this was even worse.

There was a light tap on the door and we both jumped. "Yeah?"

The door opened a crack and Anna May stuck her head in. "I'm all done, what is taking you so long?"

"I'm almost done. It's been a while, okay?"

Anna May shifted her weight against the door. "Well, do you guys want me to wait for you? I really have to get home; I have an ethics test to study for."

"No, we're fine. You go ahead."

She shrugged. "All right, see you tomorrow then." She waved and shut the door behind her.

Megan let out a big breath and sank into her chair. "Well, that wasn't so bad. I thought she was going to insist on staying."

We waited another fifteen minutes to make sure that she was gone and had no plans of coming back. I ate my doughnut while we waited and that helped calm my nerves.

Once enough time had passed, we went out to stand by the entrance and take a peek around the plaza. All the lights were switched off in the stores, and there wasn't a shop owner in sight, not even Cindy. Megan and I looked at each other without speaking.

It was go time.

CHAPTER
24

We stood outside the office, side by side, staring at the door. I was trying to figure out what the big deal was. Maybe this wasn't so bad.

I pulled the keys out of my back pocket and stepped up to the door. "Here goes nothing."

Megan watched me fumble with the keys. "Do you know which one it is?" she asked.

"No, they weren't marked."

She threw her hands up. "Lana Lee, oh my God! What if none of them work? Then what do we do?"

"Shhh," I hissed. "There's like fourteen keys on here. One of them has to be it."

I went through thirteen of the keys, and none of them fit. We looked at each other as I slipped the fourteenth key into the lock. I held my breath.

Nothing.

My head dropped. "Who has this many keys?"

Megan crossed her arms. "Well, now what?"

"I don't know. Let me think." I inspected the keys in my hand. They had to go to something. All of them looked similar to one another, except one. One key looked like it would fit into a security door. "Follow me," I said, coming up with an idea.

"Where are we going?"

"Just follow me."

We went back into Ho-Lee Noodle House, through the kitchen and to the back service door. It led out into a dingy hallway lit by fluorescent lights. The glow of lights on the dirty brick walls made it feel like something out of a horror film.

"I didn't even know this was back here," Megan whispered.

We stepped out into the hall and made our way around the bend, coming up to the door that was the back of the property office. "It's mainly for deliveries. I never come back here but Cindy from the bookstore mentioned it the other day . . ."

I chose the security key and stuck it in the lock. It fit.

Megan and I looked at each, hopeful.

Slowly, I turned the key and the lock clicked. Megan gasped next to me.

I pushed open the door and we stepped into the office. Megan shut the door behind us, locking it. Not that it would help if anyone caught us. We'd be trapped inside.

I slipped the backpack I had brought along with me off my shoulders and set it on the ground by the door. We didn't know if we'd find anything of importance, but best to be prepared. I've heard that's what they tell you in the Girl Scouts.

Megan pulled two miniflashlights out of her bag and handed one to me. "So we don't have to turn on the lights."

Taking mine, I turned it on and pointed it toward the front. "That one over there is—was—Mr. Feng's desk," I said, pointing to my left. The packed-up boxes I had seen the other day while meeting with Ian were still there untouched. Small favors.

"Okay, you look there, and I'll start looking around the rest of the office," Megan said, pointing her flashlight to the opposite side near Ian's desk.

I stared at the desk, feeling another bout of guilt for going through a dead man's things. It didn't make it easier even though I had already gone through the Feng house. After giving myself a mini pep talk, I squared my shoulders and got to work.

The boxes that had been on top of his desk didn't prove to be all that interesting. Most of it was random books and notebooks dealing with business-type stuff. There were a couple bottles of vitamins and tins of tea. If Ian had been the one to pack this stuff up, he hadn't organized it very well.

I rifled through the drawers and found papers and bank statements, nothing really that personal that could tell me anything new about Thomas. So far, all I'd learned about the man was that he kept everything and had no sense of order.

When I got to the last drawer, I found that it was locked. I pulled the ring of keys out again, looking for a key smaller than the others that would fit in a desk drawer. There weren't any. Figures.

I popped my head up, looking at the random items

on the desk. If I were Mr. Feng, and I had a locked drawer in my desk, where would I hide the key? I took another look through the random items in the boxes. Nothing stuck out. Then I rifled through the papers that were still lying out. Nothing.

"Dammit," I whispered.

"What's wrong?" Megan asked. She was standing over Ian's desk, looking through his drawers.

"There's a locked drawer in his desk and I can't get it open. None of these stupid keys work."

She cocked her head. "What about the underside of the desk, or a vase or something?"

I ran my hand under the desk. "Nothing. And I don't see any vases here."

Megan came over to help me look. "This guy seems complicated to me."

"I'm going to agree with you on that one." I stood up, placing my hands on my hips. "And I already gave my mom the keys to Donna's house, so I can't get back in."

We stood and stared at the desk. Megan turned abruptly and went over to Ian's desk. "Hang on," she said, opening his drawers and digging around.

"Don't mess up anything. He might notice." I turned back to the desk, checking the bottoms of the tea tins, just in case.

She blew a raspberry. "Like he's going to know it's . . . aha!" She produced a tiny key from the pencil tray of his desk drawer and scurried back over. "Try this one."

I rolled my eyes. "Why would that work if it's from Ian's desk?" With annoyance, I inserted the key, but to my surprise, the lock turned. I looked up at Megan, dumbfounded.

In return, she beamed at me. "See? And you didn't want to try."

Ignoring her, I opened the drawer and was disappointed to find another stack of papers. I pulled out a handful and flipped through them. "More bills," I said, defeated. "Why would you even bother locking these up?"

"Maybe there's just nothing that he's hiding."

I turned around and looked at her. "Megan . . . someone killed him, and they didn't do it for no good reason. There has to be something." I removed all the papers from the drawer and set them on the floor, shining my flashlight in the drawer. That's when I saw it. "Jackpot!"

"What?"

"There's more in here." I stuck my hand in and removed the thin wooden board. "There's a hole in here for you to stick your finger in." I showed her the plank of wood.

"Interesting . . ." she said, shining her flashlight in the drawer.

Inside, I found a manila envelope marked "confidential"; I passed it over to Megan for inspection while I finished digging through the drawer. Along with that envelope, I found another, smaller envelope stuffed with photographs, an appointment book, and another key. It was attached to a key ring that had a logo from the Hidden Den, a local bar. My eyes ran over the items I'd pulled from the drawer. We'd have to take all of it with us; I couldn't risk leaving anything important behind. And I certainly wasn't coming back again unless it was to put everything back where we'd found it. Although I doubted anyone would miss it.

I gathered everything up and stuffed it into my back-pack, careful not to bend the photos.

"Um, Lana . . ."

"What?"

"I don't really understand what I'm looking at yet, but what do you know about Donna?"

"What do you mean?" I asked, looking up from my bag.

Her eyes were fixed on the papers from the manila envelope that she held in her hand. "I think she was up to something?" She flipped the papers around for me to look at. "I don't know, but it looks like Mr. Feng was doing some kind of investigation on her . . ."

I took the papers from her hand and skimmed through them. It was some kind of background check. Why was Thomas doing a background check on his own wife?

I took a deep breath. "We're taking it with us. Let's get the hell out of here." I shoved the rest of what we had in my backpack and then straightened up the desk to the way it looked before I went digging through it. I was confident that the area was such a disaster to begin with that Ian wouldn't even know anything was touched.

We left as quietly as we'd come in, locking the door behind us. We didn't say a word as we made our way back down the service hallway and through Ho-Lee Noodle House, both of us lost in our own thoughts. Megan stood behind me as I locked the door to the res-taurant for the final time that night.

I was so distracted, looking through my purse for my keys, that I wouldn't have noticed anyone if Megan hadn't put her hand on my arm.

"Oh my God," she whispered.

We both stopped in mid-step, standing exposed in the plaza as Kimmy Tran came waltzing out of China Cinema and Song in a red sequined dress and stiletto heels. Her hair was, for the first time, perfectly straight and not up in a ponytail or bun. We stood frozen watching her lock up the store.

Megan hissed in my ear. "I thought everyone was gone."

"So did I," I whispered from the side of my mouth.

Kimmy must have sensed us standing there because she froze at the door and turned her head very slowly to face us. It took a second for recognition to set in, but when it did, her face set into an angry scowl. "What the hell are you two doing here?"

CHAPTER

25

Kimmy Tran stomped over in her stiletto heels and sized us up. She crossed her arms over her chest and eyed us with suspicion. "The plaza has been closed for a while now, what are you two doing lurking about?"

I tried to come up with a million and one excuses for why Megan and I were standing in the middle of the plaza with backpacks, looking as thick as thieves. But before I had the chance, Megan answered for both of us.

"And what exactly are you doing?" Megan pointed an accusatory finger at Kimmy. "You look like you're about to stand on a corner somewhere."

Kimmy gasped. "Did you just imply what I think you did?" She took a step closer to Megan, her hands balling into fists.

Megan lifted her chin. "If the shoe fits . . ."

"Like you have room to talk, you blond little—"

"Okay!" I yelled. "Ladies, let's not get crazy." I stepped between the two of them with my back to

Megan. I gave Kimmy an apologetic look. "I think what Megan was trying to say is that we're surprised to see you so . . ."

"So what?" Kimmy asked, folding her arms back over her chest.

"Dressed up . . ." I said.

She looked down at her outfit and back at me. "If you really want to know . . ." Kimmy smoothed the lines of her dress. "I have a date."

"Well, we wouldn't want to keep you then," Megan spat from behind me.

Kimmy's eyes narrowed. "You're lucky I have somewhere to be right now."

Megan snorted. "Yeah, real lucky."

Kimmy groaned and spun around, hitting me in the face with her hair. She stomped off toward the main entrance of the plaza leaving me and Megan standing there in shock.

After she'd left the building, both of us relaxed and headed toward the exit.

"I'm going to take a stand and say I don't like that girl," Megan declared.

I laughed. "Yeah, I kinda got that impression."

Back at the apartment, Megan and I sat on the living room floor with the contents of the hidden drawer laid out between us. On the way home we'd splurged on a pizza and were in the process of stuffing ourselves while investigating what we'd found. Kikko sniffed at the closed pizza box on the coffee table, wishing she had thumbs.

Megan had the confidential envelope in front of her, mumbling to herself as she read the report. "So, it looks like Mr. Feng started this investigation about a month before he died. Not only did he have a background check done, but someone was following her around." She passed me a few photos. "She didn't seem to be caught doing anything exciting."

I flipped through the photos, which had clearly been taken without Donna's knowledge. Megan was right, nothing about them was exciting. She was captured going to the store and meeting with other Asian community members, most whom I recognized. Not exactly anything suspicious. I handed the photos back to Megan. "What could he have been looking for?"

"Wait a minute . . ." Megan said, flipping between two pages. She put the rest down and held the pages side by side. "Look at this . . ." She took the photos from me and handed over the papers she'd been inspecting.

"What is this?" I asked, looking between the two pages. "Two birth certificates?"

"Look at the note attached," Megan instructed, stuffing the pictures back in the envelope.

The note read: "Country of Origin: China."

I looked between the two birth certificates again. "From what I remember, my mom told me that Donna came from California."

Megan tilted her head. "Well, obviously not. But why would she lie about where she was born?"

I shrugged. "I don't know, but maybe that was what Mr. Feng was trying to figure out." I gave her back the documents and she put them back in the envelope. I moved my attention to the envelope full of pictures. "Let's see what else we come up with."

Some of the pictures had been taken with black-and-white film. From their texture and style, I could tell they were pretty old. The top picture was of two little Asian boys in a park, wearing similar clothing, in front of a swing set. The back of the picture was dated 1967. "I think one of these little boys must be Thomas." I held out the picture, showing it to Megan.

"Oh, look how cute," she said, taking the picture and inspecting it. "Wow, 1967, are they all this old?"

I flipped through the pictures. "No, not all of them. There are some that look more recent."

The next ones that caught my attention were of two young-looking men and a beautiful Asian girl standing between them. One of the men was taller and resembled Mr. Feng. I didn't recognize the other man. Behind that photo was a picture of just the girl in what appeared to be a student headshot. She was absolutely stunning. Her raven hair was curled in the classic Farah Fawcett style. Her makeup was minimal, but she didn't really need it. She had a natural beauty about her. Her eyes spoke of happiness and she was so familiar to me that I felt almost as if I knew her, but I couldn't place the face.

The next picture after that was a school photo that reminded me of my own school pictures. A little Asian boy sat smiling uncomfortably at the camera. Behind him, on the backdrop, were neon blue and pink lasers. My parents had a similar photo of me hanging in their living room, despite my protests.

"Look at these." I passed the photos to Megan.

"Who are these people?" She flipped through the photos.

"I have no idea. Maybe family or something?"

I riffled through the remaining pictures and found one that intrigued me. "What the heck?" In my hands was an old faded color photo that was torn in half. Several Asian people stood huddled together outside of a nondescript building, all smiling happily at the camera. There was one white guy in the mix, and I inspected the photo more carefully. No doubt about it, I'd seen that face before. It was my dad. He had his arm wrapped around my mom and she leaned into him, her head barely reaching his chest.

There were a couple other torn photos mixed in, all taken around the same time.

Megan leaned forward to look at the pictures in my hand. "Why do you think those are ripped?"

"I don't know, but here's one with my parents in it." I handed her the picture I'd been scrutinizing.

"Wow . . ." Megan eyed the picture closely. "Look at your mom! She was a fox!!"

I gave her the rest of the pictures to look at while I went through the planner. As I flipped the pages, I realized that everything was written either in Chinese or some kind of code.

I cursed myself for not trying harder to learn how to read Chinese. I could only recognize a couple of characters, but I had a feeling I was taking them out of context. One character put with another could completely change the meaning of a word or sentence.

I skipped ahead to the day of Mr. Feng's death. He'd had an appointment that day for 12 P.M. Next to the time were a string of Chinese characters, and the letters *AC*. Below that, he'd scribbled Cindy's name, a few more Chinese characters, and 1:30 P.M.

I thought back to when I'd delivered his lunch; it had been shortly before noon. This was proof that he'd met with someone after I had delivered the food. Which meant that I was not the last to see him alive. I felt a twinge of relief. There had been someone else. Now the question was . . . what did *AC* stand for? Were they initials or an abbreviation?

"So what now?" Megan asked, breaking my concentration.

I looked up from the planner and shrugged. "I don't know. We can't start asking people questions because how would we know this stuff. It's not like we can go up to Donna and say, 'Hey, were you really born in China? We found your husband's papers hidden in a drawer.'"

"True," Megan replied. "I suppose we can try and find out from your mom. Maybe she knows something and just never mentioned it before."

"If she knew, I think she would have mentioned it already. She's made it a point to tell me where everyone from the plaza originally came from."

She looked at me, confused. "Why does that matter?"

"To some, it makes all the difference," I said, digging to the bottom of my backpack. "But what I really want to know is . . . what do these go to?" I pulled out the key ring that I'd found and dangled it in front of Megan. Kikko's head snapped up, her attention momentarily broken from the pizza box. She waddled over to give the keys a good sniff.

Megan looked between me and the keys. "That was locked in the drawer?" She took them from my hand and inspected the key chain. "The Hidden Den? Isn't that on the east side somewhere? Sounds familiar."

I nodded. "Yeah, I've heard of it too."

"Maybe we should go there and check it out." She dropped the keys back in my hand and I returned them to the bag with the rest of our lifted goods.

"Maybe we should." I zipped up the bag, propping it against the wall. I let out a groan as I checked the readout on my cell phone. "Ugh, it's already almost two in the morning, and I have to get up for the morning shift." I stretched my legs out in front of me, wiggling my toes. "I thought this would help answer some questions, but it's really just generated *more* questions."

Megan picked up our empty beer bottles and leftover pizza from the table. "Are you planning on telling your detective boyfriend about all of this?"

I snorted. "Yeah, right, I doubt he'd be okay with the way we got this information. And he's not my boyfriend."

"I don't know why you can't admit that you like him. It's so obvious," Megan teased as she put the leftover pizza in the refrigerator.

"That's simple . . . because I don't like him."

"Right, you keep telling yourself that."

"Why are you making this into a thing?"

She put her hands on her hips and stood over me. "Because you need to stop moping over good ole what's-his-name and just move on already. There are other fish swimming around . . ."

"You're starting to sound like my mother," I mumbled.

"Well, maybe she's right this time, Lana." Megan

moved to the couch, leaning forward and eying me with concern. "You don't want to hear it, but you need to. It's time you stop feeling sorry for your yourself and live your life again."

I threw my hands up. "I thought that's what I was doing."

"No, you go to work, come home, and sit in front of this TV watching Netflix all night." She pointed accusingly at the television. "How is that living? And how many times have I invited you to the bar and you never show. I swear if this murder hadn't happened, you'd never have come up there to talk to me."

I stood up. "I just don't feel like it right now, okay? Plus, we're kind of busy with this whole murder thing." I pointed to the backpack.

"Well, you better start to feel like it," she commanded. "Because this isn't cutting it anymore, Lana. I've let you mope around the house all these months, and maybe that's my own mistake, but I'm not going to sit here and watch my best friend be miserable every day."

"Where is this coming from?"

"I'm concerned about you," she answered. "If not Detective Trudeau, go out with Ian then," she challenged.

I gawked at her. "I don't think that's a good idea."

She threw her hands up. "Of course you don't. Because no one is a good idea, are they?"

Taking a deep breath, I replied, "No, because he's on my suspect list."

"How convenient."

"Look, I don't feel like talking about this right now. I think it's best if we just—"

"Ignore it?" Megan asked.

I glared at her. "I was going to say get some sleep."

"Same difference."

"I'm fine, and I don't need anybody telling me how to live my life. Now I'm going to bed, and that's the end of it." I stomped to my room with Kikko following close behind. I gave the door a healthy slam and flopped onto my bed.

I couldn't believe her. Here we were in the middle of a murder investigation, and she was talking about me going out on dates. There wasn't any time for that and I wasn't interested in either party anyway. And that's what I continued to tell myself until I fell asleep.

CHAPTER
26

I woke up grumpy, most likely due to the fact that Megan had given me the tenth degree the night before. It also might have had something to do with the fact that I had had trouble sleeping and had woken up several times. I couldn't stop thinking about the contents of the drawer and whether they would be of any use in helping us solve the great mystery of who murdered Thomas Feng.

When I opened the door to my bedroom, I found a note wedged underneath. It read: *I'm sorry.*

I found a Post-it and scribbled, *Ditto,* and stuck it on her door. We never bickered for long.

I went through the motions of my morning routine, finding myself preoccupied while applying my makeup and amazed to see that I'd gotten it on in all the right places.

In a daze, I walked the dog. The weather was mild so I let her sniff here and there for extended periods of time. Even though I knew I should rush, I couldn't shake the feeling of absolute preoccupation. There was something about the photos that was bugging me. Well, there was something about all of it that was bugging me.

The rest of the morning continued this way, and I hoped that the restaurant would be empty most of the day.

The Mahjong Matrons came in promptly at nine and sat at their usual table by the main window. Without having to ask, I brought over their pot of oolong tea and placed it in the center of the table. "Shall I get you ladies the usual?"

All four of the women nodded in unison.

"When is Peter coming back to work?" Opal inquired. "He has been gone for some time now."

"I'm not sure," I admitted. "I haven't talked to him much lately."

"If you speak with him," Helen said. "Please tell him we miss his cooking."

I smiled and headed back to the kitchen where Lou was organizing his utensils. I handed him the order slip without saying anything.

He looked down and read the order. "The Mahjong Matrons strike again!" he exclaimed in an announcer's voice.

"Uh-huh . . ." I rolled my eyes.

Lou watched me, the grill sizzling below him, the only noise in the kitchen. "Can I ask you something?" he said, sounding unsure of himself.

"Um, okay."

"You don't like me very much, do you?" He scratched the back of his neck. "Have I done something to offend you?"

"No. Why would you think that?"

He rubbed the bottom of his lip. "It just seems that way, I suppose. I know that I can be overly chipper at times, but I'm just trying to keep things upbeat. It's the best way to get through the day, you know?"

If there was one thing I was a sucker for, it was a guy who looked vulnerable, and Lou was tugging on my heart strings. I started to feel bad for all the times that I'd dismissed him or gotten snippy with him.

I put on a reassuring smile and said, "Don't worry; I've just been preoccupied lately, and it's affecting my mood. It has nothing to do with you."

He grinned. "Promise?"

"Promise."

As I headed back out into the dining area, Ian walked into the restaurant. He did a quick scan of the room until his eyes settled on me, and he smiled, sticking his hands in his pockets. Per usual, he was dressed well, in an Italian-cut pin-striped suit. The black suit fit his body as if it were specially made for him and I didn't doubt that it was. The top button of his crisp, white shirt was undone, and he looked more casual without his tie.

The Mahjong Matrons had been chatting loudly when he'd walked in, but when they noticed him, they immediately stopped talking, and you could sense in their postures that they were ready to get a little eavesdropping in along with their breakfast.

"Good morning, Miss Lee," Ian chirped, bowing his head ever so slightly. "It is a pleasure to see such beauty in the morning."

I could hear one of the matrons giggle. Trying to hide

my annoyance, I plastered on "the smile" and said, "How can I help you this morning, Ian?"

"Well, first, I'd like to get some breakfast to go, and then I'd like to discuss some business with you, if you have a minute."

"Sure, what would you like to eat? I'll place your order and then we can talk for a few minutes until your food is ready."

He told me what he wanted and I made my way back into the kitchen, handing Lou the order slip.

When I came back out, Ian was sitting at one of the two-seaters near the kitchen entrance. He stood from his chair when I came over and pulled out the chair opposite him, extending a hand. "Please sit with me."

I sat in the chair, and out of the corner of my eye, I could see the matrons watching us from their table. I'm sure this was going to feed the gossip mill.

Ian cleared his throat. "I wanted to apologize for my behavior at the memorial the other day."

"Your behavior?" I asked, thinking back to the memorial and my interactions with him. Nothing came to mind.

He looked down at his polished dress shoes. "Yes, I am so embarrassed about my speech."

Oh, THAT! I thought to myself but didn't say out loud. Instead I appeared dumbfounded . . . for his sake. "Oh? I hadn't noticed."

"Well, that makes one person," he replied with nervous laughter. "Apparently, a lot of people commented on it after the memorial."

"They did?" I said, this time with genuine surprise. And here I'd thought that everyone was going to talk about Donna passing out at the table. "What did they say?"

He avoided eye contact while he answered. "Mostly, they gave the feedback to my father and told him that I wasn't ready to run the plaza on my own."

"But Donna technically will be helping you with everything, won't she?"

He looked at me for a split second from beneath hooded eyelids and it reminded me of every evil villain in every Chinese movie I've ever seen. "She will be helping in a very limited capacity. Her name is on the paperwork for appearances. Basically, this is my show to run, as of today."

Though his voice was quiet, the aggressiveness seeped through and made the hairs on the back of my neck stand up. I tried to shake it off, but it wasn't working. Instead, I stood, almost knocking the chair over in the process. I grabbed it just in time. "Um, excuse me for a minute, I have to get food out to the ladies."

The food for the matrons was ready. I strategically placed everything on a large tray, hoping to make it out in one trip.

With my packed tray, I headed over to the Mahjong Matrons who were all giving me the same look. That "go get him" look that women give each other. I pretended like I didn't notice and placed their food on the table.

As the women dug into their breakfast, I made my way back over to Ian who had been watching all of my movements. "Your food is just about ready, too," I said, hoping he'd hurry up with what he had to say.

"Right, so, as I was saying, I didn't want you to think

poorly of my character and have it potentially affect your decision to have dinner with me," he blurted out in one long breath.

I stood looking down at him, awkwardly holding the serving tray against my chest. "I'm not sure if this is the right time . . ." I muttered. It was never pleasant telling someone no and this was no exception. Even though I thought his motives might be suspicious, I hated to reject someone.

He nodded, contemplating what I'd just said. "But you haven't completely ruled it out?"

What was with the menfolk this morning? I sighed. "It's not something I see happening in the foreseeable future."

Ian slapped the table with excitement. "Well, all right then. Best news I've heard in days."

My eyes widened. "I'm sorry?"

"Well, it's just that you said the 'foreseeable' future, and since the future can't be seen, that means that you haven't declined my dinner invitation."

"But—"

"Besides, we have a lot of work to get done around the plaza and maybe you're right, it's not the best time," he said, more to himself than me. "After the debacle at the memorial, I need to regain the trust of this plaza. It's even more crucial now that this committee I'm organizing sets the right tone."

Speechless, I turned around and went back into the kitchen to get his food. I didn't know what it would take to drop a hint to this guy, but maybe subtlety was the wrong approach. I'd have to think on that one.

After I had cashed him out and sent him on his way,

I went to check on the Matrons again. They had just finished their breakfast, plates and bowls with remnants of Chinese omelet and rice porridge pushed off to the side. They chatted with excitement over their tea. The lid to the pot was left open, signaling they needed a refill.

Pearl beamed. "You know, he's a good boy in his heart, but maybe not a good businessman." She looked at me, waiting for my response.

"What's wrong with him as a businessman?"

Helen answered for the group. "We heard he had a lot of money trouble in Chicago, and his father had to come rescue him. His family was so embarrassed. That's why he got a job with Thomas. Thomas was the only one who would take him."

"Where did you hear this?" I asked Helen.

"When you play mahjong, people talk, sometimes they talk too much," Wendy explained.

Mulling that over, I took their empty dishes and teapot. So, it was very possible that Ian wasn't the successful businessman that he claimed to be. He hid it well behind a pretty face and sharp suits. Was it possible that the speech-giving Ian was a more accurate portrayal of who he was?

Something was still bothering me that I couldn't quite put my finger on. Until I shook that, I wasn't going to be able to give this new information any of my real attention. I refilled the teapot and returned to the Matrons. I wondered what else I could learn from them.

"I figured it out!" I blurted to Megan, making her practically jump off the couch.

"Oh my God, Lana!" Megan hissed. "I almost spilled this entire bottle of nail polish all over Kikko!"

Kikko looked up at the sound of her name and sniffed the air with a snort. No doubt hating the smell of the nail polish fumes.

"I figured out what's been bothering me." I had my investigation notebook in my lap and had been filling in all the new information and my thoughts on everything we'd found, including my new intel from the Mahjong Matrons. "I almost forgot about the key."

"The unknown key we found in the drawer?" Megan asked, inspecting her nails.

"No, the key that we used to open the locked drawer," I said. "That *is* what's been bothering me this entire time. Not the pictures."

"Yeah, what about it?"

"You found it in Ian's desk."

"So?"

"So, why would Ian have the key to Mr. Feng's special locked drawer? The one with all kinds of secret information tucked away for safekeeping."

Megan delicately applied nail polish to her ring finger and shrugged. "It had a false bottom; doesn't mean that Ian ever figured that out. I mean, he's a good-looking guy and all, but from what you've told me, he doesn't sound too bright."

I wasn't convinced. "The papers that were in there were all old bills, probably prior to anything that he would be involved in. So why would he even be interested in those? And why did he keep the key and not give everything to Donna?"

Megan contemplated this by painting her pinkie nail.

"Hm, good point. I'm off tomorrow, and I planned on doing some research on our good friend Donna. Want me to look into him too?"

"I think that's an excellent idea. Maybe check on Mr. An too. Then I think we'll have covered everyone."

"You got it."

I looked back at my notebook. It was filling up pretty fast. Somewhere in this mess, the answer had to be staring me in the face.

CHAPTER
27

- - - - - - - - - - - - - - - -

After work the next day, I set out to my parents' house in pursuit of old pictures. My mother kept everything, so I knew she'd have old photos lying around somewhere. Meanwhile, Megan was hot on the Internet search, digging up anything she could find on our remaining potential suspects.

When I got to my parents' house, my mother was gone, probably out with Esther somewhere, and my dad was lounging in his favorite chair with the remote in his hands. He was flipping through stations when I walked in.

"We have about a hundred channels, and there's never a damn thing to watch," my dad said as he turned to face me. "What brings you by, goober?"

"I was wondering if I could look through some of your old photos."

"Oh, yeah?" My dad turned the TV off and stood up with newfound energy. He loved it when I wanted to look at their old things. "Well, let me lead the way." He hurried down the hallway to the spare bedroom, which was Anna May's old bedroom.

From a bookshelf in the corner, my dad removed a few photo albums and plopped them down on the bed. "How far do you want to go back?" he asked with enthusiasm.

I sat down on the bed and flipped the cover on the first one. "I was looking for stuff from when you and Mom were young."

"Oh, really?" He rubbed his hands together. "Well, in that case . . ." He took the albums off the bed and stacked them back on the shelf. From a different shelf, he selected four albums, setting them on the bed in front of me, and then grabbed a large tin with a flower design on the lid and placed it next to the albums. "These ones in the tin are the ones we haven't organized yet. I always say I'm going to do it on the weekends but . . ."

"I know, all those channels to flip through," I joked.

My dad chuckled. "Do you want anything to eat while you're here? Your mom has some fried noodles in the fridge I can heat up for you."

I already found myself preoccupied with the albums. Since they were organized by year, I decided to leave the tin for last. "Maybe later, Dad."

"All right," he replied, hovering over me.

"Dad . . ."

"Yeah?"

"What are you doing?"

"Maybe I should stay and look through them with you so I can explain stuff if you have questions."

I sighed, knowing that my dad would turn this into

an all-night event. But the look on his face made it impossible to say no. I scooted over on the bed so my dad could sit beside me, looking at the albums over my shoulder.

The first album was from when they were in college. There were a lot of pictures of them on campus and my dad stopped on every page to point out the locations and buildings that were in the background. A couple of cookout pictures showed up with my grandparents from my dad's side.

"Wasn't your mother beautiful?" my dad said, cooing at the pictures. "The minute I saw her, I knew she was the one."

We continued on to the next album, which was mostly wedding and honeymoon pictures. My parents had done a two-week vacation, spending one week in Taiwan and another week in Hawaii. The pictures were gorgeous and I looked a little longer than necessary, almost forgetting my mission. I hadn't been to Taiwan since I was little girl and I wanted to experience it with my adult eyes, to appreciate the history and the heritage. But the money was never right. And my parents, though they wanted to, couldn't spring for the trip for me or my sister. One day, Lana, one day.

I closed the album feeling wistful, daydreaming about the day when things would be right again, and I could do the things I'd always wanted to do.

That feeling didn't last for long though. When I opened the third album, I found what I'd come looking for. Pictures of the plaza when it first opened.

It spoke of a different and much simpler time. The structure of the building had been plain and looked like any other shopping cluster you've seen. It wasn't until the late eighties that Thomas had added the pagoda façade.

My father had taken tons of photos to capture everything imaginable; the stores and their owners, construction in the moment, and the restaurant as it progressed.

A picture of my young mother and another woman caught my attention. It was Esther, standing in front of her store, her and my mother smiling brilliantly to the camera. It was always odd to see my mother when she was younger. Partially because I realized then how much I looked like her, but also because it seemed like another lifetime. These pictures were taken before Anna May and I were born, and my parents had much left to experience with each other.

I kept flipping through the pictures searching for the mysterious woman in Mr. Feng's photos. "Dad?"

"Yeah, kiddo," my dad replied.

"When exactly did you and Mom meet Mr. Feng?"

He scratched the scruff that was beginning to grow on his usually smooth face. "Well, let's see, we were almost done with college, and he had already begun construction on the plaza, so 1976, maybe?"

"Did you ever see him with another woman? Or did he have any close guy friends?"

My dad's bushy eyebrows furrowed. "Why do you ask?"

"No reason," I said, looking back at the photo album.

"Goober, you wouldn't be sticking your nose into anything you're not supposed to, are you?"

Avoiding his stare, I said, "Of course not."

My dad sighed. "This is because I bought you Nancy
Drew books when you were a kid, isn't it?"

"Dad . . ." I whined.

"Look, I'm going to give you some advice," my dad
said. "Don't get involved with other people's circus
animals."

I looked at my dad. "I think you're saying that wrong."

He paused and then shook his head as if to clear the
thought. "Either way, you just worry about you, and let
the police take care of anything that may be going on."
He patted my knee. "Now, how about we look into some
of those noodles your mother left behind?"

When I got home, I didn't feel any closer to figuring out
who the mystery people were. They clearly weren't
people that had worked at the plaza when it first opened,
otherwise my dad would have gotten at least one photo
of them.

I found Megan at the dining room table with her laptop and a coffee. Kikko was underneath the table with
a bone in her mouth and a chew toy lying beside her.
"Well, don't you two look comfy," I said, shutting the
door behind me.

"Oh good, you're home," Megan said, looking up
at me.

"My parents' house was a bust," I said, walking to
the fridge.

"Well then, let me give you a little bit of good news,"
Megan said cheerily.

I pulled the leftover pizza from the fridge. I'd eaten

some noodles with my dad, but research makes me hungry. "What did you find?"

Megan turned the laptop to face me. "This is a career profile that I found online with a list of all the places that Ian worked in Chicago."

I reviewed the screen and looked back up at her. "So?"

"I happened to call all of these places."

"You did?"

"Yep, and surprise, he didn't work at any except one."

"What?" I set the pizza box down and sat down at the table to review the jobs he had listed. Two were major corporations and one I'd never heard of. In all of the positions, he had listed himself as senior management.

"This one," she said, pointing at the screen, "is the only one that actually knew who Ian Sung was. And they said he was a janitor."

"A janitor!"

Megan nodded proudly. "Yep, this guy has virtually no job experience whatsoever."

"How did you find all this out?" I asked.

"I pretended to be a potential employer that was calling for job verifications."

"Wow, so he's a fraud," I said, sitting back in the chair.

She turned the computer back toward her and nodded. "Yeah, I'm glad you turned him down. If he lied about this, then what else is he lying about?"

"So, what do you think?" I asked.

"I don't know. From what you've told me, he seems pretty adamant about wanting to take over control at the plaza. Maybe he wanted to get Mr. Feng out of the way."

I thought about what Ian had told me about the relationship with his father, and then what the Mahjong Matrons had told me. "Maybe it's possible he's doing all of this to impress his father," I suggested.

"Daddy issues are nobody's friend," Megan replied.

"What about Donna?" I asked, nodding at the computer. "Did you find anything out about her?"

"Nothing exciting," Megan said, closing the lid to the laptop. "She's mentioned on a bunch of society pages and all of that, but nothing that isn't common knowledge. I couldn't find anything juicy about her anywhere."

"Nothing at all?" I asked.

She shook her head. "Nope. If you ask me, it's all a little too clean."

I agreed with her on that. If there was nothing exciting to find, then why would Mr. Feng have hired a private investigator to follow her around? And what was up with the different birth certificates?

Megan shut the computer down and closed the lid. "You know what I want to know?"

"What?" I asked.

"Are we going to stare at this pizza box all night? Or are we going to eat some?"

CHAPTER
28

I promised Nancy that I wouldn't be gone long during my lunch break. Business had been steady that morning and we anticipated a long lunch with the amount of people that were roaming around the plaza. Holiday shopping was in full swing.

I found Mr. Zhang outside of his shop, pacing back and forth as he normally did. "Hello, Mr. Zhang," I said, trying not to sound like I was in a rush.

"Good afternoon, Miss Lana." He bowed his head and continued to pace back and forth.

"I was wondering if you could help me with something."

He stopped, giving me his full attention. "I am here to help."

"Donna told me that you recommended yellow jasmine for her migraines. And I've been having some migraines myself, do you think it would be good for me?"

"Hmmm . . ." He looked at me thoughtfully. "Yellow jasmine is becoming more popular but I do not like to tell people to take this. It is very dangerous."

"You don't?" That was definitely not what Donna had said. Add a check back to the suspicions column under Donna Feng.

"No, for Donna, it was the last thing to try. She has tried everything else, and nothing works for her. But I told her she must be careful." He shook his head. "Many people have come to ask me about this. Even Mr. An has come to see me for help. He has never talked to me before."

"I see." That stumped me. Who in this plaza didn't talk to Mr. Zhang? He was the honorary grandfather of almost everyone in the Village.

"Ah, I know!" Mr. Zhang held up his index finger and hobbled into the store. "Come try this, it's good for you."

I followed him into the store and watched him as he scanned a shelf covered in miniature brown-tinted bottles. He found the one he was looking for and plucked it off the shelf, unscrewing the cap to expose a liquid dropper.

"Come here," he said.

I stood inches away from him, and he held the dropper out. "Give me your hand."

I did as he instructed and he dropped a bead of liquid in my hand. "What is this?" I asked, sniffing my hand.

"Eucalyptus, it will help your headaches."

I winced at the smell. "Oh, what do I do with it?"

"Rub it on your temple," he said, gesturing to his own head.

To be polite, I did as he said, rubbing the liquid on my temple. Immediately my skin started to tingle and I had a flashback to when my mother used to rub Vicks VapoRub under my nose . . . a fate surely worse than death. "Oh . . . this is great," I fibbed.

"I give you this one for free," he said with a smile, shaking the bottle at me. "If it helps you, you come back for more."

"Oh, you don't have to," I said, holding up my hands in protest. "I appreciate the offer though."

"No, no, I insist." He went behind the counter and grabbed a paper bag. He dropped the small bottle in the bag and stapled the top shut. "Now, you will feel better. Mr. Zhang is here to help."

I thanked him and left with my bag of unnecessary eucalyptus oil.

As I stepped out of Wild Sage, I saw Jasmine out of the corner of my eye. She was standing in the entrance of the salon, waving at me. "Yo, girl!"

I waved back.

"No," she yelled, and signaled me to come over.

"Hey Jasmine," I said, walking over. "What's up?"

She put her hands on her hips. "Aren't you forgetting something?"

"No?"

"I told—" She wrinkled her nose. "What is that smell?"

I rolled my eyes. "Eucalyptus oil . . . long story."

She shook her head dismissively. "Anyway, the other day at the memorial, I told you that I wanted to see you, remember?"

I had completely forgotten after the ordeal with

Donna and all the events that took place after. I smacked my forehead. "Ugh! I'm so sorry . . . I can make an appointment right now." I touched my hair self-consciously.

She clucked her tongue. "Your hair is fine. I just said that because Peter was standing there listening to us and I didn't want him to wonder about anything."

"Wonder about what?"

"About whether or not I saw them talking in the bathroom hallway."

"Who?" I asked, feeling like I was missing something.

"Peter and Kimmy."

My eyebrows shot up into my hairline. "Yeah?"

Jasmine pulled me over to the corner and lowered her voice. "Yeah. They were acting pretty strange that night, and I wanted you to know . . . because . . . you know." She gave me a wink.

I looked at her, completely lost.

She leaned in. "Cindy told me that you were asking a lot of questions at the bookstore. I know what you're up to," she said, winking again.

"Me?" I asked, looking around to make sure no one could overhear us.

"I know you're trying to figure out what really happened," she whispered. "But don't worry, I won't tell anybody. I know it'll fly around this plaza in no time."

My face reddened. "Oh . . . well, I just . . ."

"You don't need to explain anything to me. I get it."

"So what did you see?" I asked, suddenly feeling very anxious.

"I was coming out of the bathroom before the memorial started and they were both in the hallway arguing. Kimmy was bawling like a five-year-old."

"She was?" I didn't think Kimmy was capable of tears. "What was she crying about?"

"I'm not sure," Jasmine said. "But I did hear Peter say not to worry so much and that he wouldn't say anything."

I thought back to my confrontation with Kimmy and how she'd accused Peter of telling me something I shouldn't know. "Are you sure that's what you heard?"

"Yes." She nodded resolutely. "Also, you probably didn't see this since you went off with that detective guy, but she and Peter left that night . . . together. And they were bickering the entire way out the door. I heard her yelling at him and she said something that sounded like 'you can't tell anyone no matter what'."

My mind was swimming with thoughts. "Thanks for telling me," I said. "I really appreciate it."

"No problem," she replied. "Just do me a favor."

"What's that?"

"If you're seriously going to do this, watch your back," she said, staring me in the eye. "Because that girl is crazy."

I rushed to the restaurant, realizing I'd been gone longer than intended. My mother and Nancy both stood hanging around the hostess booth. When she saw me come through the door, she crossed her arms over her chest with a disapproving look. "Where have you been? I had to come help Nancy and now my soap opera is over."

"Sorry, Mom, Jasmine stopped me on my way back,"

I said, trying to catch my breath. I tucked my paper bag from Wild Sage under the counter and grabbed my apron, tying it back around my waist. "I'm sure Esther can tell you all about your soap opera."

My mom sniffed the air. "What is that smell?"

"Eucalyptus . . ." I said, hoping she wouldn't ask why I had it on.

She nodded with satisfaction. "This is very good for you, but it will not help you catch a boyfriend."

Nancy nodded in agreement. "Your mother is right. This smell is not attractive to men."

I groaned. "Thanks, I'll try to remember that."

Megan had left work early and agreed to meet me in the plaza parking lot. I'd called to tell her about the conversation I'd had with Jasmine and that we had some more investigating to do.

My car was parked in the last possible parking spot and I had the lights off. I drummed my fingers against the steering wheel, feeling restless. I looked at the clock for what felt like the thirteenth time. Five minutes had passed. "Great," I mumbled to myself.

Finally I saw Megan's car pull up. She parked a few spaces away from me and jumped into the car. "Sorry I took so long, I had some tabs to close out." She sniffed the air. "What the heck is that smell? Did you open a Vicks bottle in here?"

I released a heavy sigh and told her the story about Mr. Zhang and the eucalyptus oil that he'd made me put on my temples.

She rolled down the window, leaning toward the open air. "And you didn't try and wash it off?"

"I did," I said, leaning my head on the steering wheel. "It won't come off."

"Did you find anything out while you were there?" she asked, covering her nose.

I told her about the conversation I'd had and his comments about Mr. An stopping in.

"That's weird, right? And you said he gives you the heebies."

I nodded. "He does. I feel like he's always lurking around too."

"He's already on our list, but we haven't paid much attention to him. Maybe we should."

"No one seems to know much about him either. I tried asking Kimmy some questions the same day she flipped out on me about a second job, but she didn't say anything useful."

Megan groaned, waving a hand in front of her face. "Ugh, I can't take it anymore. That stuff is nuclear. Please don't use it at home, I'll have to move out."

"Would you get serious?" I said a little bit more harshly than I meant to.

"Geez, sorry."

"No, I'm sorry," I said, pulling the car out of the plaza parking lot. "I just want to get this going already."

"What exactly are we doing again?" Megan asked.

"We're going with your idea and we're going to sit outside of Peter's apartment to see where he goes . . ."

She nodded. "It's about time. My money is on Peter

and Kimmy . . . or Ian . . . but mostly Kimmy because she's an evil hell spawn."

I gawked at her.

Megan shrugged in return. "Okay, so sue me, I don't like the girl."

"Clearly."

"What if he's not at his apartment?" she asked.

"Then we'll have to try again another night, but I'm hoping that's not the case," I said, stopping at a red light.

She turned to me. "What if you don't like what we find?"

I watched traffic pass, wondering if anyone else had to follow their friends around to find out their darkest secrets. "I guess we'll burn that bridge when we get to it."

Fifteen minutes later, we were in Lakewood, sitting a few buildings down from Peter's apartment building. The light was on in his apartment and that was a good sign.

While we waited, Megan filled me in on her work drama to help pass the time. We talked about the other bartenders and some of the regulars, but even though we had plenty to talk about, it felt like we'd been sitting in the car for an eternity. In reality, it had only been fifteen minutes. Along with my poker face, I made a mental note to work on my patience.

"I don't know what's taking him so long," I blurted out.

"Just relax, we haven't been here that long." Megan looked at her cell phone, checking the time.

I drummed the steering wheel. "I think I have to pee."

"You always have to pee," Megan replied.

Another five minutes went by and then the light in Peter's apartment went out. My heartbeat picked up. He was either leaving his apartment or going to sleep. Since it wasn't that late yet, my money was on him leaving.

Sure enough, a few minutes later, Peter came walking out. He moved with purpose as if he needed to be somewhere and my stomach did a little flip-flop. Where was Peter going to take us?

He got in his car, taking his time getting started. Finally he turned on his lights and pulled into traffic. We stayed a car length behind him to remain out of sight. I'd watched it a million times in the movies, so I felt I had some experience.

We followed him onto the freeway all the way to Brookpark Road. The area he took us to was well-known for its smattering of strip clubs and adult video stores.

He pulled into the parking lot of the Black Garter and parked. We pulled in behind him, passing his car, and found a space toward the back where we had some cover from the entrance.

I looked at Megan, "Now what?"

She took a deep breath. "Have you ever been to a strip club before?"

"No . . ." I said. "Have you?"

She looked out the window. "A few times."

"Megan Riley!" I gasped.

Megan giggled. "It's kind of funny," she said, teasing me. "Don't be such a prude."

"I don't want to spend the night looking at half-naked girls," I huffed.

"Well, too bad, you signed up for this," Megan replied. "Plus, if he *is* getting into fights at a strip club, this might be the one. So we have to see what's going on in there."

"If they kicked him out, why do they keep letting him in?" I turned in my seat to look at the entrance, panic setting in. "Are they going to think we're weird for wanting to go inside? And what if Peter sees us?"

"Stop worrying. And no, girls go all the time." She started to open the door. "Come on, you'll see."

Hesitantly, I got out of the car and squared my shoulders. "My mother would kill me if she knew."

"Good thing she's not here to see this then," Megan said, walking a few feet in front of me. "Now let's go."

We headed for the entrance and stepped up to the bouncer who was watching the door. A scantily clad girl stood at a podium behind him. The bouncer looked us over with a stern eye and then gave a slight nod, which prompted the girl to smile brightly at us. "Hi, ladies, how are we doing tonight?" She held out her hand. "I just need to check your IDs."

Megan stepped up with ease to the podium and handed her ID to the girl who viewed it under a black light. "You're good, sweetheart." She gave Megan a wink and handed back her driver's license.

Nervously, I gave her my ID. She looked it over and then handed it back to me. "First time at a strip club, honey?" she asked with a syrupy voice.

I gulped and gave her a curt nod as she handed back my driver's license.

Megan grabbed my hand and we headed inside.

"I don't even know you," I hissed.

She laughed and opened the door. Immediately we were bombarded with loud hip-hop music and a wave of smoke. The place was packed and there was hardly any room to walk. Megan held on to my hand and maneuvered us through the crowd to the bar. "You need a drink to calm down," she yelled at me over her shoulder.

While she ordered, I looked around, trying to appear casual, but I had the feeling that I had a big ole sign on my forehead that screamed FRESH MEAT. From what I did notice, the ratio of women to men was almost split down the middle, which surprised me. Megan had been right, there were a lot of women here.

Megan nudged my arm and handed me what looked like a rum and Coke.

I gratefully took a healthy swallow.

"Do you see Peter anywhere?" Megan yelled over the music.

I shook my head. "Nope, it's impossible to see anything in here." The smoke in the room was coming from a fog machine placed right by what I'd call the main stage.

"Come on, let's walk around a little," Megan suggested.

I let Megan lead the way, and tried to keep my eyes down so I wouldn't accidentally gawk. We circled around the room and we'd almost made it back to where we'd gotten our drinks when Megan stopped dead in her tracks, forcing me to run into her. She jerked forward and most of her drink splashed onto the floor.

I grabbed her arm to straighten her out. "Sorry!" I said, looking around us. "Why'd you stop?"

She didn't respond, she just pointed. I looked to where she was pointing, but it took me a minute to see it. She was pointing to one of the cocktail waitresses, carrying a tray above her head. This particular one had stopped and was leaning down, talking with a man seated at a table with a few of his friends. The seated man was smiling up at her with a devilish grin. He grabbed her free hand and said something to her that made him and his friends laugh. I watched the annoyance creep up on her face and that's when I realized who I was looking at. I'd seen that face before. It was Kimmy.

I think my jaw must have dropped to the floor as recognition flooded over me. This was Kimmy Tran, the girl I'd known since I was a little kid. The same girl I played Barbies with.

As if that weren't enough to shock me, Peter came stomping out of nowhere, swatting the guy's arm away from Kimmy. She stumbled back from the motion, and as she collected herself, she glared at Peter.

The seated man stood, and when he rose, he just kept going. The man must have been well over six feet and he towered over Peter, making him look like a scrawny teenager. However, Peter did not back down. He stood his ground, balling his fists at his sides.

The towering man took a step closer to Peter and said something through gritted teeth. I wasn't a lip reader so I had no clue what he'd said, but I bet anything that it was a threat.

Megan grabbed my arm. "Come on, we have to go over there before Peter gets pummeled."

We headed over to where they were standing. A crowd was forming around the two men, people egging them on.

Kimmy turned her head just as we were approaching and did a double take as she realized that it was us. She scowled, her drink tray falling to her side. "What the hell are you guys doing here?"

"I'd like to know the exact same thing," a voice boomed from behind us.

I turned around and there in all his detective right-eousness stood Trudeau with the most exasperated expression I have ever seen on another human being.

"We, um—" I started to come up with some kind of lie, but he didn't even let me finish.

"I'd like to speak with you outside, Miss Lee." He pointed to the door. "Right now."

CHAPTER
29

"What the hell were you thinking?" Trudeau yelled, his nostrils flaring.

We were standing outside the Black Garter practically toe to toe, with his eyes burning daggers into me, and my eyes, well, I was looking at our toes. My brain scurried for a reasonable explanation. Megan stood off to the side trying to give us some privacy, but Trudeau's booming voice was making it easy for her to eavesdrop.

I looked up at him from beneath my lashes, calling on all my powers of cuteness. "We were just having some drinks?" It came out more like a question than a statement.

He threw his hands in the air. "You're unbelievable, you know that?"

"Why? You don't think that I can—"

"Cut the cute act, Lana, I've been following you all night," Trudeau said.

My eyes bulged and I risked a look in Megan's direction. "You were following us?"

"To be more specific, I was following Peter, and I watched you and your little friend here tail him all the way from his apartment. What were you planning on doing? Confronting him?" He crossed his arms over his broad chest and stared at me, waiting for an answer.

"We . . . just wanted to see what he was up to," I mumbled.

"Oh, I see," Trudeau replied sarcastically. "You thought that he was involved in this murder so you just wanted to see. No worries about whether he was the actual killer and might try to hurt you if you got too close?"

I chewed on my lip. "Well, we figured since it was a public place . . ." I looked to Megan for help.

"A public place helps you while you're in it. This guy knows where you live, he certainly knows where you work, and I'm guessing he knows most of your habits. Were you planning on staying in the strip club forever?" With each word, his voice got louder.

"Okay, Detective," Megan said, holding up a hand. "You don't need to yell at her, we understand that it was silly of us—"

He pointed a finger in her direction. "Don't even get me started on you, young lady. You went along with this and you're just as careless as she is."

Megan's eyebrows scrunched together and she put her hands on her hips. "Listen here—"

Trudeau stopped her, holding up a hand. "You might

want to think about the next thing you're about to say. You're still talking to a police detective."

Her mouth closed and she took a step back.

Trudeau turned his attention back to me. "Now, I want you and blondie over here to go home and mind your own business. Is that clear?"

I heard Megan cluck her tongue in the dark. I nodded and we skulked to the car. I could feel Trudeau watching us the entire way.

"Want me to drive?" Megan asked. I handed over the keys and got in on the passenger side, moping like a child that had just been put in the corner.

Once inside the car with the doors locked and the windows up, Megan let out a heavy groan. "That guy is a jerk. Complete and total jerk. *Blondie. Blondie?* And he shouldn't have talked to you that way. He acts like we're a couple of criminals or something." She started the car. "It's not a crime for us to go to a strip club and look around. He doesn't know that we weren't there because we wanted to be."

"He watched us follow Peter from his apartment," I reminded her.

"Whose side are you on, anyway?" she asked.

"Okay, sorry."

"Anyway," she said, backing the car out of the spot. "He was tailing Peter for a reason, which means that we're not far off from what we were thinking."

"I don't know anymore . . ." I said, looking out the window as we passed the Black Garter. "I think it's as simple as Kimmy working in a strip club. Her parents would be mortified if they knew she was working as a cocktail waitress in a place like this."

"Yeah, but what's that got to do with Peter?" Megan asked.

"That's what we still have to find out."

Immediately upon waking up, I had the events of the previous night rolling through my head. Specifically the looks on Peter's and Kimmy's faces as they realized we had caught them in a place they shouldn't be. The only thing of it is, Peter being in a strip club wasn't really something that should be so strange for a male in his early thirties, but it was just plain out of character. Then again, what did I really know about Peter? As long as I'd known him, I'd never seen him in a relationship. He kept to himself and focused on his hobbies: video games, sketching, and karate. I didn't know him to be any other way. So, what caused this sudden change of character?

I tried calling him on our way home, but he never picked up or returned my call. My guess was that he wasn't exactly thrilled at having to explain what was going on, especially if Kimmy was on his back about it. I assumed that's what all the arguing was about during the memorial. She must have thought that Peter had confided her secret to me. I kind of wished he had . . . it could have saved my first experience at a strip club from becoming a reality.

It was still early and my room was dark. I could feel Kikko under the covers, her fur pressed against my leg. I gave her a little nudge and she popped up, snorting her way out of the blankets.

After I got dressed in a thick sweater and bundled up, we went on our morning walk, which lasted about two minutes. The temperature had dropped drastically from the previous day. Kikko and I weren't much for winter weather. When we got back, Megan was moving around in the kitchen, getting coffee ready.

"Morning," she mumbled. "I slept like hell."

I unleashed Kikko and she scampered into the apartment. "Last night bugging you?"

"Maybe the detective is right," Megan said, filling the coffeepot with water. "Maybe we should just forget this whole thing. I mean, what are the chances we're actually going to figure this thing out?"

My jaw dropped. "You're joking, right?"

She turned to face me. "We're going in circles, and things just keep getting more confusing. Don't you think?"

"You can't give up on me now. What about all the time we've already put in? And the lectures you gave me on how we don't have to be professionals to figure this out?"

Megan smirked. "I'm glad to hear you say that."

"What?" My confusion was bordering on agitation. I knew that smirk.

"I just wanted to make sure you were still serious about this and that the detective didn't persuade you to stop looking into it."

"So, you're not being serious about giving up?"

"I wanted to make sure that you were telling me the truth."

I put my hands on my hips. "You could have just asked."

"I like to be creative," she said, waggling her eyebrows at me. "And tonight . . . tonight, my friend, I think we should look into that mysterious key."

I would have strangled her right there, but my cell phone rang. It wasn't typical for me to get calls this early in the morning and I rushed to find my phone. Calls this early in the morning usually meant that something bad had happened. And if there was anything that I didn't need, it was another incident.

I didn't recognize the number on my phone, and I paused before answering, thinking that I should let it go to voice mail. But my curiosity won out. "Hello?"

"Lana?"

It was Donna Feng.

"Yes, good morning," I said with hesitance.

"Sorry to call so early, but I'm on my way out for the day, and didn't want to forget to give you a call. Do you think you could stop by my place after work today?"

"Sure, is anything wrong?" I asked, alarm bells going off in my head.

"Nothing like that, dear, just wanted to talk to you about something. Come by around six-thirty, okay?"

"Um, okay."

"See you then, dear." She clicked off.

I sat on the edge of my bed dumbfounded, holding my phone, staring at the blank screen.

"Who was that?" Megan asked, coming into the doorway of my bedroom. She held out a cup of coffee.

"It was Donna . . ." I said, taking the cup from her hand.

"Donna? What could she possibly want this early in the morning?"

"I have no idea, but she wants me to come over after work. Say, around six-thirty."

Six-thirty couldn't come fast enough, and I kept an eye on the clock through my entire work shift.

When my shift was over, I left so fast I almost forgot to take my purse. Vanessa gave me a weird look as I rushed out the door.

When I pulled into the driveway, I did a quick rundown of all the possibilities. Did she know I'd been snooping around? Had someone from the plaza told her that I'd been asking questions about her husband?

I hurried up the driveway and onto the steps. Before I could ring the doorbell, Donna opened the door with a pleasant smile. "Come on in, my dear."

I smiled back, but wasn't sure how convincing it looked. I was a ball of nerves.

She led me into the same sitting room we'd spent time in the day after Mr. Feng passed away. The room was perfect, as it always was, and she had set out a service of tea on the coffee table. She gestured to the chair. "Have a seat."

I sat down, uncertain of myself, setting my purse on the floor at my feet. "I hope you don't mind me cutting to the chase," I said, my voice a bit shaky. "But why did you ask me to come over?"

Donna took her time getting comfortable, and poured two cups of tea. She handed one to me and I took it, cupping it in my hand, the heat traveling through my fingers.

She sat back on the couch and looked at me with perfect calm on her face. "I have known your family for a long time," she started. "For as long as the plaza has been around, I have known your parents and have been friends with them for many years. And when they had you girls, I couldn't have been happier for them." She paused, blowing on her cup of tea.

I looked down at my own teacup and a thought passed through my brain about yellow jasmine. I didn't feel very thirsty at the moment.

"And they've brought you up right. Both you and Anna May are exemplary models of what children should be. Even if you may be a bit of a rebel yourself . . . underneath it all, I know that you're a good person, with the best of intentions." She stopped and looked at me, watching my reaction.

"Donna, I—"

"So you can imagine my surprise, when I find you have been snooping through my house."

My heart sank . . . dropped . . . imploded . . . I didn't know the word for it, but I was starting to wonder what the chances were of a twenty-seven-year-old having a heart attack out of the blue. "I'm sorry . . . I don't . . ."

"Don't play dumb with me, young lady," Donna said with venom in her voice. "I know you were snooping around my house while I was in the hospital. And I know you know my secret . . ."

CHAPTER
30

I set the teacup down on the coffee table and rubbed my hands on my jeans. "I don't know anything about secrets, I only brought in your mail, I swear."

Donna sneered, setting down her teacup as well. "At least have the respect to tell me the truth, Lana. We're both intelligent women."

"I promise; I only came to put your mail away." My eyes glanced toward the entrance, and I wondered how long it would take me to run out. She had heels on, so that would slow her down at least.

She smiled sarcastically to herself. "So I suppose my surveillance cameras are the liars then?"

Surveillance cameras? I took a moment to process that information.

She laughed. "You know, at first when I watched the tape, I laughed to myself, thinking you were just curious about what the rest of my house looked like." She paused. "But then I realized you were taking too long. You must have gotten into something."

The fact that she didn't know for sure relieved me. It also told me that the cameras must not have been anywhere that would give away what I was really doing. "I had to use your bathroom," I lied, hoping she would buy it.

"I know that you went through my vanity, and I know you saw my birth certificate!"

My heart was racing at full speed. So there *was* something strange going on with her birth certificate. While I thought of the possibilities, she continued to rant.

"You have no idea what this information could do to me, if anyone knew that I'm not really who I say I am." She stopped and looked at me, her expression desperate. "It could ruin everything and jeopardize my kids."

"Wait . . ." I said, finding myself more confused. "Jeopardize your kids?"

"Yes! I can't have anybody coming after my family." Her voice was shrill as she said it.

I didn't know what her birth certificate could have to do with her children. But I knew by what she was saying that I had her at a disadvantage. I only had two options. The first was to act like I had no idea what she was talking about and stick to my bathroom story. The other . . .

"I promise I won't tell anyone about your birth certificate if you agree to trade information with me."

"What kind of information?"

"Tell me about this birth certificate angle, and I'll tell you what I was doing here."

She took a deep breath, closing her eyes. "I need you to explain to me what you were doing here first."

If there was any one moment that I needed to be honest, it was now. "I'm looking into who really killed your husband. All I did was go into Mr. Feng's office upstairs to look for a key to get into the office at Asia Village. I promise I didn't go through any of your personal things."

Her eyes widened and she shifted on the couch. "Lana! That is dangerous! What are you thinking?"

Careful to leave out certain details, like the information I had found in Mr. Feng's desk, I filled her in on what I had been doing and the odd things that had been going on with Mr. An, Peter, Kimmy, and even Ian. She sipped her tea as she listened, soaking in everything I was telling her. "I thought maybe if I could get into the office and find something, I would be able to figure out what really happened to your husband. I was just trying to help . . ." I said, feeling silly now that I'd explained the story in full.

For a few minutes after I'd stopped talking, we sat in silence, and I'm sure that she was thinking of what to say next . . . or what to do with me. Now that my story was out, she could easily renege on our agreement of sharing information with me.

I decided to break the silence. "Please don't tell anyone what I've been doing. I promise I'll stop and I'll give you the keys back."

She glanced up at me. "Did you find anything in my husband's things?"

I left out all the parts about how Megan and I had taken certain things from Mr. Feng's drawer. In my current position, I felt it was best she didn't know it existed. I did tell her about the appointment book and that Mr. Feng had scheduled a meeting with someone other than Cindy that day.

"Well, you can take Ian off your suspect list," Donna replied dryly.

Her response took me by surprise. "How can you be sure? He's gaining quite a bit from your husband being out of the picture. Especially with you taking a backseat in running Asia Village."

She laughed. "He's too incompetent to come up with something quite so clever."

I cocked my head. "But if he's so incompetent, then why are you letting him run the plaza?"

She waved a hand. "It's a promise I made to his father. Ian has had a bad run, and his father is just about done with him. He almost refused to help Ian when he called from Chicago. That's when I offered a solution to their problems," she explained. "I suggested he work with Thomas, and gain experience. Once Thomas was ready to retire, we planned to let Ian handle affairs at the plaza. I thought under our guidance he could be molded into an excellent businessman. Ian needs someone who still has patience left for him. He's screwed up too many times and there's not very many people who are willing to take a chance on him like I am."

"But why would you want to set him up with me then?"

She chuckled. "He needs a good woman with a strong head on her shoulders, someone to guide him and keep him on track."

I sat back, shaking my head. "Well, that's not me, because I'm still trying to get myself together."

She smiled with understanding. "Lana, you need to stop being so hard on yourself. These things happen over time, and you'll find your way. Right now, you are doing what any modern twenty-seven-year-old would be doing . . . you're finding yourself."

I thought that over and wondered if she had a point. Was that what this was? I was finding myself? Is this what they called a quarter-life crisis?

"Now, while I'm relieved to know that you weren't trying to expose my secret like I originally thought, I suppose a deal is a deal. But you must swear to me that you will tell absolutely no one. If you do . . ." She paused. "If you do, then I will be forced to tell the authorities that you broke into my house. Is that clear?"

I nodded.

She leaned back on the couch. "I am not from California like I've made everyone believe. But it is very important that everyone continue to believe I am Donna Feng from San Francisco, California. No one must find out that I am actually from Shanghai."

"But why?" I asked.

"For them." She looked at the mantel that sat to the right of us. Her eyes focused on the pictures of her family. "My father was not a good man, and had many enemies. My mother had to make a difficult decision when I was young. She chose to protect me, so she made a deal and brought me to the U.S. where we could start over. Just me and her."

I thought back to the only time I had met her mother, and the hard look that rested on her face. It made me wonder how many secrets that woman carried with her.

"The only way for my mother to be sure that we

would be safe here was to pretend that we had been here since the beginning. So the story goes that I was born in San Francisco, and shortly after, my father died in a car accident, leaving her to raise me on her own. And the man who killed my father in this supposed car accident was extremely wealthy, giving us more than plenty of money to live an above-average lifestyle."

"So where did the money really come from?"

Donna looked down at her hands. "Let's just say that my mother has taken care of all our needs and kept me on a need-to-know basis. The less we all know, the better."

I thought this over. "Do you think this has anything to do with Mr. Feng's death?"

She shook her head. "If anything were to be found out, the first person they would go after would be my mother. They know how much she means to me."

"I see . . ." I had no idea what else to say. This was not what I had expected to hear.

"Now that I've told you, do you understand why it's important that no one find out the truth?"

"Yes, but then why keep a copy of your birth certificate where it can be found?"

She sighed, looking at me with sadness in her eyes. "Sometimes it's hard to be someone else. It's the last thing I have to remind me of who I once was."

We sat together for a short while, and I even took a sip of tea. My worries of her being guilty of anything had mostly withered away. I doubted she knew that Mr. Feng had found out her secret, and for her safety, and her family's, I decided I would burn the papers that Megan and I had found from the private investigator.

She walked me to the door when I'd decided to call it a night. "I'm still quite upset with you for not telling me what you were up to," she lectured. "Don't you think I want justice for Thomas too?"

Instead of admitting that I thought she was a potential suspect, I said, "I didn't think you'd want me to meddle in this, but I had to do something. You seemed so sure that Peter was guilty. And I can't understand why."

She pursed her lips. "Well, I have my own reasons for that. But if you think that this is worth looking into, then I will accept that."

"You will?"

She laughed. "Honestly, Lana, you're a bright girl, and I think you're capable of figuring out who killed Thomas."

"You do?" I asked in amazement.

"Yes, I do. You're able to see a side to these people that the police can't uncover so easily. And what's more, I'm willing to keep your little secret under one condition."

"Okay . . ."

"Tell me what you find before you go to the police. I would prefer not to be surprised by the outcome of anything you may uncover."

I tilted my head in contemplation. Not wanting to create unnecessary conflict, I conceded. "That seems fair . . . it is your husband after all . . ."

"So, she's a fraud too?" Megan hissed through the phone.

I was driving home and couldn't wait the twenty minutes it would take to get there, so I'd called Megan to fill her in on what happened. She was still at the bar waiting for the next bartender to come in.

"I know," I answered in disbelief. "I mean, it shouldn't have been that big of a shock since both of us saw those birth certificates, but it's still pretty wild."

"She must have said or done something bizarre to make Mr. Feng look into it," Megan concluded. "So, who is she then?"

"I'm not sure, but I made it a point to leave out that we'd found a copy of the birth certificate in his office. I don't think she'd be too thrilled to find out that her husband hired a private detective to follow her around."

"Figures that the evidence was right under his nose the entire time. In their own freakin' bedroom," Megan said. "But I have to ask . . . do you think she's trying to pull one over on us? I mean, she seemed to flip switches with you pretty fast. Maybe she's faking?"

I shrugged as if she could see me through the phone. "I don't know about that either, but my main priority was getting out of there. I'm lucky she didn't turn on me after I told her what I was really up to. She does have me on camera after all."

"I see your point."

"So what time do you think you'll be home?" I asked as I made my way off the freeway into North Olmsted.

"Who knows," she said with exasperation. "Robin has been late every day this week, so I can't even guess anymore."

"Okay, well, text me when you're on your way home, and I'll make sure that I'm ready."

An hour later, I hopped into Megan's car and we

headed toward the Hidden Den. We weren't sure if it would turn into anything, but I wouldn't feel that it was resolved until we at least had a look. It could just be a random key chain he decided to use.

The Hidden Den was located on the corner of a predominantly residential street and looked like it might be out of business. The brick structure was small and unattractive. The flat roof made the building look shorter than it was, and I tried to imagine someone the size of Detective Trudeau fitting in the door.

Megan parked the car close to the main entrance, which was on the back side of the building away from the street. An unexceptional building like this one, with an entrance in the back, gave me the feeling that a lot of shady dealings could go on here.

"You ready for this?" Megan asked me over her shoulder as she opened the door.

I shrugged. "Do we really have a choice?"

She snickered and pulled open the door, letting me walk ahead of her. It was dim inside and it took a minute for my eyes to adjust. When they did, I was struck by a sense of mediocrity. The room itself was a small rectangle with a low ceiling and the perimeter of the room was decorated with multicolored Christmas lights that I imagined hung there all year long. A small wooden bar with about ten stools stood to our right, and to our left were the bathrooms and a scattering of tables. The place smelled like a mixture of backed-up sewer pipes and French fry grease. I had a hard time imagining Mr. Feng coming to a place like this.

The bartender was an older, jolly-looking man with a full head of bright white hair. He had on a plain white shirt and a towel was slung over his shoulder. He smiled warmly at us as we made our way up to the stools. "What can I get you lovely ladies this fine evening?"

"I'll have a vanilla vodka and Coke, if you have it," I said, hopping up on the stool.

He smiled. "I don't have any of those fancy vodkas here, but I have some cherry Coke that I can mix in your vodka."

"Okay, that works."

"Same for me," Megan threw in.

The bartender went to make our drinks, and I took a casual look around the bar. Hardly anybody was there. An older man sat at the other end of the bar, his eyes fixed on the TV screen just above his head. Behind us, a young couple sat together at a small wooden table for two, holding hands across the tabletop. Country music was playing softly in the background.

The bartender came back and slid our drinks in front of us. "That'll be four fifty." My eyebrows shot up at the low price and he chuckled. "One of the perks of not having anything fancy around here."

I pulled out a ten to pay him. "I was wondering if I could ask you . . . do you happen to know anybody named Thomas Feng? We think he might've come in here on occasion."

He looked at me knowingly, and leaned against the bar as if to confide his greatest secrets. "Listen, sis, if you have to wonder if your fella is cheatin' on ya, then he's probably not worth the trouble."

I gave a nervous laugh. "Oh no, it's nothing like that. He was a friend of mine who got in some trouble and I've been trying to figure out what he's been up to."

"Most people that come in here, they don't mention their names to me. Usually they're here hiding from something . . . or somebody." The bartender nodded in the direction of the couple sitting behind us. "You see them two over there?"

Megan and I nodded in unison.

"Their relationship probably isn't entirely on the up-and-up. If you look closely, you'll see they both have wedding rings on, but it's not likely they belong to each other."

I chanced a quick look over my shoulder and sure enough, watching the couple for a few minutes gave me the distinct impression that they were just seeing each other for the first time in a long time. I turned back around to face the bartender. "So, if I told you what this guy looked like, would that help?"

He shrugged. "Worth a shot."

I gave my description of Mr. Feng the best I could. I started out with the fact that he was Asian because I thought that might help narrow it down. Not a lot of Asian men going into dive bars that play country music. Was I stereotyping my own ethnicity? Yes.

"Wait a minute," the bartender said, a lightbulb no doubt going off in the recesses of his brain. "Is that the Chinese guy that did all the community work and owned that plaza over there on the west side?"

"It is . . ."

"Yeah, he used to come in here all the time with this real beautiful Chinese lady. I think he had an apartment somewhere in the area. I always thought it was real strange that he'd come in here with all the money he had, but hey, I don't ask questions, or turn away business."

So Mr. Feng had been coming in here with someone and I highly doubted it was Donna. Partially because I couldn't imagine a woman of her status coming to a hole-in-the-wall bar like this one, and also because she was often featured in the papers with Mr. Feng, which would make the bartender most likely call the beautiful Chinese lady his wife. "Did he ever talk to you?" I asked, holding on to hope that we'd find out something else.

He thought on it for a minute. "Not really, he'd make small talk while he waited for the woman to show up. They'd stay for about an hour and then they'd head off to wherever they went. He never drove here, so I'm assuming that wherever he was coming from was within walking distance."

The bartender walked away to get my change, and I sat thinking about what all of this could mean. I don't know why I hadn't thought about it before, but Thomas did own a few apartment complexes in the area. So it was entirely possible that he was taking his mystery woman to one of those apartments. And if that was the case, how would we narrow down which one? The keys I'd taken from the drawer had no symbols or numbers on them to give any clues.

Megan must have been reading my mind because she asked, "How are we going to find the apartment?"

"Maybe if we figure out which of his buildings have vacancies? And then we can check those out? See if the key fits in any of those locks?" I asked. Another long shot, but so far the night was looking up.

"But if he was using an apartment on a regular basis, would it be up for rent?" Megan asked skeptically.

"No, you're probably right about that, he'd want to keep it for himself." I drummed my fingers on the side of the glass. "If I was walking here, it would be because it was the closest place to get to . . ."

"Especially if you didn't want to be seen roaming the streets," Megan added. "He could run into someone . . . he's pretty well known."

"So, let's figure out which buildings he owns in this neighborhood and find the closest one." I pulled out my phone. "We'll start there."

Megan looked at me with wide eyes. "You mean, you want to do this tonight?"

I started my search for any property owned by Thomas Feng and said, "Might as well, we're already out this way."

CHAPTER
31

After a little bit of digging on the Internet, we located a small apartment complex that Mr. Feng owned about a block away. Perfect walking distance.

We thanked the bartender for his help and went on our way.

The old stone structure was well kept, but looked to be about a century old. At this time of night, the building was mostly dark, and only a few lights were on in the three-story building.

Megan parked the car in the street a little away from the building so we could walk past first and check for activity. It had dawned on me while we were driving the short distance here that the mystery woman might live in the apartment we were looking for.

We had our flashlights and a backpack in case we needed to take anything with us. We made our way up to the entrance of the building, which was surrounded by boxwood shrubs that needed a good clipping. There was a small entryway and it was cramped with just the two of us standing in it. I checked for a security camera, but found none and gave a sigh of relief. No more cameras.

On the right wall, there was a pad with twelve buttons and an apartment number listed next to each. Twelve metal mail slots sat to the right of it, all of the mailboxes had names listed on them except for two. That would be our starting point.

With shaky hands, I rang the first buzzer and waited for a reply. Nothing.

Megan looked at me. "Well, that's a good sign, right?"

"Maybe," I said. And I pressed the second buzzer with no listed name. And again, nothing. Of the two keys on the chain, I picked the larger one that resembled the kind of key we had for our security door. The lock stuck a little bit, but I got it open and we hurried inside.

The first apartment with no name was on the second floor, and both of us tiptoed up the stairs. TVs could be heard in the hallway, and I was thankful for the lack of total silence.

We read the numbers on the door and found apartment 203. I pressed my ear up to the door and listened. Silence.

Megan, who was keeping an eye out, turned to me. "Well?" she whispered.

I shook my head. "I don't hear anything." I straightened and braced myself, putting the key in the lock. It fit, but wouldn't turn.

Megan sighed and gestured up the stairs. I nodded in reply and we made our way quietly up the steps to the third floor. We stood in front of apartment 301. This had to be it. Unless we had the wrong building altogether. I kept my fingers crossed that we wouldn't have to search for another apartment building.

I went through the same routine of putting my ear to the door, and I heard nothing on the other side. Just to be sure, I gave a light knock, hoping that none of the neighbors would hear the noise and come out. When there was no response, I put the key in the lock, and turned it slowly. The door started to give. Megan and I exchanged a look, and I pushed the door open just enough so we could sneak in.

Once we were inside, I shut the door gently, and turned the lock. We stood in the dark for a few minutes, listening, and absorbing our surroundings.

I heard Megan rustling around in her bag, and when she was done a small beam of light hit the floor. "Let's do a quick walk-through to make sure no one's in here with us," she whispered. I could hear the nervousness in her voice.

I nodded in agreement, not sure if she could even see the gesture. I felt around in my bag and found my own mini flashlight. I switched it on so it would light up the floor, and I made my way through the living room, careful not to make too much noise.

The apartment was cozy, with a decent-sized living room and small kitchenette. There was a short hallway that I assumed led to the bedroom. We headed for the hallway and thankfully there weren't any shut doors. At the end of the hallway was a small bathroom, and to the left was the bedroom. I crept up to the doorway and slowly shone the flashlight over the perimeter of the room near the bed. As far as I could tell, no one was in it. I breathed a sigh of relief.

The room had one window covered in miniblinds. I moved along the side of the bed and twisted the handle to close the blinds tight. Megan and I stood in the room catching our breath.

"Do you think anyone is living here?" Megan asked, waving her flashlight around the room.

"Let's hope not. I'm going to make sure all the blinds are closed in the living room too."

"Okay, I'll look around in here."

Before heading out into the living room, I stopped in the small bathroom, and took a look around. There was nothing extraordinary about the bathroom, and I felt a slight touch of claustrophobia standing in the small space. There wasn't even a window. I stood in front of the sink, and stared at the mirror of the hanging medicine cabinet. The glow of the flashlight lit up the edges of my face and dread washed over me as I recollected every urban legend about standing in front of mirrors in the dark.

I shook away the fear that was creeping up my throat and slowly slid the mirror to one side. The inside of the medicine cabinet was nothing exciting. There was a tube of toothpaste, a bottle of generic aspirin, and a small bottle of mouthwash. I closed the cabinet and moved back to the living room.

There was a sliding glass door in the living room and it was covered with vertical blinds. I made sure they were closed and worked my way around the kitchenette and the living room.

I don't know what possessed me to check the fridge, but I felt my body ease as I searched through the contents. A carton of milk was on the top shelf with an expiration date of two weeks ago. So, either the person living here didn't clean out their fridge too often, or no one had been here in at least a few weeks.

Megan came out into the living room. "There's nothing exciting in the bedroom. A couple of women's shirts are hanging in the closet, but the drawers are practically empty. Nothing under the bed either."

I told her about the milk and she let out a sigh of relief. She plopped down on the couch and held her head in her hand. "This whole thing is stressful. I hope we find something here . . . then at least it'll be worth it."

"I couldn't agree more," I replied as I opened all the drawers in the kitchen, which also contained nothing exciting. A lot of the drawers were empty or had minimal supplies in them. I found chopsticks in wrappers and mismatched napkins that must have come from takeout orders.

I went over to the couch and sat down gingerly on the edge next to Megan. I was feeling defeated and the whole ordeal was draining the life out of me. I felt like I could sleep for a week.

"Maybe we should just go," Megan suggested. "The longer we're here, the creepier I feel."

"Not yet. There has to be something."

To our right, there was a small credenza that hugged the wall. I hadn't noticed it when we walked in because I was so busy worrying about open windows and sound sleepers tucked in their bed. So preoccupied, in fact, that

I hadn't noticed the picture frames placed on top, or the stack of papers lying next to it.

Megan watched and followed my line of sight. "What are you looking at?"

"There are pictures over there," I said, swinging the flashlight to the desk. I got up to get a better look, and what I saw couldn't have shocked me more. It was Peter's mom, Nancy. I picked up the frame and shone the light on the portrait. Smiling back at me was Nancy; slightly younger, but it was definitely her. "Holy . . ."

"What?" Megan asked, springing up from her seat on the couch. She looked over my shoulder at the picture. "Is that . . . ?"

"Yup, Peter's mom." I stared at the picture. I was having a hard time absorbing and processing all the potential scenarios. From the look of things they were still seeing each other. Did Peter know? Was he the killer after all? Or was it Peter's mom? Thomas was supposed to be happily married to Donna. So why did this apartment even exist?

"You know what's even more strange?" Megan said, breaking me out of my thoughts.

"It really can't get weirder, Megan . . ."

"Wanna bet?" she asked, reaching around me and lifting the other frame to eye level.

"What . . . ?" I stared at the frame she held in her hand; it was one of those folding frames with two slots for five-by-seven photos. One side was a picture of Peter in a cap and gown, his graduation photo. And the other was a picture of a younger Mr. Feng with a toddler on his knee, and Nancy standing behind the two with her hand on Mr. Feng's shoulder.

"Didn't you tell me once that Peter never knew his father?" Megan asked.

"Yeah . . ."

"Do you think—"

"No." I shook my head. "No, this can't be right. He probably just took him under his wing or something. You know, since he didn't know his own dad." I turned away from Megan, clutching the photo.

"Lana . . ." Megan said softly.

Before I could venture further into denial land, we heard a door slam in the hallway, and both of us jumped. I dropped the picture frame I was holding in my hand, and it made a loud thud against the table.

Megan swore for both of us.

We stood frozen in place, listening for more sounds in the hallway. When we didn't hear anything, Megan crept to the door and put her face up to the peephole.

"Nancy?" a muffled voice called through the door. "Is that you?"

Megan jumped back from the peephole, her hand flying up to her chest. She turned to me and put a finger to her lips.

"Nancy?" the voice called again. Then there was a light knock at the door.

My heart was thudding so loud in my chest, I thought for sure the entire city block could hear it. We stood in place for several minutes until we didn't hear anything anymore. Megan quietly stepped back up to the door, placing her face near the peephole and held it there for several minutes.

She must not have seen anything because she turned

to me and hissed, "Bring that picture frame. We need to leave!"

Back at home, we both sat on the couch with a beer in our hands. We hadn't talked the whole way home. Half of the car ride was spent catching our breath, and the rest of the silence, well, I didn't know about Megan, but I was lost in my thoughts about everything we'd learned since leaving the house earlier that night.

What we had found opened up even more possibilities than we'd had before, and now that I had more time to think about it, it could even put Donna back on the suspect list. Did she know that her husband was being unfaithful to her? Was everything she'd told me earlier that evening a lie?

And Peter . . . did he know that Thomas was his father to begin with? Or had he just found out and that's why he'd started acting so strangely? Furthermore, if he'd just found out, why had Nancy or Thomas decided to tell him after all this time? Either way, I didn't want to believe it.

"I think it was Peter," I blurted out into the silent room, shocking myself in the process. Did I really believe that?

Both Megan and Kikko turned to look at me. Both with equal surprise.

"You sound pretty sure of yourself," Megan replied.

I stood up and started to pace. "It has to be. He must have known that his mom was sleeping with Mr. Feng . . . or doing whatever they were doing." I had a cringe moment thinking about it.

Megan leaned forward, balancing her elbows on her knees. "I don't know, something doesn't feel right about it being Peter . . ."

"What makes you say that?" I asked, stopping in the middle of my pacing.

"With everything we've found between the office and this secret apartment . . . I think there's more to it. I don't think it's as simple as Peter being mad because Thomas Feng was his father."

I threw up a hand. "Of course there's more to it."

"Aha! So you admit there's a possibility that Thomas is Peter's father."

I grunted and continued to pace. "I don't know."

"Don't be stubborn, Lana, there's a family photo to prove it."

"We don't know that. I've taken pictures with you and your family before, doesn't mean that we're related."

"We just left their love nest, Lana. I mean, come on, that was obviously their secret meeting place."

"We don't know anything," I repeated.

She huffed. "Okay, fine, we don't know that to be a hundred percent true. What are we going to do now?"

"I don't know yet   "

"Well, one thing's for sure, we can't tell Donna any of this. No matter how much she wants to help."

"Agreed," I replied. "She could be guilty after all, I mean, her whole story could be made up to throw me off track."

"A woman like Donna . . ." Megan shivered. "I don't even want to know how she'd react if she found out her husband was cheating on her."

"I need to find a way to talk to Nancy about this. I

need to find out what the extent of their relationship was and if she thinks Peter may have found out. Jeez," I said, throwing my arms up. "I need to talk to Peter too." I thought about the times I had tried getting him to open up to me, and how close he'd come the night that Kimmy interrupted us. His behavior couldn't all be because of Kimmy's workplace situation. There had to be more to the story.

"Do you really think either one of them will tell you anything?"

"I'm not sure about Peter at this point, but I might be able to convince Nancy that it's best to tell me, so I can help her before anyone else finds out the truth."

"Help her?" Megan asked, confused.

"Yeah, you know . . . so Donna doesn't come after her."

That night I had weird dreams about Mr. Feng, Donna, and Nancy, all sitting together at a dinner table. In front of them were plates and plates of shrimp dumplings.

The trio talked cheerily to each other, but their voices were muffled and I couldn't make out what they were saying. I watched as they laughed, throwing their heads back as if they didn't have a care in the world.

Mr. Feng sat between the two women, his arms hung loosely around both of their chairs. They leaned close to him and whispered. Donna picked up a pair of chopsticks and grabbed a dumpling, bringing it to Mr. Feng's lips. He took a bite and smiled lovingly at her.

I yelled to him, trying to warn him not to eat the shrimp. But he couldn't hear me.

I woke up screaming. My body was slick with sweat and I gasped for breath. Kikko poked her head out from under the blanket and looked at me with doggy concern.

I couldn't do this anymore. Now this whole thing was invading my dreams. This had to end.

CHAPTER
32

It is my firm belief that every once in a while, the universe will present you with a gift. It could be something very small and seemingly insignificant, but it will lead you down the right path. And usually, it's when you least expect it.

So that's why when at the end of my shift that day, Nancy Huang walked casually into Ho-Lee Noodle House on her day off . . . the very next day after Megan and I found the secret apartment, I sent thank-you vibes to the universe. Here was my chance, so conveniently laid out before me. I couldn't pass it up.

Nancy smiled pleasantly at me as she walked up to the hostess station, and I tried my best to return the smile. But, as I had suspected, I failed. Nancy immediately picked up on it, and cooed her concern. "Lana, what's wrong? Such a beautiful girl should never look so sad."

"I would like to talk to you about something, if that's okay." My tone came out flatter than I meant it to.

She nodded. "Of course, anything."

I looked over my shoulder. "Not here. Maybe we could talk out in the plaza. My shift is over in fifteen minutes."

Concern spread on her face. "Is everything okay with Peter?"

"As far as I know, everything's fine with Peter," I assured her. "I wanted to talk to you about something else."

"Okay, I'll go wait for you by the bench near the koi pond." And with a furrowed brow, she exited the restaurant.

The minutes dragged on as I waited for Vanessa. At five on the dot, she came in like a flurry of wind. "Sorry, I'm here, I'm here," she said through gasps of breath.

"It's fine," I said and grabbed my things. "I have to go."

"Um, okay . . . see ya then," she said.

I hurried out into the plaza, and saw Nancy sitting, as promised, on a bench near the koi pond. Even in her modern clothing, she reminded me of a traditional Asian painting. I thought back to that particular painting in Mr. An's store and thought how much she resembled the lovelorn woman.

When she saw me coming, she gave a weak smile, and patted the bench next to her. "Lana Lee, you are worrying me."

"I'm sorry, I don't mean to be like this, but I have to," I said, setting my bag down next to me.

"What is this about?" She looked at the bag and then at me.

I dug around in my bag, and pulled out a few photos.

"I'd like you to look at these," I said, handing them to her.

She looked at me with worry in her eyes and then down at the pictures, taking them from my hand. "I don't understand . . ."

"Just look," I encouraged, nodding at the pictures.

She flipped through the pictures I had kept with me in my purse. The first one was of the young girl that I had recognized but couldn't quite place. Now I knew it had been Nancy when she was a young girl, still in college. The second was the one that Megan referred to as the "family photo," and the third was the torn picture I had found in Mr. Feng's secret drawer.

Nancy's eyes began to moisten. She touched the photo of Mr. Feng with a delicate finger. "Where did you get these?" she asked, looking up at me. The photos shook in her trembling hand.

"Around," I said.

She turned her head from me. "Are you going to tell Peter?" she asked in a shaky voice.

"Tell Peter what?" I asked, wanting her to say it out loud. "I was hoping you'd tell me what all of this is about. I believe it has something to do with Thomas Feng's death."

Her head whipped back around to face me. "What? No, it couldn't."

"Nancy . . ."

Her shoulders sank. "Thomas is Peter's father."

Well, bully for Megan. She was right on that one. I took a moment to process that. "Does Peter know?"

She shook her head. "No, I never wanted to tell him." She wiped a tear away.

"So . . . how did all of this happen?" I gestured to the photos. "Why did he end up with Donna instead of you?"

She began to cry, and I imagined that it was in memory of days long gone. Days that she had buried in the back of her mind until I so callously brought them back to the surface. I felt a twinge of guilt . . . but only a twinge. I reminded myself that a man was dead, a close friend, and it might have something to do with their affair.

"Nancy, I need you to tell me."

She nodded through her sobs. "Thomas and I were very much in love . . . it happened by accident. He and I became friends through Charles . . . and we didn't mean to . . . fall in love."

"Charles?" I asked.

She looked at me blankly. "Charles An."

My mind fled back to the photo of the two young boys on the playground. So, the other boy was Charles An.

She continued. "Charles and I had been dating, but he was always so quiet. He never laughed and he barely smiled. He was shy, and I wanted excitement. I wanted to feel in love."

I nodded with sympathy, urging her to go on.

"I started to spend more time with Thomas, and soon we began to see each other in secret . . ." She gave me a pointed look, and that was all I needed to know. As far as I was concerned, my whole generation came from storks.

"And then Mr. An found out?"

She started to cry more. "He caught us together . . .

and . . . I could see it in his eyes . . . I had broken his heart." She paused. Her shoulders shook as she continued to sob.

"It's okay," I assured her, placing a gentle hand on her back. "Then what happened?"

She laughed, almost maniacally, and waved her hands around. "Then this plaza happened."

She must have read the confusion on my face because I didn't have to ask her to explain.

"Thomas loved this plaza more than me. More than anything. Then Donna showed up and she had a lot of money. She comes from a rich family, and I do not . . ." she said with spite in her voice. "My mother was a seamstress at a factory and she hardly made any money. I was lucky even to go to college."

I thought about my previous conversation with Donna and her need for people to believe that story. "So, he left you for Donna?" I asked, but hated to do so. I could see the pain on her face.

"Things were going on that I didn't know about," she said. "Things were already in place and Thomas had made promises to her for money."

"And he didn't know you were pregnant?" I guessed.

She shook her head. "No, and I did not want to tell him. I knew that this was his dream, and I would just get in the way."

"So what did you do?"

"I went to live with my mother, and she took care of me. After she died, I had to take care of myself and things were very hard because I did not have much money. That's when Thomas found out."

"You told him?"

"No," she said. "He figured it out by himself when he first met Peter." After that, he helped me with money and we started to spend time together again.

The tears continued to flow and I hoped that part of those tears came from relief. She had kept this secret for over thirty years. I took a moment to contemplate the weight of something like that. It seemed unfathomable.

"Nancy . . ." I said softly. "I'm so sorry about all of this."

"I am too." Her eyes became wild. "If this has anything to do with why he died, I will never forgive myself."

"You can't blame yourself. You did the best you could."

She looked off into the distance at Ho-Lee Noodle House. "Every day I am thankful for having Peter in my life. Even though I am sorry for the way things happened, I would never take it back."

We sat in silence for a few minutes, and I thought about how complicated life could be. The holes we could so easily fall into. And even though I was convinced that falling into my own holes and seeing things pan out for myself was the right way to go, I could see through Nancy why people tried so hard to protect their children from the pain of most realities. Some things were better left unknown.

"Does anyone know the truth about Peter?" I asked.

"Your mother and Esther know, but that is it," she confided.

"My mother!" I fumed. Here she'd known this whole time. And she didn't think once to mention it.

Nancy could read the anger on my face. "Please do not be mad at your mother for keeping my secret. She is a very good friend to me."

She had a point. If Megan had a secret like that, I wouldn't tell anyone either. As much as I wanted to be mad at my mother, I really couldn't blame her.

Wiping away the tears on her face, Nancy said, "You can't believe that it was Peter. He would never hurt anyone."

"Are you sure that he doesn't know?" I asked her, keeping his strange behavior in mind.

She shook her head. "I didn't want him to find out after all these years. Thomas wanted to tell him about it, and we fought about it a couple of weeks ago."

"Fought about it where?"

"What?" she asked.

"Where did you fight about not telling Peter?"

"We were in his office."

Puzzle pieces started clicking in my brain. Nancy must have been the woman Yuna heard and mistook for Donna. And it also might have explained Peter and Mr. Feng's argument that Cindy had witnessed that day outside of the property office. Maybe that was why Peter didn't want to see Mr. Feng and stuck me with delivering the food. But that didn't necessarily mean that Peter was the one who killed Mr. Feng.

"What will you do now?" Nancy asked, watching me.

I sighed. "I don't know . . . something is missing . . . I just can't . . ." I looked down at the photos in her hand. "I almost forgot . . . can you tell me why some of these pictures are torn in half?"

She looked down at her hands and plucked the torn

photo from the stack. "It looks like these ones had Charles in them. Their fighting was very bad. Charles moved away to California. I don't know why he came back . . ."

As Nancy continued to ramble about the falling-out between the two men and all the events that took place after, more things began to fall into place and I realized that I'd been looking at this all wrong. There was just one more stop I had to make before I could say with certainty that I knew who killed Thomas Feng.

After I left Nancy, I drove straight to Peter's apartment. If he could just answer a few questions for me, I could have the peace of mind I needed.

He answered the door, surprised to find me on his doorstep. He stepped aside without saying anything.

I whipped around to face him after he shut the door. "Did you know?"

Peter tilted his head. "Know what?"

"About Mr. Feng."

He walked past me into the living room and slumped on the couch. "I'm not ready to talk about this, okay?"

I was done playing nice. "We need to talk about this now!"

"Why?"

"Because I am trying to clear your name, and I can't do that if you don't tell me the truth."

Peter let out a heavy sigh and in place of the little boy he had appeared to be only a few days ago, he looked like he'd aged about ten. "If you're trying to ask me if I knew that Thomas Feng was my father . . ." He stopped, folding his arms across his chest.

"You did know!"

He looked up at me with surprise. "How did you know?"

"Trust me," I said, sitting on the arm of the couch. "It's a long story . . ."

We sat in silence for a few minutes. I tried to think of something to say, but came up empty.

Peter saved me from racking my brain any further. He turned to face me. "A few weeks ago, Mr. Feng . . . Thomas . . ." He threw his head back on the couch. "He ordered takeout like he always did, and I took it over there like I always did.

"Only this time, he told me he needed to talk to me about something. He said he couldn't take me not knowing anymore and that he felt bad I had grown up without a father."

My heart lurched.

"He told me all about him and my mother and how they fell in love." He laughed to himself. "He told me more than I needed to know.

"So I yelled at him and told him to leave me alone. But he wouldn't. A few days later, he cornered me again and said he wanted to make things right."

"That must be when everyone saw you guys fighting."

"Yeah, man, it was totally embarrassing. Everyone came out of their stores to see what was going on . . . Esther . . . Mr. An . . . even the Yi sisters."

"And that's why you didn't want to deliver his food that day?"

"Yes," Peter admitted. "I told him I needed more time

and he wouldn't listen. I thought the only way for him to leave me alone was if I avoided him."

I nodded. "Makes sense."

"I'm sorry that I got you into this mess, Lana."

"It's okay," I told him. "I just don't understand why you didn't tell all of this to Detective Trudeau?"

"It wouldn't have mattered, man. I would still look guilty." Peter brushed stray hairs from his eyes. "Plus, I didn't want anyone to find out about my mom and . . . Thomas. I don't even know what to call him . . ."

"You need to cut your mother some slack, by the way. Imagine how hard this was for her."

He huffed. "I know . . . I just need some time to get things straight in my head."

"Well, I think you should come back to work," I said. "Things aren't the same without you, and it might be better if things go back to normal in your life." I looked around the apartment. "You can't hide in here forever."

He laughed. "What are you talking about, dude? This place is a palace."

After we'd made amends and the air felt clear and breathable between us again, I got up to leave. I stopped at the door, turning back to look at him. "Just one more thing . . ."

"What?"

"This whole thing with Kimmy? What's that all about?"

He blushed. "I started hiding out in strip clubs to get away from everyone. I knew no one would think to look for me there. I never expected to run into Kimmy."

"So, all the strange behavior between the two of you?"

"She's worried I'm going to rat her out or whatever. She thinks I told you about it. She mentioned something to me about you snooping around asking about her second job."

"Oops." I winced. "Well, her secret is safe with me. I plan to take that secret with me to the grave. The fewer people who know I've gone to a strip club, the better."

I left Peter's with all the confirmation I needed. I reworked the puzzle pieces swirling in my head as I drove home. Despite the number of people I had suspected along the way, there was only one person who seemed to keep showing up at the most interesting moments. I thought about the times he had stopped at the restaurant or the times he had shown too much interest in what was going on with me or Peter for no apparent reason. I thought how he just so happened to be at our banquet table right before Donna had her episode at the memorial. He'd been standing right there at the seat he'd thought was mine. I hadn't thought much about it at the time.

My hands gripped the steering wheel tightly as I thought about the things Mr. Zhang had told me about him stopping by the herb shop to ask questions about yellow jasmine. But it was when I thought about the appointment book from Mr. Feng's office that I could have really smacked myself.

The letters *AC* were initials!

Because of the way I was brought up, I didn't think in terms of Asian versus American, which reminded me of the time Esther had told me she still thinks in terms of the way she was brought up even though she's been in the U.S. for decades. So it wasn't until that moment in the car that I realized Mr. Feng had written the initials the Chinese way . . . the surname initial first. To someone like me, it would have read *CA*.

And there was only one person I knew with those initials . . . Charles An.

CHAPTER
33

I should have called Trudeau the very minute that I came to my conclusion. But there was that niggle of doubt and denial that crept into my brain. That annoying voice that said, no, you have it all wrong.

So instead, I compiled everything I knew and wrote it down in my notebook, preparing all of my facts and ensuring that I hadn't missed anything. Kikko sat diligently at my side, watching my pen fly across the page. I had meticulously written out everything I'd learned from start to finish in an outline of sorts, ready to present to Trudeau.

Part of why I didn't want to talk to him right away was because of the way we'd left things outside the Black Garter. He had told me to mind my own business and stay out of trouble, and I'd failed to do so.

The next morning, on my way in to the restaurant, I called the number he'd given me. He didn't answer, so I left a message telling him I needed to talk and asked him to meet me at the restaurant when he had a chance. I was hoping to hear back from him before I even got to the plaza, but my drive ended in silence.

Absentmindedly, I opened the door to the restaurant and shuffled through my morning tasks. As I busied myself with wiping down tables, lost in thought, I didn't hear the door open and shut behind me. The bell tinkled, but I was so preoccupied that the sound didn't fully register.

The next thing I heard was a gun being cocked. "You couldn't leave things alone, could you?" an angry voice accused from somewhere behind me.

I whipped around, fearing that I knew who was behind me, and sure enough, there he was . . . Charles An.

I held my hands up in defense and backed away. He matched my steps and gave me a *tsk*. "Stay right there."

"Okay," I said, eyeing the kitchen door. "Just calm down . . ." If I could make it through the swinging doors, I could at least barricade myself in my parents' office and call for help. I cursed myself silently for not having locked the door behind me. "You don't need to use that."

"Don't tell me to calm down," he spat. "I have been calm for a long time now. I have watched you be nosy." He took a step forward. "Asking too many questions . . ."

I took another step back. "I don't know what you mean . . ."

"Oh, just shut up," he yelled. "I saw you talking with *my* Nancy yesterday. That is when I knew you know too much, little girl. You should have minded your own business."

"Nancy and I were just—"

"Don't lie to me! I'm not stupid."

"I didn't say you were. I'm just trying to explain—"

"Explain it to someone else!" He laughed to himself, his gun shaking with the movement. "But you will never get the chance. It really is too bad too. I liked you very much when you first came here."

"You can't shoot me," I said, trying to sound rational. "They'll figure out it was you."

"Oh, no they won't," he replied smugly. "And you know why? Because they are going to think it was Peter. I have plans for him too. He was supposed to take the blame for Thomas dying. That bastard."

I stared at him. "You knew?"

He laughed. "Yes, I knew. That stupid traitor, he took away my girlfriend, and then he got her pregnant." His lip curled in disgust. "Then he would leave her to be a mother by herself? For what?" He held his arms out. "For this plaza?"

I eased myself around a table while he had his gun pointed elsewhere.

He continued to rant, fixing the gun back on me as he noticed my movement. "And I left for so many years. But it followed me. Everywhere . . . everywhere I went, I saw her . . . and him . . . together. It makes me sick."

"Well, now you can have her back . . . now you can go find her and be with her . . ." I offered.

He snorted. "I tried, but she doesn't want me. Not anymore. Not after him. I thought, maybe if he goes away, she will change her mind." He looked off in the distance, and I took it as another chance to make further progress. "So I came up with a way to get rid of him," he admitted. "I asked him to have lunch with me.

I told him I wanted to make up, that we should not fight anymore. All these years . . ." He cackled. "All these years . . ."

I took a small step back.

"I came to your restaurant early that day and ordered shrimp dumplings. I already knew he would have his own dumplings from your restaurant. Every week, he orders the same thing. So boring of him. And I knew that Peter would deliver them . . ."

A thought passed through my mind that Trudeau had only checked the to-go receipts and Mr. An had ordered in that day.

"But you had to get in the way." His eyes slid back to me. "I thought it would ruin everything, but you making the delivery helped Peter look even guiltier."

I inched my heel back a little. "So, you did want Peter to take the blame . . . not me."

"Of course, how perfect for the son to kill the father, right? The father he didn't know all his life."

"But how did you switch his dumplings?"

"I spilled my tea. He got up to get me napkins," he said, laughing. "And when he turned away, I switched my dumplings with his. No one would know, they all look the same."

"What about his EpiPen?" I asked. If I was going to get shot, I at least wanted to know the full story.

"He tried to use it. He tasted the shrimp right away. I took it from him before he had the chance!" he said, staring off again. "I did it for her . . . I did it for my Nancy. But that only made it worse . . . now all she does is cry for him. She cries more for him than his own wife does."

My leg bumped a chair and the sound brought him back to reality.

"Stop moving!" he yelled.

"Okay, okay . . ." I said, surrendering. My legs shook uncontrollably and I felt like I would collapse at any moment. Right then, I made a promise to myself that if I made it out alive, I would change my life. I would listen to Megan and my mom and stop moping around the house watching sad romantic movies. I threw the promise out into the universe, hoping that someone out there was listening.

"I hope you know this is your own fault. You should have minded your own business. Everyone else does. No one will miss Mr. Feng. People will forget about him." He focused the gun at my chest. "Now you will learn your lesson for being so nosy!"

I squeezed my eyes shut. This was it. I was done at twenty-seven. I was going to die a server at my parents' restaurant with no man to call my own and a dog named after soy sauce.

"I'd put that gun down if I were you," a voice said calmly from somewhere near the entrance. I popped an eye open and was both surprised and relieved to see Trudeau standing behind Mr. An with a gun in his hand. "I've got one just like it pointed at your head, and I can guarantee you, I'm a hell of a better shot than you."

Mr. An seemed to weigh his options. His eyes burned into mine and I imagined he was trying to decide if I was worth it. With a disgusted look, he swore to himself and set the gun on the table in front of him.

"Hands up!" Trudeau barked.

In slow motion, Mr. An moved his hands over his head.

Trudeau moved in a flash and removed cuffs from his belt as he shoved him forward on the table. He slapped the restraints with force around Mr. An's wrists.

I watched in amazement as Trudeau read him his rights and Mr. An groaned against the table. The door was flung open behind Trudeau, and with his free hand he flashed his gun at the intruder.

Peter jumped back. "Dude," he shouted, holding his hands up over his head. "What's going on?"

After that, everything went black.

When I came to, I was lying on the couch in the back room and someone was holding an ice pack to my head. It took me a minute to realize it was my mother. She looked down at me with a worried expression that eased to relief when she noticed that my eyes were open. "Ai-ya! Lana, you scared Mommy half to death!"

My father came running out from the office with Megan and my sister following close behind. "Hey there, goober, welcome back."

"What happened?" I took hold of the ice pack and tried to sit up.

Megan sank down next to me, squeezing my shoulders. "You fainted during the arrest . . ."

"Of all days, Peter finally decided to come back to work today," Anna May reported, laughing. "He called us right away."

"Where is Peter?" I asked, looking around the room, not seeing him.

My mother answered. "I told him to go see Nancy. I told him they need to make up before he comes back to work."

"But what about the restaurant?" I had no concept of time, but I was guessing we were supposed to be open right about now.

"Restaurant is closed today. Today we celebrate," my mom said happily.

Anna May shook her head. "Who would have thought it was Mr. An that killed Mr. Feng? I didn't even think they knew each other."

I looked at my sister. "If you only knew."

My mom stood up, clapping her hands. "Okay, noodles for everyone! I will cook." And she rushed off toward the kitchen. As she made her way to the swinging door, Trudeau came through and practically got smacked in the face with the door. "Detective!" my mother said as she jumped back. "Why does everybody hide by this door? Mommy will have a heart attack one day." She smacked him on the shoulder and continued on into the kitchen.

Trudeau snickered and came to stand at the foot of the couch. My sister and Dad looked at each other. "Come on, ladies," my dad said. "We'll go set a table in the dining room."

Megan got up, pinching my arm, and followed my dad and sister out.

Trudeau looked at me with something like exasperation on his face. "Obviously, I got your message. You really push the limits, you know that?"

I looked up at him, feeling slightly embarrassed. "So I've been told."

"What you did was dangerous . . . and foolish . . ."

I glanced up at the ice pack on my head. "In case you haven't noticed, I've been injured. Maybe save the lecture for another day?"

He chuckled. "That's fair. But just remember," he said, turning to leave. "You've got it coming to you."

"Trudeau . . ."

He stopped. "Yeah?"

"Will you stay and eat with us? It would probably make my mother happy."

Smiling, he said, "Oh, your mother, huh?"

"Well, yeah . . ."

He seemed to think on it, and then turned around to face me. "Under one condition . . ."

"Oh, brother." I rolled my eyes. "Okay, what is it?"

"Call me Adam."

EPILOGUE

Two weeks later, things around the Village were almost back to normal. The story of Charles An's arrest had made front-page news. The headline featured in the *Plain Dealer* was titled I DID IT FOR LOVE. And unfortunately for Nancy and Donna, a lot of things that had been hidden were no longer so. Donna, ever resilient, managed to make a few graceful statements about water being best kept under a bridge. She sent sympathies to Nancy whom she labeled an innocent bystander in the whole mess. Somehow during the whole thing, she remained classy as ever. She never came right out and said it, but I knew she'd known the secret about Peter all along.

Mr. An admitted to the police that the yellow jasmine was originally intended to shut me up. And if Donna and I hadn't switched seats, it might have worked. Because she had been taking it this entire time, she had built up a tolerance and it would have required a lot more to actually be fatal for her.

I had to appreciate the fact that she had inadvertently saved my life.

Peter and Nancy made up with each other just like my mother had insisted. Peter came clean and told Nancy all about Mr. Feng and his shocking confession. They had a lot to work through together, but I knew that all would be well in the end.

Kimmy Tran's secret life as a cocktail waitress at the Black Garter remained secret. After a heart-to-heart sit-down with her, I managed to convince her I had no reason to expose her secret. She confided in me that it was her plan to help her family with their money problems.

She wouldn't admit that she and Peter might have a thing for each other, but I felt it was almost too obvious to not be the truth. I'm sure the Mahjong Matrons would uncover any potential love story should it arise.

Things with Ian Sung seemed to mellow out, and whether he was still embarrassed from his stage performance at the memorial or not, I didn't ask. For the time being, he was keeping things strictly business between the two of us. We even had our first committee meeting. For someone who wasn't very good at business dealings, he had a lot of great ideas, and I thought that perhaps Donna was right in that he just needed a little bit of patience.

As for me, I was still reeling from the experience of being held at gunpoint. Sleep was rough and I often woke up in cold sweats. I was thankful more than ever that Kikko was there to snuggle with me when my imagination started to run away.

And despite that struggle, I didn't forget the promise I made to myself about living life and getting over the jerk who'd stolen so much of my time and thoughts. No, this was a new beginning for me. Which is why I was headed on my very first date since my breakup.

The doorbell rang, and my stomach lunged into my throat. With one last look in my full-length mirror, I smiled to myself. *You've got this, Lana.*

I grabbed my coat and opened the door. There he was, staring back at me, handsome as ever. "Right on time, Detective . . ." I blushed. "I mean, Adam."

His eyes crinkled with laughter, and I felt myself melt like crayons on a hot sidewalk. He offered me his arm. "Are you ready to go?"

It was just one date. What could it hurt?

ACKNOWLEDGMENTS

While the act of writing a book is solitary, the creation of one is not. When following a dream, you meet a lot of wonderful people along the way. Some of them help steer you in the right direction and others help make who you are today. It is those people I wish to thank.

First and foremost, I would like to graciously thank my agent, Gail Fortune, for helping my dream become a reality, and for letting me squeal on the phone. My deepest appreciation and gratitude goes to my editor, Hannah Braaten, and all of St. Martin's Press for allowing me to be a part of their amazing family of authors. I feel so fortunate to have been given this opportunity.

Three cheers for Sisters in Crime, whose existence helps so many in achieving their aspirations in the mystery-writing genre. I would have been lost without you. A special shout-out to my local sisters and misters in NEOSinC who have not only provided me with an amazing support system, but also have become people

I'm proud to call friends. Special thanks to my fairy godmother, Casey Daniels (who also writes as Kylie Logan), for the encouragement she has provided and the wisdom she's shared. And to our chapter president, Irma Baker, who has taught me so much about writing and style in the short time I have known her. Thank you from the bottom of my nerdy heart.

A big thank-you to Chief Erich Upperman of the Fairview Park Police Department for taking the time to answer my questions about local law enforcement. And much appreciation goes to Gage Roberts for helping me with general police procedure. (Any errors or changes to procedure belong to yours truly.)

Thank you to my amazing dad, Paul Corrao, for being my rock, and for entertaining all my wild ideas (in real life and in fiction). *Xie xie ni* to my mother, Chin Mei Chien, for showing me an amazing culture I am proud to be a part of, and for teaching me the value of laughter. Kudos to my sister, Shu-Hui, for taking me under her wing and putting up with me all these years.

I would be remiss if I didn't send much love and respect to my milestone friend, Rebecca DuBiel, whose confidence and support has inspired me to push past my limits for the past twenty years. Hugs and gratitude to Tiffany Holliday for encouraging me to follow my dreams and always believing in me. Many hugs to Alyssa Danchuk, Lindsey Timms, Mallory Doherty, and Robert J. Moore for being my constant cheerleaders every step of the way.

For the unnamed family and friends who have shown me their love and support, I salute you.

Read on for an excerpt of

- - - - - - - - - - - - - - - -

Dim Sum
of
All Fears

- - - - - - - - - - - - - - - -

Now available
from St. Martin's Paperbacks

CHAPTER
1
- - - - - - - - - - - - - - -

"Ai-ya!" my mother bellowed from across the crowded restaurant. She stood up from the table, her hands squeezing her hips. My sister and father turned in their chairs to see what she was looking at with such disdain.

It was me. Lana Lee.

The gawking eyes of just about everyone in the room—including staff—followed me as I slunk across the restaurant to the table where my family was seated. Of course, they had to be sitting all the way in the back.

The best way to describe our family of four is similar to the game "one of these things is not like the other," with my dad—the solo white guy—being the odd man out. Even though my sister and I are only half Taiwanese, you wouldn't know it by looking at us. If I had a dollar for every time someone said, *"That's your dad?"* well, I probably would never have to work another day in my life.

On Sundays, the four of us gathered for our traditional dim sum outing at Li-Wah's on Cleveland's east side. And, because of this, we opened our own restaurant, Ho-Lee Noodle House, at noon. This gave neither my sister nor me an excuse to skip out on family time.

"Shhh!" I hissed at my mother as I slipped into the empty seat next to my sister. "People are staring at us!"

"Your hair is blue!" my mother screeched, ignoring my plea. "Why is your hair blue?"

My mother, though petite, did her best to tower over the table. At times it was hard to take her seriously because she was so darn cute with her chubby cheeks, but it was all in the eyes. And today, the eyes let me know that she was not amused.

I lifted a hand to my head, running my fingers through the freshly dyed hair. "Not all of it."

Ok, so maybe it wasn't the best time to dye my hair with streaks of blue. I hadn't really thought that part through when I'd set up the appointment.

Not only was I springing a daring new hairstyle on my parents who were both on the old-fashioned side, but I was also getting ready to tell them that I had been interviewing for a new office job in hopes of quitting my stint as server at our family's restaurant.

Most of the positions I had been looking into were for data entry jobs, but there was one company that stood out amongst the others that I had applied for and the position was a little higher on the totem pole. It was for an office manager and the pay was great. The benefits package was great, the office itself was great . . . everything was great. And, added bonus, it came with three weeks of paid vacation.

I'd interviewed with them the week before and it had gone exceptionally well. They had called this past Friday to set up a second interview for this upcoming Thursday and I had a good feeling that by the end of it, the job would be mine if I wanted it. Which, of course, I did. After all, a gal can't peddle sweet and sour pork her entire life. So, alas, it was time to let my parents know they needed to start looking for new help.

"Betty." My dad, the calm and collected one of the family, put a gentle hand on her forearm, nudging her back into her seat. "Let's all sit down."

Anna May—older sister and picture-perfect daughter—gave me a once over. "And you did this . . . on purpose?"

After stuffing my purse under the table, I shimmied out of my winter coat and hung it on the back of my chair. "Yes, I did it on purpose. Not all of us want to be so plain all the time." I gave her a pointed look.

"Interesting." My sister ran a French manicured hand through her pin-straight black hair. It fell just below her shoulders, gleaming. "I suppose you're right though, not all of *us* can pull off a classic look."

My own nails, painted teal, were chipping. I hid my hands under the table before she could notice. "If that's what you want to call it . . ."

My mother continued to analyze my hair; her eyebrows scrunched low over her eyelids. "Why did you do this?" Her lips pursed as she landed on the question mark.

With a shrug, I replied, "I don't know. I felt like it." *Lie*. I did know. However, I didn't want to admit to them, or to anyone, that it was because of what happened to me only a few short months ago. Of course, I'm sure that no one would say anything once I explained that it was because my life had been threatened at gunpoint, but part of me didn't want to say it out loud. Saying it out loud made it more real.

Since then, I've decided to stop putting things off until the elusive 'tomorrow.' Procrastination is nobody's friend.

My savvy stylist, Jasmine Ming, was more than thrilled to swap out my gold peek-a-boo highlights for some bright blue ones. I don't want to go overboard, but I'm pretty sure I saw a glint in her eye when she added the first touch of blue.

I reviewed the plates on the table and avoided eye contact with my mother. Placed in front of me were plates of baby bok choy in garlic sauce, noodle rolls, turnip cakes and pot stickers. I busied myself with unwrapping my chopsticks and grabbed a rice noodle roll stuffed with shrimp.

My dad looked at me with a soft smile. "Is this because of 'what's his name'?"

"No, Dad," I huffed, my chopsticks involuntarily tapping my plate. "I could care less about him."

OK, that wasn't totally true either. "What's his name" was my ex-boyfriend, who we did not mention by name. Ever. Not unless you wanted me to sprout snakes out of my head a la Medusa.

Anna May snickered. "No, Dad, she's dating Detective Trudeau now, didn't you know?" She clasped her hands together next to her face and batted her eyelashes. "He's sooo dreamy."

"Would you all stop it?" I jabbed the noodle roll with my chopsticks. "You're making a big deal over nothing. I've been thinking about doing this for a while, and I decided to stop putting it off. That's all."

I twisted in my chair, to properly face my sister. She looked a little too amused at my expense. "And, for your information, Adam and I have only been out on two dates. I hardly call that dating. Not that it's any of your business."

Anna May turned her nose up. "Well, I won't be looking for my wedding invite any time soon, but still, close enough."

"I kind of like it . . ." My dad cocked his head at me, nodding in acceptance at my hair. "Now, about this Adam character . . . he's a cop, so he's no slacker. Does he drive American?"

"Bill," my mother clucked her tongue. "This is no good. My daughter looks like a cartoon."

"Oh honey, she looks fine," he said, squeezing her hand. "Let's just enjoy our lunch before we have to head to the restaurant." He tapped his watch. "Besides, we still have the news we need to tell the girls, remember?"

My sister and I glanced at each other.

"What news?" Anna May asked.

My mother set down her chopsticks and shifted in her seat. "Your A-ma called this morning. She is very upset and has been crying for many days now." She shook her head. "Your uncle does not know what to do with her."

My "A-ma" is my grandmother in Taiwan. Because of her declining health she was now living with my mom's younger brother and his wife, along with their three children. Two of the children are close to the toddler range, so I'm guessing the living quarters were starting to feel a little cramped.

"So . . ." my father started, urging my mother along.

"We are going to Taiwan for a couple of weeks to help take care of A-ma." My mother said this in one long blurt while avoiding eye contact with my sister and me.

"A couple of weeks?!" I screeched. No, no, no. They couldn't leave now. Not when I'd just found the perfect office job.

"Right before Chinese New Year?" Anna May looked between the two of them. "Can't you wait until after it's over?"

My parents looked at each other.

"Who will run the restaurant?" I asked, fearing the answer. Any way you spun it, it wouldn't be good.

Anna May perked up beside me, straightening in her seat. "Well, that's obvious . . . it's—"

"Lana will run the restaurant," my dad announced before Anna May could continue. He put his arm around my mother and gave her another squeeze.

"What?!" My sister and I shouted in unison.

My dad held up a hand. "This makes the most sense. Lana is already working there full-time. And besides," my dad said, eyeing Anna May, "you've got school. You don't have a lot of time to run a business."

I threw up my hands. "Oh, of course, Anna May and her law school stuff again. What about my stuff? Does anyone ever think of what I have going on in my life?"

"Lana." My mother gave me her masterful look of disapproval. "This is something to help Mommy. Why would you not want to help Mommy? I changed your diaper when you were a baby."

I sighed. The diaper argument. Every time.

"I can't believe you're leaving her in charge." Anna May slouched in her seat. "Lana isn't responsible enough to manage the restaurant unsupervised. I'm going to end up putting in extra time to help anyways."

"Are you kidding me?" I turned to glare at her. "I'm sitting right here."

She returned my glare with one of her own. "I know."

"OK, girls," my dad interjected. "That's enough bickering. This is our decision and it's final. Anna May, you have too much going on in your life to give the restaurant your full attention. Lana has more time than you do right now and this makes the most sense. End of story."

Anna May folded her arms over her chest. "Yeah, I suppose you're right. She doesn't have anything going on besides hanging out at that stupid bar where Megan works."

I stiffened in my seat. "First of all, Megan's bar is not stupid. And I have stuff going on. Just because I don't tell you every single thing I do doesn't mean I'm not doing anything."

"Right . . . want to tell us what that supposed stuff is exactly?"

My dad shushed my sister and then turned to me. "Lana? Is there a reason you don't want to be in charge of the restaurant while we're gone? If there's something going on, Goober, you need to tell us."

If I didn't speak up now, it would be too late and I

could kiss my chance of leaving the restaurant good-bye. By the time they were back from their trip, the position I was hoping to take would more than likely be filled. I contemplated and weighed my options as my family continued to stare at me, waiting for a justifiable answer.

My mother finally got to me. Her typical stoicism usually drove me crazy because I never knew what she was thinking. But, today, her emotions were written all over her face.

I looked away, feeling defeat. "No, there's not."

"Good, then it's settled," my dad said, rubbing my mother's back. "See, Betty? I told you everything would work itself out."

"When are you guys leaving?"

My mother looked down at her plate. "We leave in three days."

"Three days?!"

Anna May chuckled beside me.

Great.

I'd like to say that this was my biggest problem, but unfortunately, this was going to turn out to be one of my better days.

CHAPTER
2
- - - - - - - - - - - - - - -

After dim sum, I headed home, a little on the blue side. The hope that I'd been holding on to for reinstating my former life was starting to slip away. In the past smattering of months, things had progressed from bad to worse, starting with the breaking up of 'what's his name' and drifting in a downward motion towards walking out of a more-than-decent job, a mounting pile of credit card debt and an obsession with donuts that gained me a pant size. (In the wake of emotional disaster there is nothing I find more comforting than pastries and retail therapy.)

The uphill battle had been a difficult one and I gave in to taking a job at my parents' Chinese restaurant so I could get caught up with my bills again. Turns out bill collectors are not very sympathetic to your break-up induced depressions.

Don't get me wrong, some people like being in the service industry, and quite a few people even love it. But me . . . well, I'd had my fill. Ho-Lee Noodle House had been a part of my family since before I was born. There wasn't a time I remembered it not being there. I needed a change of pace.

I don't think it had originally been my mother's dream to open a restaurant, but regardless, she and my father poured everything they had into making their business succeed. The plan was to keep Ho-Lee Noodle House alive for as long as possible, which for them meant keeping it in the family.

With two daughters, you wouldn't necessarily think that the burden would be left on my shoulders. You'd think that it would go to the eldest. But, you'd be wrong.

Anna May, the scholar of the two of us, had her whole life planned out in a detailed outline that she'd started when she was around sixteen and read her first John Grisham novel. From there, talk about criminal law existed in the Lee family household just as much as noodle recipes.

Of course at that time, being two years her junior, I was still concerned with rock band posters and how I was going to get out of third period gym class. I had no such ambitions that could compare to that of my sister's legal dream.

And perhaps, it was the pressure of comparing to her that led me down my eventual path of idealism. I became the dreamer of the family, the lover of arts and literature, taking joy in things that were made with creativity. I wanted to do something meaningful . . . to be driven by passion. I wanted to have something more than just "a job." I just wasn't sure what that entailed exactly. I had my interests, but nothing had stuck in terms of "life-long."

And, as most twenty-somethings come to realize, having a dream doesn't pay the bills in the adult world. After college, I floundered around aimlessly looking for jobs that would at least sustain my life as an adult, all the while knowing that if I didn't find a grand career scheme like my sister, my fate would be chosen for me. "Pre-destined" did not sit well with me.

All of this devastation tumbled through my head as I walked into the two-bedroom apartment I shared with my best friend, Megan. It was a modest, garden-style apartment in North Olmsted, which was only a hop, skip and jump away from Asia Village. It made my commute easy and was one thing I could put on the "pro" side of my list.

Kikko, my black pug, waddled to the door to greet me. Her curly tail wiggled as she spun around my ankles. I knelt down to give her a pat on the head. She approved and scampered off in search of something acceptable to bring me.

Meanwhile, I found Megan sitting at the kitchen table with a cup of coffee in hand and paint swatches scattered in front of her. She was still in her pajamas, makeup-less, and her blonde hair was swept away from her face by a thick black headband. Without looking up she said, "Oh good, you're home. I was just about to text you. I was thinking we could go to Home Depot today. I've decided on this mermaid theme for the bathroom, and this teal is the perfect color to paint the walls." She held up a swatch to show me her recent selection. "I also need to grab a new flashlight and some window cleaner."

"A flashlight? We have one under the sink."

"I want one for my car. I'm putting together a whole kit of tools to keep in the trunk."

I studied the paint swatch. "This works for me," I said, with little emotion. I was too bogged down with my current pity party to give a more enthused answer.

"It kind of matches your hair." She looked up and frowned. "What happened? Did your mom give you a hard time about your hair? Because you were anticipating that and we decided you weren't going to let it get to you, remember? We both know she doesn't do well with change."

I nodded, sitting across from her, still in my coat. "Yeah, but that got overshadowed real fast."

"With what?"

"My parents announced that they're going to Taiwan for a couple of weeks to help take care of my grandmother."

Megan sipped her coffee, unimpressed with my news. "What's the big deal with that?"

"They're leaving me in charge of running the restaurant. They leave on Wednesday." I slouched in the chair.

"Wednesday?!" Megan shouted.

Kikko came barreling into the dining area, stuffed duck flapping in her mouth. She dropped it at my feet and looked at me in anticipation.

I knelt down and picked up the duck, throwing it into the hallway. Kikko happily scuttled after it. "Yes, Wednesday, the day before my interview. The interview I'm not going to make because I now have to work."

"But, didn't you tell your parents that you were trying to get this job?"

I looked at the floor.

"You did, right?" Megan insisted.

"I didn't think it was a good time . . ."

"Lana! How else are you going to get out of that place if you don't speak up?"

"It wasn't a good time to bring it up. It's really important to my mom that she go to Taiwan right now, and I didn't want to cause more problems for them," I said, trying to justify my actions. "I can always try again when they get back."

"What about Anna May? Can't she run the restaurant?"

"They think it would get in the way of her school stuff. And, it probably would."

Kikko came back with her duck, dropped it on the floor, and nudged it with her nose.

"Of all the times for your parents to choose to go to Taiwan, of course it's now." Flustered, Megan stood abruptly, startling Kikko who in turn grabbed her duck with indignation and pranced into the other room. "Well, we'll figure out a plan together. You have to get that job. It's not going to wait around for you." She sighed. "In the meantime, I'm going to get dressed and then we're going to Home Depot . . . getting into this bathroom project will cheer you up."

"What will cheer me up is if we stop at the donut shop on the way."